Lagrange Shining

A Cuss Abbott Novel

Doug J. Cooper

Also by Doug J. Cooper

Crystal Deception (Book 1)
Crystal Conquest (Book 2)
Crystal Rebellion (Book 3)
Crystal Escape (Book 4)
Crystal Horizon (Short prequel & sampler)

Bump Time Origin (Book 1)
Bump Time Meridian (Book 2)
Bump Time Terminus (Book 3)

Lagrange Rising (Book 1)
Lagrange Calling (Book 2)

For info and updates, please visit: crystalseries.com

Lagrange Shining
Copyright © 2025 by Doug J. Cooper

Published by: Douglas Cooper Consulting

Beta reviewer: Mark Mesler
Book editor: Tammy Salyer
Cover design: Damonza

ISBN-13: 979-8-9999637-0-3

Author website: www.crystalseries.com

Acknowledgement

Lagrange Shining is my tenth science fiction novel. Three people have helped me on my journey, and I am grateful to them.

Tammy Salyer has edited all of my books, sharpening the prose and ensuring consistency across each series. You can learn more about her exceptional editing services at: www.inspiredinkediting.com

Dr. Mark Mesler has been my trusted beta reader, offering sharp insights and candid feedback that strengthen each story in its earliest stages.

And my muse — who patiently listens each evening as I recount the day's writing, her reactions subtly shaping the chapters to come.

From the bottom of my heart, thank you.

Chapter 1

Something woke Moby Navarro from his nap. A bump. A thud. It seemed to be coming from outside, which was very concerning because he was riding a delivery van through space, ferrying a load of equipment from Earth to Lagrange.

Clunk.

"What was that?" he asked the ship as he sat up. "That sound?" He'd dimmed the lights to sleep and now brightened them as he swung his feet to the floor.

"Investigating," replied the ship, its voice crisp, midrange in pitch.

Boom! An explosion shook the vessel with enough force to shift Moby on the bed. Alarms blared. A red light began flashing above the door out to the main deck, signaling that the other side no longer supported human life. Opening it without a pressure suit would be fatal.

His suit hung in a cargo hold locker at the other end of the ship.

"What's going on?" he hissed.

A hoverview appeared at the foot of the bed, the display showing the action right outside his room. The camera zoomed in on the ship's hatch, now severely damaged. The oval hatch was ajar, its center distended. The bulkhead frame where it had sealed tight was fractured, shards of metal poking out around the edge like daggers.

The deck was now exposed to the vacuum of space. And because Moby was horrible about safety procedures, rarely closing pressure doors because of the hassle of doing so, pretty much all of the ship was venting air.

"We have experienced a catastrophic containment failure," said the ship. "You must remain in your cabin until hull integrity is restored."

Dazed, Moby watched as someone in a heavy-duty pressure suit, the dark green kind worn by a host of trades when working in space, climbed through the hatch opening. A second person in a similar suit followed.

"Buckets," Moby called to the ship's bot. "Come to the bridge and repair the main hatch. Top priority."

The invaders stood on the deck facing each other, the ship's acceleration keeping them grounded. The big one turned to survey the cabin, pointing, talking over private comms. The small one fiddled with an electronic box held in a gloved hand.

"Attention intruders," called Moby using a broad-spectrum transmission. "This ship carries no valuables. Our cargo is industrial equipment."

Moby was certain they heard because both turned toward the row of doors, the leftmost one being the door to his room.

Buckets appeared behind the invaders, approaching from a ladder up to the deck, a toolbox gripped in one hand. He was a helper bot, humanoid in shape, gray synthetic skin, designed for lifting and assembly and cleaning. Buckets motioned to the damaged hatch. "Excuse me. I'm here for repairs."

The larger of the two invaders—Moby assumed a male based on size and build—had a laser rifle hanging by his side, the barrel pointing down at the deck. The man pushed the rifle stock back with his elbow, causing the weapon to swivel on a bracket mounted to his hip, raising the barrel in front. He moved his hand to the grip and pulled the trigger.

Moby saw a brilliant flash. A hole the size of a plum appeared in Buckets' chest, so clean you could see right through it.

Remaining upright, Buckets tilted his head forward to view the damage to his chest. The man fired the laser again. The second discharge cut through the bot's chin, severing his neck. Buckets collapsed to the floor, his head hanging by a few wires.

"What do you want?" Moby called, fighting fear. "I'll cooperate. There's no need for violence."

The hoverview display he was watching vanished. He called to the ship but his comms were dead. Isolated in the pilot's quarters, he couldn't see what was happening outside his room.

On the deck, the man with the rifle turned to the wall with three doors. Stepping to the one on the right—a door leading to a combination galley, eating area, and meeting room—he fired his laser into it, the flash of a single shot.

Moby felt and heard a *whump*. He figured it was the laser, its fearsome bolt of energy punching through the hull, creating a tremor through the substructure of the ship as it did. But he couldn't imagine what they were trying to achieve.

The gunman moved to the second door—the bathroom—lined up his rifle, and fired again.

Moby experienced another *whump*. This one closer, the tremor more powerful. Overwhelmed by fear, his body began to shake.

The third *whump* was paired with a beam flashing across the room right in front of him, the brilliance of the light momentarily blinding him.

A turbulent roar dominated everything as his vision returned. The beam had burned an entry hole in the door and an exit hole in the back wall, one that continued out through the ship's hull. The roar he heard was the sound of life-giving air rushing from the room out into the vacuum of space.

Now in full-on panic mode, his first thought was emergency putty, stuff from a squeeze tube that, when lathered over tiny cracks, would get pulled into the crevices and seal them. But he could fit two fingers into these holes. The putty would be sucked out with the air.

His desk had a flat plastic mat on top. He snatched it up, spit on one side to lube the surface, and pressed it over the hole in the door. The air pressure inside his room pushed against the sheet to hold it in position, much the way pressure from water in a kitchen sink will press on a plate that has slipped over the drain.

With the hole in the door sealed, the roar of air out through the hull dominated everything. Hurrying toward the rear wall, he cast about for another flexible sheet to use as a second plug. Seeing no good options, he pulled his T-shirt over his head, twisted a portion into a tight cone, and stuffed the wad into the hole, turning the shirt cloth with both his hands to wedge it tight.

His efforts reduced the exit of air, but a hiss confirmed that he'd only slowed the pace. He looked for something to bolster the plug, feeling dizzy from the thin air.

Then the laser beam blasted through the room with another *whump*, creating a second set of holes.

Moby stared in disbelief, already feeling faint, knowing he couldn't plug the new holes in time.

Under normal pressure, air dissolves in water much the way salt does when stirred into a glass. A vital example is when air in our lungs dissolves into our bloodstream, feeding the biochemical dance our cells use to sustain life.

With the loss of air pressure all around him, oxygen and nitrogen in Moby's bloodstream boiled back out as a gas—a froth of bubbles erupting inside him. It was a worst-case form of the bends, the ailment that plagues scuba divers who surface too quickly.

The delicate membranes of his lungs began to swell and blister. As he struggled to breathe, the fluid in his eyes vaporized, causing them to bulge before blinding him. Every joint screamed, and he sensed his skin would explode.

Then, darkness.

. . .

The gunman led the way into the cargo hold. The smaller one followed and, once inside, stopped at the operator's station against the wall and signaled for the cargo bay door to open. The gunman continued ahead to the ladder, descending the rungs as he counted the load. As expected, there were eight chest-high crates, each a sturdy white protective shell housing intricate mechanisms.

"Grab something," called the smaller pirate. "I'm killing the drive."

The gunman could sense a lightness in his stomach as he became weightless, a feeling like riding a roller coaster over a rise.

He held on to a rung and watched the cargo bay door open. Like the rise of a theater curtain, the door moved upward to reveal a breathtaking field of stars. The gunman's ship floated a hundred meters away, lost in shadow, its outline barely visible from the starlight it blocked.

It was a smaller ship, about half the size of the van, its hold big enough for perhaps three of the white crates. But that wasn't the plan.

An oval of light appeared near the front of the pirate's craft, the glow showing at the edges of the hatch. The hatch swung wide, and in the wash of light, a construction bot appeared, a gangly creature made of dark composite and synthetic muscle, its six arms suggestive of a monstrous insect.

The bot pushed off from the pirate ship and out into open space. As it floated across the gap toward the van, a second construction bot followed.

The pirates watched as the automatons unstrapped the crates from the deck of the van and floated them out of the hold. With the crates hovering in space between the two ships, the bots worked as a team to lash them together into a single long stack.

Next, the bots unfurled a fine lattice netting and used it to wrap the stack. The gunman had a moment of anxiety when the fabric became tangled. But the bots persevered, eventually covering the crates with the mesh material and snugging it tight. The netting served as a modern-day Faraday cage, blocking any tracking devices hidden inside the crates from communicating with electronic sensors searching for them.

To complete their task, the bots attached a small propulsion device to the tail of the bundle. They oriented the stack so it pointed away from Earth, away from the Moon, and fired the engine.

It was almost comical the way the mini-drive sputtered, moving the crates ever so slowly. But over a period of minutes, the mummified stack was fading into the distance, gaining speed, its own independent spacecraft.

Back in the pirate ship, the gunman tracked the bundle until the engine ran out of fuel. At that point, the crates became another piece of space junk, detritus in the ever-growing cloud of trash littering the orbits of Earth and the Moon.

He took a final reading on the stack and recorded everything needed to track it through space. After confirming that his partner and the bots were aboard, he sealed the hatch and made for home.

Chapter 2

Interworld Marshal Cuss Abbott floated through the waiting area, hugging the wall to avoid the crowd.

"You're looking for *Dependable 8*," said Ygo, his partner and friend. "It's a black delivery van."

Cuss heard Ygo inside his head, a private conversation no one else could hear. For Ygo to hear his words, however, Cuss had to speak aloud. "I'm glad they parked it on this side."

Hermes, like the other three tube cities of Lagrange, had a spaceport at each end. One was a passenger port designed for families, luggage, and pets traveling to and from the city in noisy throngs. People on that side would take vids of him if they learned he was an Interworld Marshal working a case. Others would ask questions out of curiosity. It would force him to be civil. Maybe even smile.

This end of the tube held the industrial port, a facility that handled the vast amounts of equipment, supplies, and bulk goods needed to sustain a thriving metropolis hovering in space between Earth and the Moon. He preferred the industrial port because it was filled with working stiffs too busy to gawk.

He also liked that he could tell something about the people by the color of their grav suits, coveralls that were attracted to the deck, keeping workers grounded while they toiled. Cuss should have been wearing a blue-and-white grav suit, colors reserved for law enforcement personnel. But he didn't expect to be more than a few minutes, so he chose to ignore protocol, save the time it took to climb into the bulky outfit, and just float.

He passed through a security door at the back of the shuttle waiting area and moved out to the massive flight deck. Grabbing a railing on the wall, he held himself steady as he sorted through the collection of spacecraft—freighters, tankers, express carriers—searching for the *Dependable 8*. There were dozens of vessels across the expanse, tall and squat, new and worn, colorful and drab. Auxiliary trucks—machines used to move cargo, fuel, and supplies on and off the various craft—crowded the deck, complicating his search.

"A little help?" he asked Ygo.

Cuss wore an ultra-high-tech lens in his right eye that enhanced both sights and sounds. Ygo, who worked from the hold of their Interworld Marshals Service spaceship, the *Nelly Marie*, could access it remotely. He did so to highlight a craft off to Cuss's left, midway across the deck. It was a newer vessel with a slick corporate paint job, black with a stylized Dependable Delivery logo emblazoned in white and red on the side.

"Got it," said Cuss.

Still holding the handrail, he placed his feet against the wall and checked both directions for hazards. Seeing none, he pushed off with his toes and flew above the flight deck, something the deckmaster frowned upon but regulars did anyway.

Painted lines scrolled beneath him, marks on the deck showing where it was safe to move and boundaries not to cross, clearly visible because the lights high overhead kept the place lit like the sun. Growls and rumbles and whines of machines all around him warned of danger.

After thirty meters or so, he could see that he was drifting to the right of his goal. He reached out and snagged the handrail of a portable stairway, swung to a stop, refined his aim, and pushed off again. He arrived moments later at a yellow docking post near the *Dependable 8*. He held on to it while he studied the craft.

Set lengthwise on three short legs, the *Dependable 8* was as big as a small commercial airliner, only instead of broad wings midway along, it had two stubby fins. He couldn't see a hatch on this side of the ship, but he could see three small holes burned into the expanse. Ygo highlighted the fourth, a hole in the center of the curly loop on the second *D* of the Dependable Delivery logo.

"It takes a powerful beam to punch a clean hole like that through a modern ship's hull," said Ygo. He was viewing the vessel through Cuss's lens, enhancing the image using feeds from nearby security cameras.

"You said it was carrying industrial equipment?" asked Cuss, recalling details from the briefing Ygo had given him on the way down from Luna Deck.

"That's right. Eight big pumps and their control electronics. Complicated things, each worth over three hundred thousand common, two and a half mil for the load."

"What do they use 'em for?"

"These were supposed to be for the water revamp project here in Hermes."

Cuss pushed off the yellow pole, floated under the belly of the ship, and grabbed a rear landing strut on the other side. He saw that a stairway had been pushed up to the hatch near the front of the craft. "Why do they cost so much?"

"The Hermes water system services a half million residents, plus thousands of businesses, the farms, the ports. It takes sophisticated equipment to regulate such a complex network."

Cuss still couldn't picture it but moved on. "They must have known what they'd find. I can't imagine an organization risking a crew and ship to stop a random delivery van where they're just hoping to find something good."

"You're thinking a special order?"

"Which would mean they had a buyer lined up in advance." He paused. "I suppose another reason could be to disrupt the project on Hermes. Protesters of some sort."

"Or maybe the doers want the pumps for themselves."

"Don't they have tags embedded?"

"It's standard."

"So now the equipment is linked to a murder. What do the doers say when a repair tech runs a scan and that fun fact pops up on their display?" Cuss shook his head. "And why kill at all? Wasn't the pilot trapped in his quarters?"

"According to the crime scene report."

"Why bring that kind of heat to a forgettable robbery?"

"Maybe murder was the point and the theft is misdirection?"

Cuss pondered that while he studied the craft. On this side of the ship, the cargo bay door ran half the length of the fuselage, providing easy access to items in the hold. He saw the ship's hatch at the front of the craft. According to Ygo's briefing, it led to the living and working compartment for the pilot, the only real deck of the ship. Above that was a small cockpit for navigating the craft. Everything else was cargo bay.

He floated over to the stairway and guided himself hand-over-hand up the railing. The stairs led to a misshapen ship's hatch, a twisted oval of metal composite with the *Dependable 8* logo in the middle. He counted eight fist-size hollows around the perimeter of the opening, the gray substrate of the hull exposed beneath the polished black finish.

"What happened to *Dependable 1* through *7*?" asked Cuss, making conversation while he studied the damage.

"Probably still in operation. It's a fleet business. They have sixty ships."

"Any ideas about these?" He indicated the hollows, imagining a coordinated explosion that cut the door pinions and forced the hatch.

"Shaped charges of some sort. An explosives expert is due later today to see what they can learn."

That's when Cuss realized there was no yellow crime scene button stuck to the hull—a Community Patrol device that served a number of important functions: telling civilians to stay away, defining boundaries not to cross, and warning of legal peril for those who did. The ship had been escorted into port the night before. If there was still evidence to be collected, the device would help protect scene integrity.

"Why no button?"

"There should be one. Techs have processed the scene. From what I understand, the explosives expert is all that's left."

Cuss huffed in annoyance, hoping it wasn't a sign of things to come. Sloppy police work made everyone's job harder.

Careful to avoid the sharp projections jutting out around the hatch frame, he floated through the opening and into the living compartment. It was a modest-size space, empty but for a headless bot floating near the far wall, an automaton with a matte-gray synthetic skin. A strap around its waist kept it anchored to the wall. A bag made of netting material held the bot's head to the strap.

Cuss drifted over to the bot and turned his head sideways to peer through the hole in its chest.

"Behind you!" shouted Ygo.

At that same moment, he heard a different voice. "Keep your hands where I can see them."

Cuss's senses spiked to full alert. He cooperated by moving his hands out from his waist, elbows bent so they didn't get too far from his body. He was no longer holding on to anything, so he began to turn slowly in the air.

He considered the voice. A woman. Commanding. Hint of an accent. No one he recognized.

Ygo fed an image of her to his lens. "She has masking tech of some sort. I didn't see her in my scan."

Cuss's rotation turned him toward her. He shifted his focus from his lens to the person floating in front of him.

She was medium height, medium weight, solid build, dark hair cut short. Smooth skin. Warm complexion. A cute nose with a faint bump on the bridge, perhaps an injury from her youth. High cheekbones that framed her face.

And oversized sunglasses that blocked her eyes. Until he could see her without them, he couldn't get a proper read on her. He guessed late thirties or early forties but needed the glasses off to refine the estimate. She wore gray slacks and a white blouse. Nice material. Quality clothes. Her right hand was behind her back near her waist as if she were reaching for a gun in her waistband.

"Got her." Ygo sent an ID to Cuss's lens: Mia Moreau, agent for the Lunar Organized Crime Unit. Forty-two, Cuss's age. Five foot seven. Proficient with a dozen different weapons. An impressive resume of past postings, accolades, and achievements, a list he chose not to review at this heightened juncture.

He knew about LOCU. They were elite agents selected for their intelligence, skill, and determination; specialists charged with taking down large criminal enterprises that threatened Nova Terra and its citizens. And that meant her sunglasses were something like his lens: enhancing views, boosting comms, providing information.

She could see he was a big guy without her glasses. Fit. But her eye-tech was likely informing her that he was an Interworld Marshal, that he packed two hundred twenty pounds in a six-foot, one-inch frame. That he, too, was qualified with a catalog of weapons. Trained in a mix of fighting forms. Had fewer job hops than she did but an equally impressive work history.

"Hold the wall," she said, tilting her head to his left.

He grabbed a pipe run where she indicated and righted himself.

"Who are you?" Her accent was European. Not Spanish. Not Italian.

"Cuss Abbott, Interworld Marshal. But you know that. Who are you?"

"You may call me Mia, Marshal Abbott. May I ask your role here?"

She spoke in a loose, sloshy way, as if she had a mouth full of saliva. Between that and the name Mia Moreau, he decided her accent was French.

"Here's the thing, Call Me Mia. I'm investigating this crime scene with the authority of the Interworld Marshals Service *and* at the personal request of Michael Belnick, governor of Lagrange."

He smiled, deciding to reveal a bit of his knowledge in an attempt to shift the dynamic. "Not to put too fine a point on it, but we are on Hermes' flight deck, a city in Lagrange. Definitely not the Moon. And this is a murder scene that involves parties from Earth and Lagrange, which explains why I'm involved. But I'm curious why LOCU cares?" As he finished the statement, it clicked. "This is a piece of a larger puzzle, one that reaches Nova Terra?"

She didn't move for several seconds. He imagined her reading him, trying to decide how to answer. But the sunglasses were effective at hiding her expression and intentions, frustrating his information-gathering.

"Would you consider a truce?" She brought her hidden hand around front so he could see it was empty. "Maybe work the scene together? Share observations?"

"I can't find useful background on her to guide you," said Ygo. "LOCU works hard to keep their agents as unknowable as possible."

Cuss couldn't see much downside to casual cooperation. "Sure. Since I just got here, maybe you can show me what you've learned and I'll add what I see as we go."

He watched her think some more, and then she said, "Let's start at the front and work our way back." She motioned toward the accessway to the cockpit. "After you."

He turned his back to her and made his way forward, a signal of trust. But Ygo was watching her for him. Cuss counted on it.

The cockpit was tight. As they squeezed in, their shoulders touched. He smelled her for the first time. A spicy floral. Not a strong scent like perfume. More subtle like a shampoo. Maybe a skin cream. Still, he liked it.

He looked around but there wasn't much to see. A pilot's seat in front of a black wall. Simple and unadorned. Clean and modern. There was a yellow crime scene button on the seat cushion. He picked it up and held it for her to see. "Really?"

But when he tried to meet her gaze, her sunglasses blocked his view. He knew they let her see everything clearer, more alive, augmented with all manner of extras. But they hindered his ability to assess her. That was the point, of course. Still, it bothered him.

"It's fully automated," she replied.

He frowned, confused.

"The ship. It's fully automated. There's really nothing for a pilot to do but watch." She made a motion, and a hoverview display came alive in front of the chair, a floating holo-image asking for authorization. When she didn't provide it, the display disappeared.

He understood that she was ignoring his annoyance over the crime scene button. Changing the subject. Yet he found the new topic intriguing. "Then why have pilots? What are their duties?"

"To be present if the ship needs rescue."

She turned and exited the cockpit. He followed, carrying the crime scene button with him.

Back on the deck, she expanded her answer. "If a ship is adrift and no humans are aboard, Space Watch will leave it as a private matter. That means either the owners recover it themselves, or their insurance company pays a third party."

Cuss made the connection. "But a human gets a rescue."

"Exactly. It's cheaper to a pay someone to be aboard than to pay for salvage insurance."

"Except insurance doesn't get murdered," said Ygo.

"Is it a common practice in the industry?" Cuss asked her. "Using a human in place of insurance?"

"It's common in the cargo delivery business. Maybe two-thirds of the companies put a person on board. It's a great gig. Take a nap. Eat some food. Watch some shows. Maybe help with something in rare situations. What's uncommon is a pirate killing one."

"What are the quals for the job?"

"It varies from company to company. For some, it's a warm body. Others want retirees from the industry. A few want ex-military. My sources say Dependable Delivery hires their own retirees."

Mia pushed off the wall and drifted over to the bot. "Its name was Buckets. Crime Scene says it was shot here on this deck. You have any thoughts on that?"

"There's no damage to the ship's hull behind it," said Ygo. "Their laser was powerful enough to make a clean hole in the bot, and had advanced smarts capable of cutting the beam the instant it pierced the target."

Cuss passed along the observation.

Mia brought a hand to her sunglasses like a teacher about to look over the top of her specs at a precocious student. She stopped herself. "Nice. Anything else?"

Cuss looked around, aware he was being tested, unconcerned because he was there to survey the scene anyway. She'd already provided information that would benefit his investigation, so he was happy to play along. For now.

He scanned the common area, but it was pretty much open space. The deck had a speckle-patterned coating that appeared new except near where the hatch had been blasted. There were pipes and conduits in raceways along the wall in a manner typical of a spaceship, with everything coated in an off-white glaze so it blended together.

His attention was drawn to a line of three doors behind Mia. Floating past her, he stopped his drift at the nearest one. The laser hole was centered in the door slab when measured left to right, and was waist-high off the floor. It was a clean puncture like the one in Buckets' chest.

He signaled for the door to open and then moved into a small space that proved to be a combination galley, eating area, and meeting room. The laser had pierced the door, drilled through the backrest of a chair, and continued out the rear wall, creating a hole in the hull.

He drifted across the room and peered through the opening, seeing out to Hermes' flight deck with its bright lights. "Their laser had at least two settings. Here it was set on the full-bore option."

The next door was to a bathroom. Another sequence of holes that pierced the hull.

The last door was the pilot's quarters. Cuss saw a round hole in the door, a second one in the wall two steps along.

He turned and looked down the row. "All the holes are the same waist-high distance off the floor. That tells me they had gravity during the assault, which means the ship's drives were engaged."

Mia looked up and down the row of doors. After a moment, she nodded. "I agree."

Cuss signaled the door to open and entered the pilot's quarters, a small room with modular components. Along the wall to his right was a molded slab projecting from the wall, a mattress resting on top, a blue bedspread floating above the mattress, a set of drawers beneath. Next to it was a smaller surface projecting from the wall, this one higher than the bed. The chair tucked underneath suggested its use as a desk or table.

"The pilot plugged one with a shirt," said Mia, tilting her head toward the back wall. The hole to the right had a tight knot of green fabric filling it, a dangling tail of cloth waving slowly in the weightlessness.

She looked back toward the door. A net bag attached to the wall held a plastic mat. "Crime Scene thinks he may have tried to use that sheet to plug one of the holes on that side."

"Was he wearing a shirt when they found him?" Cuss pointed at the green cloth. "Was that off his back or something he picked up in the moment?"

"Good question to ask the medical examiner, though my instinct is the information won't move the case forward. A curiosity, though."

"Dr. Shawna Lewis is both the coroner and the ME on this case," said Ygo. "You're meeting with her today at thirteen thirty."

"I have an appointment with the ME on Luna Deck this afternoon," Cuss said to Mia. "Saint Luke's Hospital. She's examined the pilot and is giving her report. You're welcome to tag along." He reasoned that if she solved the theft, he'd solve the murder. He wouldn't wait for her. But it was win-win no matter who got there first.

She paused to think.

"Have you noticed the pauses?" said Ygo. "She's working with someone. But is it a person or an AI?"

Ygo was both—a man, for sure. But one with a quantum link surgically implanted into his parietal lobe. Through it, AIs were connected into his brain, giving him instant access to the world's archives and feeds, raw data and processed information, private comms and public monitors, plus the processing power to digest it all. He never left his special bed in the hold of the *Nelly Marie*, but from his den, he watched over his partner twenty-four seven, protecting him, guiding him.

"That's very gracious," she replied. "Will there be time for lunch? My treat, of course."

"Only if you take off your sunglasses."

This time she answered immediately. "We'll see."

The rest of the tour yielded little. The hold of the ship was empty save for straps floating up from the floor, their ends cut.

The closest thing to excitement came when Cuss stopped at the operator's station at the front of the bay. Guided by Ygo, he used the interface to access the ship's archive. "We might be able to see the intruders in action," he said to Mia, using finger flicks to work his way through the interface. But he learned moments later that the record was empty. Not just for this event. The display showed zero items in the entire archive.

"Any way a forensic effort could reconstruct it?" asked Mia, looking over his shoulder.

"An empty archive means they've taken a piece of hardware," said Ygo. "It's gone."

"It's worth asking the case detective," Cuss told her.

As they exited the craft, Cuss stopped to reattach the crime scene button, placing it in the center of the Dependable Delivery logo on the distended hatch.

Mia watched him work. "You're a straight arrow, Marshal."

"I like hearing that. Some have accused me of being morally ambiguous."

"Really?"

She sounded surprised, but he couldn't tell if she thought he was teasing her, or maybe she was just skeptical of the claim. He didn't bother looking at her face for clues to sort it out, though. Her sunglasses had already driven his annoyance level to its maximum.

Or so he thought.

They started down the stairs. But before they reached the bottom, she called "C'mon" and pushed off without warning, gliding under the ship, doing so with barely a glance for oncoming danger.

Cuss resisted the urge to shake his head in judgment as she zipped across the flight deck toward the entrance to the transport shuttle service. Looking both directions, he confirmed the path was clear and followed at a more measured pace.

"Working with her is going to be a challenge," he said to Ygo as he floated past a brawny brown tanker. It squatted on four grasshopper-style legs, hoses writhing next to it as it disgorged enough industrial lubricant to fill an Olympic-size swimming pool.

"In what way?"

"Everything she does annoys me."

"Good. I was afraid you'd crush on her."

"Not likely. That said, I do want to see her with those damned glasses off. I'm curious."

Chapter 3

The perimeter wall loomed, and Cuss caught himself with both hands, letting his hip thump against it to complete the stop. He pulled himself along a handrail and joined Mia at the door to the shuttle waiting area. With her leading the way, they entered.

A row of silver poles ran through the room, the floor-to-ceiling kind that people in line could use as handholds. They moved to the first open pole at the back of the line. Cuss counted fourteen people ahead of them. Each shuttle carried ten passengers on the quick hop up to Luna Deck.

A rumble filled the room, one powerful enough to vibrate the floor. Machinery growled and thumped, followed by a *whoosh*. Shiny double doors slid open at the front of the queue. Passengers moved out and the people in front moved in. The doors shut. Cuss and Mia drifted forward and were now at the third pole.

They didn't speak while they waited. Cuss spent the time trying to decide if he wanted to work with her. Her growing list of cons threatened to swamp her modest number of pros. He hadn't reached a decision when the *growl* and *whoosh* repeated. The doors opened and passengers exited.

They climbed into a flying-saucer-shaped craft, took their seats in a ring around the perimeter, and strapped in next to each other. The door slid shut. The shuttle started forward on a track. This time minor jolts accompanied the familiar growls and rumbles. The lights blinked off. A *clunk*. And they were adrift in space.

Through the big windows above the seats, Cuss saw Hermes. They were so close to the structure that all he could see was an enormous dark wall, with seams and flanges and an assortment of electronic devices protruding here and there. The shuttle was turning slowly as it hovered in space, and the wall moved out of view, replaced by a field of stars. The rotation continued, and he saw three shimmering logs floating in the celestial sea: Athena, Demeter, and Apollo, the other tube cities of Lagrange.

Thrusters hissed, and Cuss felt a tug on his straps as the shuttle began to chase the spin of Luna Deck, the ballet necessary because the tube city rotated but the spaceport didn't.

Each tube city was formed from twelve enormous cylinders of different sizes, one snugged inside the next like Russian nesting dolls. The tubes were massive things, thirty kilometers long, the largest cylinder measuring five kilometers in diameter. The tubes were fastened together and spun as a single unit, the motion creating centrifugal gravity on twelve huge decks where people lived and worked and played.

The speed of rotation, about half the speed of a second hand moving around the face of a clock, was just enough to create Earth's gravity on the surface of the outermost tube. This was Terra Deck. Each deck inward had a slightly weaker gravity because the cylinder wall was closer to the center of rotation. Twelve decks in, centrifugal gravity decreased to that of the Moon. This was Luna Deck, Cuss and Mia's destination.

A wheel rotates on an axle, a stationary pipe that runs through a middle hub. For the tube cities, the axle was one last cylinder down the center, smaller than the others but still plenty big enough to fit a spaceport at each end. It didn't rotate, allowing spaceships to take off and land on a steady platform. The Lagrange design engineers chose shuttles to solve the problem of moving people from a spaceport that wasn't rotating up to decks that were.

Thrusters held the shuttle steady as a snakelike tentacle slithered out from the massive wall, the end approaching them like the head of a serpent, sunlight flashing off its silvery surface. Mia chirped in delight at the sight, turning in her seat to get a better look. The wonder on her face made Cuss think this was her first trip to Lagrange.

The tentacle latched onto the shuttle, and then it curled inward, pulling them toward an opening in the wall and the docking bay inside. Mechanical grips *thumped* as they grabbed the craft. Lights came on. The doors opened.

Cuss followed Mia out of the shuttle, out of the station, and into the hustle and bustle of Luna Deck. She paused on the steps in front of the shuttle station and scanned the plaza, absorbing the view.

It was an impressive sight, especially for first-timers. The sun appeared high overhead, an illusion that nevertheless radiated warmth, that traversed the sky, that mingled with clouds, that set at night. Buildings lined the square, six- and eight-story constructions, each one pressed against the next to ensure there was no wasted space. The buildings themselves wore pastel colors—pale reds, yellows, greens, blues—with brightly colored oxygen-producing foliage draped down the exterior walls. A steady stream of people moved in and out of the shops and markets at the ground level of the buildings, talking, laughing, contemplating life.

She pointed to a restaurant on the far side of the plaza. "The Agrodolce has private booths. That work for you? I made reservations."

"Of course she did," said Ygo with rare sarcasm.

Cuss knew of the Agrodolce. It was an Italian-American place with a menu designed for tourists, a little pricy, automated, commercial, devoid of character. He would have guided her to a homier place on a side street, one with personal attention, a relaxing atmosphere, and wonderful food.

"Lead the way," he said.

Surveying the market square, she didn't move, instead saying, "There are about two hundred eighty people in the plaza. How many are wearing sunglasses?"

Ygo used his lens to highlight everyone with dark eyewear, the numbers changing because people were entering and leaving the square. He fed the result to Cuss, who reported the tally. "Between twenty-five and thirty."

She nodded. "Ten percent wear them and none need them."

While he contemplated the point of her words, she descended the steps and took bounding leaps across the plaza. For a moment he was impressed with her athletic skill in the low gravity, but then he remembered that she lived in Nova Terra. Luna gravity was normal for her.

He caught up with her most of the way across the plaza and together they approached the door to the restaurant, slowing so an older couple could exit. Cuss used the time to scan the area and consider the kinds of people wearing sunglasses. Though his knowledge of couture was limited, most paired their dark eyewear with clothing he would call fashionable or stylish.

Except for the guy off his right shoulder wearing oversize sunglasses. When Cuss's gaze swept past, he saw a man sitting on a park bench studying them. The man realized Cuss was staring back, and he looked away, doing so with a casual turn of the head.

Cuss did the same, turning to the restaurant, pretending to study the façade. But he was actually using his lens to study a holo of the man.

The guy's sunglasses matched Mia's to the smallest detail. And, like her, he was dressed in conventional business clothes, in his case a sport coat, dress shirt, and dark slacks. Pretty much what Cuss wore. He had a small build but looked wiry, with facial features that hinted at

East Asian heritage. Cuss guessed he was somewhere in his mid- to late-forties, but as with Mia, the sunglasses made assessment difficult.

"Is he teamed with Mia?" asked Ygo. "Or tailing her?"

Cuss wondered the same thing.

"I'll reach out to MFOD and see what they can learn." Ygo pronounced it em-fod, which was the Marshals Field Operations Desk, a twenty-four-hour support service for agents on the job.

Cuss's curiosity got the better of him. So while Ygo worked that route, he decided to be more direct.

He followed Mia into the restaurant. The moment they were across the threshold, he said, "Grab the booth. I need to call my boss. Be back in a flash." Without waiting for her to respond, he stepped outside, doing his best to use an entering party as cover.

With each building pressed against the next, there weren't alleyways for him to slink through. And while the plaza had a scattering of plantings, sculptures, and feature walls that could provide cover, none were near the Agrodolce.

He emphasized speed. With three bounding strides, he reached the entrance to the shop next to the restaurant and ducked inside. It proved to be a women's boutique with displays of shoes, belts, and other clothing accessories.

Building code required that every commercial establishment in Hermes have at least two public exits. He saw it on the far wall, a door leading to the adjacent shop. He hustled through the boutique, through the far doorway, and into a gift emporium filled with Lagrange-themed souvenirs. The second exit from that shop led out to the plaza at a point near the park bench, the one where Cuss had spotted the mystery man.

But when he reached the door, Cuss saw the bench was empty. Given his clumsy approach, he wasn't surprised.

"Behind you!" called Ygo.

"Marshal Abbott." Cuss heard his name and turned around.

"This is Royale Anderson," said Ygo. "Also LOCU."

"Why are you following us?" Cuss snapped, his clenched jaw reflecting his aggravation, in part because he'd been caught off-guard twice in just a few hours.

"Mia can't be trusted," said Royale. "If you work with her, watch your back."

A customer entered the shop through the front door. Royale shuffled his position to make way and kept moving, exiting the store in a smooth motion.

Cuss followed Royale outside in time to see him take three bounding strides, plant a foot on the seat of the park bench where he'd been sitting, and launch himself upward. In a remarkably athletic maneuver made possible by the one-sixth gravity, he soared aloft and landed on the patio of a second-floor apartment. The patio door was ajar. Royale disappeared through the opening.

A passerby gasped and pointed.

Cuss considered pursuit just long enough to admit he couldn't make the leap. He was too big and it was too far. So he turned and headed for the Agrodolce.

"Sorry about the late warning," said Ygo. "It seems LOCU agents are using a new blurring tech. Now that I understand how it works, I can filter for it. It shouldn't be an issue going forward."

"Good to hear." He slowed before entering the restaurant, wondering how to behave with Mia. "Any news from MFOD?"

"Nothing yet."

Cuss entered the Agrodolce and followed a holo-greeter to their table. Mia sat in a booth enclosed by floor-to-ceiling walls on three sides. When Cuss slid into the bench seat opposite her, she wiggled her fingers and a partition closed across the front, sealing them in.

He scanned his surroundings. The walls were treated to look like dark wood. The bench seats were covered with an attractive patterned cloth. The tabletop was a polished slab of metamorphic rock, pale white with veins of green. The whir of a circulation fan hummed in the background providing them fresh air combined with the occasional waft of delicious-smelling food. A hoverview menu at the end of the table invited them to place an order.

A glass of water was on the table in front of him, Mia's already half gone. Cuss took a sip as he considered what to say.

She turned to the menu and began scrolling. She was viewing sandwich choices when she said, "Royale

Anderson can't be trusted. If you work with him, watch your back."

He stared at her, uncertain how to respond. Ygo provided the missing piece. "MFOD has learned that the commander of the Lunar Organized Crime Unit has accepted another job. Mia and Royale are competing for the position and are using this case to distinguish themselves."

"What's good?" she continued, still studying the menu.

Cuss decided to take it slow. "This is my first time here. Let's see if they can make coffee."

He placed an order for a cup of black brew. While he reviewed the choices for burger toppings, the coffee arrived in the delivery slot below the display. He took a sip and found it to be full-bodied and hot. One point in favor of the Agrodolce.

He continued the slow roll. "So, you and this guy have a history?"

"Unfortunately." She continued studying the menu, now looking at holos of hot sandwiches. She selected a grilled cheese with tomato and moved on to the choices for bread and cheese.

He kept at it. "Working organized crime?"

She pointed her sunglasses in his direction. "Gina Giovanni, the current LOCU director, is resigning. She's moving to Detroit because her mom is sick or something and she wants to be nearby. Anyway, I had the position locked up, and then Royale Anderson ass-kissed his way into contention. Now we're competing."

"And this case is a deciding factor?"

"Maybe." She tapped the tabletop with open palms, a pause to organize her thoughts. "Piracy is the highest-profile irritant in Nova Terra right now, a half-dozen projects disrupted by raiders in the last year alone. We think there's one group responsible for, like, ninety percent of all activity. If I can take them down, or even slow them up, then I believe I'll get the job. Royale has come to the same conclusion."

"How much time do you have?"

"To solve the case? The superintendent makes his decision in ten days."

"What do you have for leads?"

"Tons of background data but no clear target."

"You don't have a suspect?"

"I have the name of someone who will lead me to their shooter."

"She's talking about you, pal," said Ygo.

Cuss had already concluded that and his face flushed with annoyance, made worse knowing he'd planned on using her in the same way. To hide his pique, he turned to the menu, gave it a final scan, and chose a Total Burger, a hamburger that came heaped with all the extras.

"You have quite the reputation, Marshal," she continued. "The moment I learned it was you on that ship, I became hopeful. I just might have a chance."

"I appreciate the vote of confidence, but I work alone."

"I'll hang back and let you do your thing. I won't get in your way."

Ygo said, "I suggest you excuse yourself to use the bathroom and keep going out the front door."

Cuss suppressed a laugh, hiding it by sipping his coffee. The cup had a lid on top to prevent spills from the inevitable sloshing that occurred in low gravity. It was a common item in Nova Terra, and it made him think about her reactions of wonder during their brief shuttle ride. He returned to the slow roll. "How is it that you've never been to Lagrange?"

"I've been in your spaceports several times, a quick stop passing through. But Earth is where pirates do their organizing. At least, that's where my cases have taken me so far."

"No visits here as a kid?"

"We didn't travel much as a family." She gave a careless shrug when she said it, making him wonder if there was more to the story.

"Now that you're here, what do you think?"

She sat back. "The aura of Luna Deck is completely different from Nova Terra. It feels more upscale here. All shiny. No dirt roads. As for the gravity, those big leaps I took across the plaza? That's what I was testing. I can feel the structure rotating in my stride when my foot lands. The tiniest push sideways when the shoe first connects. Is that the Coriolis effect?"

"That's more about tangential velocity and conservation of angular momentum," said Ygo. "Coriolis is something different."

"Could be," Cuss said to her.

Ygo continued. "We should invite Royale to the autopsy discussion with the ME. More eyeballs means faster progress. And do we care who gets the promotion?"

Cuss drained his coffee, giving a single slow blink as he tilted his head back, signaling to Ygo, "Yes, let's invite Royale."

Then he asked Mia about her earlier behavior. "What was the point of counting people wearing sunglasses?"

She tapped her eyewear with an index finger. "When LOCU developed these glasses, they gave tremendous capability to our agents. Unfortunately, they also made them easily identifiable. So LOCU paid for a couple of designer eyewear companies to promote similar-looking sunglasses as a fashion statement. With ten percent of the populace now wearing them in Lagrange and a bit more in Nova Terra, we no longer stand out." After a pause, she added, "On Earth, of course, they wear them because of the actual sun."

If she were going to take them off for Cuss's benefit, now would have been an appropriate time. She didn't.

Their food arrived in the delivery slot. Cuss's burger looked and smelled delicious. He took a bite and savored the mix of flavors and textures, thinking he may have been wrong about the Agrodolce.

After two more bites, he slowed down and shifted his focus to the murder. "Can you share your background data? If we have ten days, I need to hit the ground running."

Mia chewed for half a minute before answering. Cuss guessed she was consulting with her attendant.

"Some of it needs to be redacted," she said finally. "Insider information that LOCU doesn't want circulated. I can send the bulk of it now and the rest as it's cleansed."

She went quiet, and Cuss was happy for the calm, enjoying his meal while Ygo sifted through the incoming treasure trove.

"It's mostly junk," Ygo reported, "but there are a few gems here and there. It'll take me a bit to sort through it."

For the remainder of the meal, they exchanged polite chitchat. As they organized themselves to leave, Cuss asked Mia the same question he'd asked others in her position. "Why would you want to get involved in management?" It was an ambition he couldn't relate to. Who would want to spend their day confronting behavioral issues, or fending off meddling superiors, or struggling with too-small budgets?

"It's not all management. I'll still have cases, ones that *I* choose. That's a huge plus. As for why?" Her head tilted as if she were looking into the distance. "I don't know. I was raised to be ambitious, to set my sights high. I suppose this is a manifestation of that."

She took a last sip of water and then signaled for the panel across the front of the booth to open.

Back outside in the plaza, Cuss pointed to the pedestrian thoroughfare, the main road running the thirty-kilometer length of Luna Deck. "The medical examiner's office is in the basement of Saint Luke's, maybe four kilometers up the way. We can walk or we can ride a pod."

He'd been leaning toward taking a pod, a hovering carriage they could ride anywhere in the city. Mia answered by starting down the thoroughfare, taking the broad, bouncing strides possible on Luna Deck.

Watching her recede, Cuss sighed. "Any news from Royale?"

"MFOD passed the message up through LOCU's main office. We won't get a specific reply. Either he'll be there or he won't."

Cuss pushed off and accelerated into a long, loping gait, chasing Mia while also scanning the crowds for Royale. He didn't see him. When he finally caught up with Mia, they were a half-kilometer away from the hospital.

Chapter 4

S aint Luke's Hospital was a stately structure, eight stories of condensate material formed to look like granite block. Cuss and Mia approached through the forecourt, passing between two stone statues before entering the building. On the left was Hermes, a young man holding a scepter, naked but for a cape hanging from one shoulder. On the right was Saint Luke, a wise old man dressed in flowing robes.

Inside, they made for the main hallway, followed it to the end, and took stairs down to the basement. There, Cuss saw the same tiles on the floor as those on the main level above. The same white walls. The same brown trim. But the chips and stains and wear on the different surfaces made it feel older, like they'd skipped the basement during the last renovation.

They stopped at the third door on the right, a sturdy thing with a frosted glass pane in the top half. The words *Office of the Medical Examiner* were written across the window in black font, easily readable because the room inside was well lit. Below that was a short list of sub-offices: Forensics, Toxicology, Crime Lab.

Cuss squared up in front of the door, Mia at his shoulder. A chime sounded, letting them know the occupants inside had been notified of their presence. After a short wait, the door opened.

"If it isn't my favorite Interworld Marshal," said a stocky woman in blue medical scrubs. She was medium height, had a kind face, and seemed to project happiness as her default state of being. She stepped back so they could enter.

"Hello, Shawna," said Cuss, greeting her with a warm smile.

He ushered Mia ahead of him and switched to Shawna's formal title for the introduction. "Dr. Lewis, this is Mia Moreau. She's a LOCU agent from Nova Terra. Mia, Dr. Lewis is Hermes' chief medical examiner."

"Shawna, please," said Shawna, shaking Mia's hand. "Good to meet you." She made a "this way" wave and led them through the room.

The group passed between two rows of lab benches loaded with boxes, tools, documents, and more, making Cuss think that the room hadn't been used for scientific purposes in some time.

"The others are already here," said Shawna over her shoulder.

The plural in "others" gave Cuss pause. His best guess was that Royale had brought his partner.

At the back of the room, Shawna stopped in front of a polished silver-metal door and pointed to a row of white coats hanging on wall hooks. "Grab one. It's chilly inside."

As Cuss and Mia dressed, Shawna slipped into a white coat that had been draped over the back of a chair. She snugged a cap on her head, the kind with a light in front that pointed wherever she looked. Tugging the door's heavy latch handle, she pulled it open to a sigh of air. They stepped into a bracing chill, condensation puffing from their mouths when they exhaled.

To the right, Cuss saw a lab bench along the wall, neatly organized, with columns of polished drawers across the front, a line of cupboards above it. To the left, rows of shiny square doors were positioned on a white-tiled wall, four across and two high, each big enough to hold a slide-out drawer with a corpse. Straight ahead was an operating table. One end had a wash station with hose, faucet, scale, and drain. Overhead, a light fixture on an adjustable arm bathed everything in white light.

A body covered in a thin green cloth lay on the table.

Royale stood on the far side of the table. When Mia saw him, she huffed in frustration.

A woman stood next to Royale. She wasn't wearing sunglasses, which meant she wasn't with LOCU.

"I don't know who knows who," said Shawna as she approached the table. "I'll leave it to you all to make your own introductions."

As Cuss followed Shawna, he nodded an acknowledgement to Royale and then studied the new face. She looked familiar. He used his lens to identify her: Julie Kapoeta.

He had known a Julie Kapoeta twenty-something years ago in high school. She'd been a smarty-pants, a junior taking some of the same classes he'd been taking as a senior.

They'd chatted back then, mostly when she was helping him rush through homework he hadn't finished. He'd graduated, and they hadn't spoken since.

The passage of time had been kind to Julie. She looked terrific. She was older, obviously. She'd been a couch potato in high school, but from the way the white coat hung on her frame, she'd leaned out nicely. She was prettier than he remembered. Smooth skin, high cheekbones, button nose. Bright blue eyes that drew him in. Brown hair with blonde streaks. Full lips tinted with a hint of red.

"Julie?" he said as he approached her. "Cuss Abbott. Remember me?"

She tilted her head to the side as if trying to recall, her smile revealing perfect white teeth. He could tell she was teasing him.

Then she nodded. "I have this hazy memory of someone with that name. But he was your classic jock, the kind who led with his muscles more than his brain. There's no way that guy would have gone on to become a somewhat renowned Interworld Marshal."

Then she surprised him by stepping forward and giving him a hug. After the briefest hesitation, he hugged her back. She felt firm under the coat. Tight.

Before he could ask about her role in the case, Shawna interrupted their reunion, speaking in a voice meant for the entire group. "Let's get started. I have another appointment right after this." She was standing next to the table, a hand on the green cloth covering the body.

They all shuffled closer to the table and she peeled back the top quarter of the cloth, revealing a man's head and shoulders. Gray hair, bushy eyebrows, wrinkled face; he looked like somebody's grandpa. His eyes were closed. If not for the pallor of the skin, Cuss might have guessed he was asleep.

"I've examined Santiago Navarro, the pilot killed in the recent raid on the *Dependable 8* delivery vessel. He went by the nickname Moby. Eighty-two years old. In good health before his demise."

Her voice lowered into a kind of chant as she intoned her observations and conclusions. "He died of pulmonary barotrauma: rapid decompression leading to asphyxiation. There is no sign of external trauma beyond skin discoloration due to the pressure loss. Organs appear normal. Blood toxicology rules out any foreign substances. Histology shows no tissue abnormalities beyond that associated with the barotrauma. Same with lung damage. Same with hemorrhaging in the eyes and mucous membranes."

Cuss listened with one ear as she droned on, spending most of the time wondering about Julie and her role in all this.

Ygo was right there with him. "She works for her dad. He founded Capit, a private firm specializing in corporate loss prevention. I'd guess she's here because a client has given up hope that the authorities will ever stop the piracy, like maybe it's time to take things into their own hands."

It was Julie who brought him back to the present when she asked, "How long did he live?"

"The hull breach caused a catastrophic pressure drop," said Shawna. "He lost consciousness in less than a minute and died soon after."

"Some people who know they're dying will scratch out a clue or say a final goodbye," said Royale. "Any evidence of that behavior?"

"Not that I saw," said Shawna. "You should confirm that with the case detective, though."

"Does he have any old dental work?" asked Mia. "Or surgeries that speak to his background?"

Cuss thought it was a good question. Dental work can hint at where a person was raised. Same with how an injury was repaired.

"Nope. He lived a good life in that regard. Clean teeth, no surgical scars."

"Any skin markings?" asked Cuss.

"One. A tattoo on his left shoulder." She tugged the blue cloth down to his waist and pulled his shoulder up, an easy maneuver in the low gravity.

The artwork was three geometric shapes, each a simple line drawing placed one inside the next. The outer shape was a circle. Inside that was a triangle. Inside that was a cross. Not like an X. This was more like a Christian cross.

The image wasn't familiar to Cuss. He glanced at the others' faces, looking for signs of recognition. But they all were leaning forward with scrunched brows, studying it themselves.

"The MFOD database doesn't have anything that's similar," said Ygo. "Plenty with circles and triangles and crosses, but nothing like this. I can't find an obvious link to any military unit or native tribe or gang membership."

"Other questions?" asked Shawna.

"Anything else we should know?" asked Julie.

Shawna shook her head. "How he died is clear. I can't comment on whether he was collateral damage during a robbery or the target of a murder. Nothing I found points one way or the other." She lifted the cloth back over Moby's head. "You all have access to the autopsy holos if you want more details." She glanced at a clock on the wall. "Sorry, but we're on a tight schedule today." She made a shooing motion, urging them to move to the warmth and clutter of the outer room.

After thanking Shawna, Cuss led the group out to the hallway and up the stairs. As they climbed, Ygo said, "Turns out it's Juan Luisa coordinating the case for Lagrange. When I contacted him, he said he wants to see you but was booked into the evening. You'll probably need to call him yourself."

Juan Luisa was a detective with Hermes' Community Patrol. He and Cuss had worked a tough investigation together the previous year. They'd bonded then, and Cuss had expected that their friendship would now give him priority access for a brief meeting. But he also appreciated that cops were pulled in different directions by competing demands.

He'd made it out to the hospital plaza at that point, Julie following at his shoulder, the two LOCU agents a dozen steps behind. He turned and spoke to the group. "I'm going to see an old friend now. A private meeting. I'm sure our paths will cross again soon. Until then, happy hunting." He gave a quick wave and resumed walking, now taking longer strides.

"Do you have time this afternoon to spend on the case?" called Julie, scurrying to keep up with him.

Cuss stopped again, wanting to be polite both for old times' sake, and also because he was attracted to this new version of her. "My friend is the case detective for Lagrange, so I'll be working this afternoon." He caught her eye. "Juan is a buddy, Julie, so I want to catch up with him alone. Maybe we can connect after? I'll brief you on what I learned."

"Juan Luisa?"

"That's right. Do you know him?"

"I've heard his name in connection with this case. Why don't you team with me this afternoon?"

Her determined expression was so cute that he found himself melting. For the briefest moment, he entertained the notion of letting her tag along. But if Juan was crazy busy, then a higher priority was to keep their meeting short and focused. "Maybe we can team at dinner?"

She pressed her lips together and pointed to a food kiosk with a half-dozen people waiting in line. "I'm going to grab a coffee. You have that long to change your mind."

As Julie walked away, Ygo said, "She's up to something, but I can't tell what."

Then a chime told Cuss that Juan was answering his call.

"Hey, Juan. It's been a while." After an exchange of pleasantries, Cuss got to it. "I'm chasing the doer on the *Dependable 8* murder. I hear you're looking at the theft. I was hoping you had time to compare notes. See if we can help each other."

"The short answer is yes, but probably not today. Believe it or not, I'm stuck on a piracy task force until late. The kickoff meeting starts in an hour and they've asked me to speak second. I'm scrambling to organize my notes."

Juan's "believe it or not" comment was a reference to rants the two of them shared when they'd worked together. They would disparage the committee-style approach to law enforcement, bragging of the lengths they'd take to avoid task force duty.

But Cuss was struggling to get his arms around the pirating hydra, saw Juan's involvement in the task force as an endorsement of sorts, and wondered if the gathering might help him get up to speed faster. "Any chance I can tag along?"

"It's not my meeting, so I'll have to ask. It's being organized by some hotshot from Earth who runs a corporate loss prevention company."

Cuss looked across the plaza at Julie, who was standing next to the food kiosk holding two coffees in disposable cups. She held one up with a smile, offering it to him.

"Would the hotshot be Julie Kapoeta?"

"That's right. How did you know?"

"I'll see you at the meeting." He closed the call.

Humbled, Cuss walked over to her and accepted the coffee. "You enjoyed that, didn't you."

"How many times did you copy off me in high school?"

He shrugged. "I don't know. A lot."

"How many times did I copy off you?"

He didn't respond, but the answer was "never."

"It's just like old times." She pointed across the pedestrian thoroughfare to a pod station. "I can't be late."

As they walked, Cuss could feel Mia's and Royales' eyes burning into the back of his head. "Would you consider inviting the two agents from the Lunar Organized Crime Unit? They're working the case as well."

She stopped and looked back at them. "I'm annoyed as hell because I sent invites to their director *twice* and never got a response. They aren't team players."

"I wouldn't disagree. But in their defense, the director just stepped down. Mix-ups happen during transitions."

"Whatever." She paused to think and then shook her head like she was denying her own words. "I want LOCU's participation. If these are good reps, let's go for it."

They turned to face the agents, and Cuss was momentarily distracted by Shawna Lewis scurrying past, calling "See you there" to Julie. The chief medical examiner would be in attendance.

Mia and Royale were staring at him through their sunglasses. Cuss waved them over. They approached warily, staying on opposite sides of him. He had to turn his head left and right as he spoke. "You are invited to a piracy task force meeting that starts in an hour up on Terra Deck." He looked at Julie. "At the Community Patrol station?"

She shook her head. "The Orini Hotel, room 114. It starts at sixteen hundred, so really closer to fifty minutes from now. There will be plenty of food and drink, a nice spread, no need to eat beforehand." Then her voice took on an edge. "After a few others speak, I'm going to be asking both of you to update us on what LOCU knows and what you have planned. If you attend, be ready to share. Do *not* play the 'it's confidential' or 'I have to check with my boss' game. Nothing like it. Spend the next fifty minutes getting permission or whatever else you need so you can speak freely." She flashed a tight smile. "See you there."

Turning, she led Cuss up the ramp and into line to catch a pod. The line was short. Shawna was already gone.

When it was their turn, they moved out on the loading platform. There, in the same way that a ski lift stages gondolas for skiers, the pod system presented much smaller travel cabins for people to ride in. Each pod could seat four in a compact open-air compartment, whisking passengers along special lanes to any location in the city.

The pods had facing seats designed to accommodate normal-size people. Julie climbed in first. Cuss scooted her all the way over and he sat in the facing seat, offset from her so he would have room to stretch his legs. As the pod got underway, he snugged himself into the corner, his body angled toward her, his huge arms draped across the top edge of the cabin, his hands hanging inside.

Julie sat back and looked at him like he was a piece of meat. "Goddamn, Cuss. You were an Adonis in high school and you've only gotten hotter. Since we'll be eating at the meeting tonight, can I accept your dinner invitation for tomorrow?"

He took a moment to study her. She was wearing a light blue top with black slacks over a trim figure. He'd thought of her as a nerd when they were younger, and while she still had that nerd vibe, her current style had a simple sophistication he found appealing.

"How have you been, Julie? What's happened in your life since way back when?"

She picked a piece of lint off her pant leg as she considered her response. "I grew up. Fell in love. Had a kid. A beautiful son, Glen. He's fourteen and thriving. His father got remarried six years ago." She looked into the distance and then returned her gaze to him. "I've mostly focused on work since then. I got a law degree after college, practiced for a couple of years, and then started working for my dad at Capit. Anyway, fast forward to today where I run the company."

She paused again, this time rubbing her fingers over her pant leg where the lint had been. "This task force leadership role is a big deal for me. It's a whole new business segment, one we hope to grow in the future. I'm all-in on making it work and am happy that you'll be participating."

"Who is your client?"

She nodded as if approving his thought process. "The one paying the bills drives the agenda, right? Here, that would be the Gastrow Group, a conglomerate that controls four shipping companies, two of which have been hit pretty hard over the past year. They're big enough to self-insure, which means they've been absorbing all the losses themselves."

"Are they the ones who put people on board their ships so Space Watch will rescue them?"

"They're not alone. It's common in the industry."

"If they just rescued the pilot and left the craft for the company to salvage, it would stop that game short."

"It's a practice that's been around for years. I think in the end, politicians enjoy campaign contributions more than common-sense laws. And it's far cheaper for the big players to pay lawmakers than it is to pay for salvage ops."

The pod entered the interdeck shaft and started the spiral climb up to Terra Deck.

"What's the plan for this afternoon?"

She shifted so her knees were pointing at his, almost touching. "It's based on the idea that if you get the right people in a room, someone will know the answer. Or a good process to follow to find one. So we share and brainstorm until we hear it."

"How do you know when that is?"

"That's the whole game. It's a mixture of gut feel, confidence in yourself, the buzz of the room, and dumb luck." She crossed her arms. "This will be my fourth task force. By that I mean where I organize it and guide the agenda. The first three were smaller. More local. This one is a test of everything I've done up to now."

"Are you nervous?"

"Scared to death. Who am I compared to the talent that will be in that room?"

The statement surprised him. She was extremely capable, and he never pictured her as anything but confident. "Do you have investigative experience? Or at least some training?"

"Some, but the job here is to act as a facilitator. I encourage participation and keep us centered on the goal. I don't offer solutions, *per se*. But when someone makes a good suggestion or important point, I highlight it to make sure the others hear it. Then I help the room distill the ideas down to next steps." She gave a quick grin. "I'm going with the old 'motive, means, and opportunity' structure from back when I read mysteries. Do you think that'll work?"

"Sure, why not?" He didn't have a better suggestion.

"I'm curious," asked Ygo. "Why did Shawna invite her to an autopsy review?"

Cuss wondered the same thing. Normally they were limited to investigators working a case. He chose not to ask. "How does Gastrow measure your success?"

She gave a broad smile. "These questions are so on point. It's fun to see your detective skills in action." Then she bit her lip. "You're going to hate this as a cop, but I've been hired to reduce piracy, not solve crimes. If I can achieve that with operational changes alone, then I will. That said, my approach will be to support law enforcement's pursuit of criminals because that's the more likely route to success. In the abstract, it's three steps: define the problem, develop a strategy the group thinks will solve it, and then ensure that plan is a priority for the government leaders who need to execute it."

He found himself being charmed by her manner. She had supreme self-confidence. But then a moment of self-doubt would peek through, a crack in the façade. And while her approach to stopping a crime spree that had stumped whole law enforcement agencies seemed naïve at best, somehow, he believed in her.

He let his eyes drift down her body, taking her in, enjoying the journey. When he returned to her face, he saw that his inspection had not gone unnoticed.

She didn't miss a beat. "What about you? What's been going on in your life?"

Cuss rarely opened up. But their common past and current affinity prompted him to share.

He'd been a young detective in Tallahassee, Florida. Married a year. Was driving through town with his wife, Becca, when a doer he'd been tracking ambushed him. Shots were fired. He killed the guy. A stray bullet from the doer killed Becca.

"Oh my God." Julie shifted seats so she sat next to him and began to stroke his arm. "I am so sorry."

"They say time heals all wounds. The truth is that it just dulls the pain."

Julie stayed quiet for most of a minute and then asked in a soft voice, "Is that why you became a murder specialist?"

The Interworld Marshals Service had grown to fifty-one field agents, and all of them did whatever was necessary in the moment. But each agent had a specialty or two that the director would use to guide individual assignments if he had the luxury of time: murder, kidnapping, terror, blackmail, espionage, theft. Cuss had never thought much about how Becca's death had shaped his current trajectory. But when Julie framed it the way she had, it made him wonder if there was something to it. He acknowledged her question with another shrug.

She slumped back in the seat. "We won't be spending any time on the murder in the meeting. I need the room to focus on the piracy."

"I'm pretty sure my doer is one of the pirates. We can help each other."

She chewed on her lower lip as she thought. "I can see that they're linked, so maybe we can work it in as a subitem. But the room has to push it there. I have to be neutral on everything."

Chapter 5

The pilot kept his eyes glued to the cockpit display, gauging the ship's progress as it converged on the bundle drifting through space: three big crates lashed together and wrapped in fine lattice netting. A tiny rocket engine was strapped to one end of the stack. It was cold, empty of fuel.

He heard pops and hisses as guidance thrusters edged his ship next to the crates. When he could see the bundle hovering alongside, seemingly stationary even though it and his ship were hurtling through space at thousands of kilometers per hour, he issued the command, "Open the cargo bay door."

The cockpit display switched to a view from inside the back of his craft. There was a different noise, the whirring hum of a motor lifting the big door that ran along the side of the craft. Through the opening, he first saw a bright field of stars on a pitch-black backdrop of empty space. As the door continued to rise, the crates came into view, floating in nothingness some twenty meters away.

A six-armed construction bot sat at the ready in the cargo bay. When the door motor quieted, the pilot gave the command to fetch. The bot pushed itself out of the cargo bay and across open space, a lightweight line trailing behind it. When it reached the bundle, it attached the line, signaled success, and held on as a winch reeled the bot and the crates back to the ship.

With the cargo bay door closed, the bot secured the load with heavy straps to prevent it from shifting in flight. As a safety precaution, it disconnected the rocket engine from the bundle and stored it separately. Finished with its tasks, it squatted into its carrier and turned off the lights.

"Mission complete," the pilot called to base, feeling a sense of accomplishment. "On my way home."

His partners had stolen the items sixty-eight days earlier, taking them from a delivery ship bound for Nova Terra. After strapping the crates together and wrapping them in netting, they'd used a custom rocket to send the bundle on a lazy ride away from the Moon. Like throwing a ball into the air, the tug of lunar gravity eventually slowed the bundle, turned it around in space, and pulled it back.

His partners had recorded the details of the flight path at the start of the journey, so his nav system could compute exactly where the crates would be on this celestial journey. And as he'd just proven for the umpteenth time, retrieving them was no more complicated than showing up on schedule.

His flight plan home appeared on the cockpit display. When he approved the details, the main drives fired, the thrust pushing him back into the seat cushions.

He'd arrive home in time for happy hour, the high point of his day. Settling back, he closed his eyes to nap.

Opening them again, he fished a flask out of his pocket and took a good pull, relishing the burn as the fiery liquid spilled down his throat. "I'm sure it's happy hour somewhere," he said before taking another swig.

. . .

Sitting at the back of the upscale hotel meeting room, Cuss noted furnishings that conveyed a certain elegance: tall doors, crystal chandeliers overhead, botanical tapestries hanging on the walls. As a counterpoint, practical features of the conference business were also evident: commercial carpeting, stackable chairs, a low stage in front that could be tucked away when not in use.

Detective Juan Luisa sat to his right, fidgeting, nervous. He was a small, muscular guy in his early fifties. Short, curly hair. Neatly trimmed mustache. Julie was about to call him up to speak and he was hating the delay, anxious to get it over with.

Up on the stage, Julie wowed the crowd with her charm. She'd done an impressive job of gathering law enforcement agencies. More than thirty representatives from nine organizations, fourteen people attending in person and the rest participating through hoverviews.

"It's wonderful to have the participation from Lagrange's Community Patrol and Nova Terra's police force," she began, motioning here and there in the room to acknowledge those in attendance.

Cuss agreed that both were key players for the group. They were involved in almost every case, whether it be receiving the first report of a crime, dealing with the locals who lost their expected delivery, chasing down leads on their respective worlds, or coordinating with off-world agencies also trying to solve the crime.

Since neither was equipped to chase criminals across the solar system, Julie had already invited the Interworld Marshals Service. She acknowledged Arron Gutierrez and Sara Beagley, both competent specialists in organized crime and major property theft. She didn't introduce Cuss, and he was happy to avoid attention. But since he'd chatted briefly with Arron and Sara when he'd arrived, he felt a moment of awkwardness at being left out.

Next, Julie acknowledged Space Watch, a division of the Near-Earth Monitoring Agency. They were a large quasi-military unit funded by the International Assembly of Earth, the present-day iteration of Earth's United Nations.

Space Watch was the service that rescued stranded ships if a pilot was aboard, putting them first on the scene in most cases of piracy. This meant they were the ones who saw evidence in its rawest form. The ones who asked the first questions. And, Cuss thought, his suspicious nature coming to the fore, the ones who could take a bit of this or that from the scene and not record it. Or even leave something behind that sent the investigation down a particular path.

Julie continued by acknowledging people from what Ygo called "alphabet agencies," organizations that went by acronyms. These tended to be based in a specific country or region and had a narrowly targeted mission. She began with LOCU, the Lunar Organized Crime Unit. Both Mia and Royale stood, Mia waved. Julie finished with a handful of esoteric agencies, two that Cuss had never heard of.

Done with the introductions, she summarized with "We assembled this group because, whether we know it or not, one of us has the answer. Over the next couple of hours, we'll have discussions where you'll get the opportunity to share your thoughts. Make suggestions. Brainstorm solutions." She waggled an index finger. "But no criticisms of others' ideas. We all need to listen carefully so we'll hear the answer when one of you makes that brilliant suggestion."

She paused, her hands clasped together in front of her as if she intended to take questions. She scanned the room, and her eyes fell on Cuss.

"Heads-up, buddy," said Ygo.

"Oh, and I'd like to introduce Cuss Abbott of the Interworld Marshals Service. He's the only one in the room assigned specifically to capturing Mr. Navarro's killer. Mr. Navarro was the pilot killed in the most recent robbery. Perhaps Marshal Abbott's perspective can inform us as we go. Or maybe our ideas will help him." She beamed at Cuss from across the room.

He blushed.

"Okay," said Julie. "Let's get started,"

Juan cleared his throat several times in a row as he prepared to stand.

"But before we start the formal agenda, I want to welcome Deputy Chief of Community Patrol Golda Kaetzel of Lagrange." She turned to the side stage and swung out an arm, moving it in a broad, sweeping motion that reminded Cuss of a game show hostess revealing a prize. A dignified woman joined Julie, midforties, small frame, brunette hair up in a tight bun, perfect makeup, smart uniform.

There was a smattering of applause around the room and a low groan next to him, the sound of a wild animal in its death throes.

"She's Juan's boss's boss's boss," said Ygo. "He's realizing she'll probably be here for his presentation."

Cuss felt the guy's pain. As a lieutenant in Hermes, Juan reported to a captain. His captain was in the audience, a dozen seats away. There was one captain on each of the city's twelve decks, and they reported to a city commander. Juan's commander was watching via hoverview. There was one commander for each of the four tube cities, and they reported to the deputy chief of Lagrange. She was now on stage.

The deputy chief spoke briefly, offering platitudes and encouragement with assurances of support from all levels of government. She finished with "I'm meeting with the governor later this evening over in Apollo to brief him on this important event. So unfortunately, I'll have to leave after the first presentations. I'll be participating as I travel, though, so I can deliver the latest updates to the governor when I report."

She took a seat in the front row.

Julie looked at Juan and nodded. "Let's begin our presentations with a report from Detective Juan Luisa of Lagrange's Community Patrol."

Juan sat unmoving for two heartbeats. When Cuss heard him whimper, he stood up and moved in front of the man, using his bulk to block the view from the crowd. He grabbed Juan by the arms and lifted him to his feet, moving his elbows to make it look as if he were smoothing the man's jacket.

"Listen up," Cuss hissed. "Begin by thanking the deputy chief. We all appreciate her support. Her leadership is vital to our success. Pile it on thick." He moved to the side and patted Juan on the back, pushing him forward at the same time.

As Juan zombie-walked to the stage, Cuss headed for the food table in the back corner. He ignored the display of sweet and salty snacks, skipped over the fruits and veggies, and made for the drinks. Specifically, the coffee urn.

The coffee cups were the dainty ceramic kind used at tea parties. Filling one with hot brew, he leaned against the back wall near the coffee urn. The cup looked tiny in his ham hands. He drank and watched the action.

Juan took the stage. To Cuss's delight, he succeeded in improvising a few suck-up lines for the deputy chief. Then he began his formal presentation with a definition of space piracy: acts of robbery and violence committed by shipborne attackers on another ship and its crew during spaceflight.

A big hoverview display opened behind Juan, and he worked through a series of charts and tables that detailed the last eighteen months of piracy—the timespan of the surge—focusing on those incidents that impacted Lagrange in some fashion. He'd organized the data in different ways for people to view: the categories of goods stolen, the businesses impacted by the loss, the points of origin for the ships, the shipping companies involved…

Cuss found it mind numbing. And Ygo had already sliced and diced the data every way possible. He drained his cup and went in for a refill.

"What did you decide about Mr. Navarro?" asked Shawna Lewis as she approached the table. She picked up a coffee cup, waited for him to finish, filled hers, and began a cream-and-sugar ritual.

"What's to decide?" he replied.

"He didn't set off any bells in your head?"

"Not so much. He did you?" A question like that from the chief medical examiner definitely set off bells. Now he was interested.

She stirred her drink and tasted it before answering. "My intuition says the doers didn't kill a random pilot. They were targeting him specifically. But I can't tell you why I think that. Maybe because it seemed so deliberate and unnecessary." She shrugged and looked back at Juan on the stage. "It's just a feeling."

"Did this feeling come from someone at the autopsy?" asked Ygo.

Cuss took the thought in a slightly different direction. "I've never been to a criminal autopsy review where someone wasn't law enforcement or a government official."

"You're talking about Julie?" Shawna pointed to the floor. "She'd invited me to this meeting and I hadn't responded, so she came to my office to persuade me." Shawna leaned over the table and viewed the assortment of cookies. "She was honest enough to say my title was important to the cause and that the food would be worth it. Somewhere in there I let on that I'd be doing the Navarro review. She said she wanted to meet the people who were coming, possibly to invite them to this meeting. I teased her by suggesting she'd have to be there to meet them. Goddamn if she didn't accept."

She made her selection, took a bite, and continued as she chewed. "Anyway, I've had researchers, academics, and family members come to autopsies. Let's see, at least two reporters. It's mostly law enforcement and government types, but not exclusively."

They chitchatted a bit more while she refilled her cup and loaded a plate with cookies.

As she returned to her seat, Royale rose and approached the table. He picked up a coffee cup but didn't make any effort to fill it. He moved near Cuss. "It hadn't clicked with me that you're tracking the killer. I was aware that you're a specialist. But with the task force and all, I figured they'd pulled you in on the larger effort."

"We can all work together," said Cuss.

Applause drew their attention to the front of the room. Juan had finished his presentation, and Julie, now standing next to him, was calling for questions and discussion.

"Don't you think it's just a robbery gone wrong? Maybe the pilot surprised the doers. Or a new guy let his nerves get the better of him?"

"Is that what you think?"

The LOCU agent shook his head. "I'm just trying to make sense of it."

"Who are you liking for the thefts?"

"Trust me, if I knew, I'd be chasing them there, not hanging around here." Royale put the coffee cup down, unused. "People are acting like you're sure to solve it. Who are *you* liking?"

Cuss studied Royale while he thought how to answer, hating the sunglasses on him as much as he hated them on Mia. "I only caught the case yesterday, so I'm still getting up to speed. You're way ahead of me on this."

Royale nodded. "I'm sure that won't last. Happy hunting." He returned to his seat.

While Cuss reflected on the awkward conversation, Juan made a beeline for him from the stage. He was grinning, clearly happy to be done. He grabbed a doughnut from the table, took a bite, and washed it down with a glass of juice. "Thanks for the kick in the butt."

"You did a great job," said Cuss. "You had the attention of the group. I'm sure the deputy chief was pleased."

"Think so? It's hard for me to tell from up there."

"You did well. You can relax."

Julie announced the next speaker, a detective from Nova Terra's police force.

Cuss drew Juan's attention back to him. "You were the first onto Moby Navarro's ship. Mind if I pick your brain?"

"The first one aboard after it was brought here. Space Watch made the virgin run."

"Had they worked it?"

Juan tilted his head in a kind of shrug. "When they discovered a body, they did a basic scene scan, backed out, and piloted the ship here. I reviewed their feed and didn't see anything unusual in their procedure."

"The ship's archive was empty. Did you remove any hardware?"

"You know me better than that." He sounded hurt. "The feed tray was missing when I boarded. The ensign running the escort ship swore none of his crew touched it. I'm assuming it was the pirates covering their tracks."

"It was a good move," said Cuss.

"They're all broadcast feeds," said Ygo.

"Why doesn't corporate have copies?" asked Cuss.

"I'm no expert on this," said Juan. He'd finished his doughnut and was scanning the assortment for his next selection. "Dependable Delivery is a subsidiary of the Gastrow Group, and apparently their central archive has been plagued with a bug. Feeds are getting mislabeled, even disappearing. They first thought it was incompetence by a new hire. Then they were sure it was faulty electronics until they replaced a bunch of equipment. Now they think it's something malicious."

"And the feed from *Dependable Delivery 8* is gone?"

Juan nodded. "The piece from this last trip."

"I'm going to contact Gastrow," said Ygo. "I wonder if the ship thefts and deleted feed segments match one-for-one."

Cuss liked the idea. Leads were sparse and it was somewhere to start.

On stage, the Nova Terra cop was presenting information similar to what Juan had discussed, only noting the impacts to the Moon instead of Lagrange. Cuss saw an item on the display that mentioned modes of forced entry. It sparked a thought. "Did the explosives expert learn anything from the hatch?"

Juan nodded. "She thinks it was something called a seeker. You stretch this flexible loop around a hatch frame and activate it. The charges move around, searching for the pin points on their own, center over them, and then blow." He mimed an explosion with his hands.

"The police and military have a version for tactical entry," said Ygo. "There's also an industrial version for precision blasting."

"Was there a tracer?" Cuss asked Juan. The tactical versions had microscopic bits in the specialty explosives that were detectable after detonation. The bits identified the product, the lot number, date purchased and, most important, the name of the purchaser.

Juan shook his head. "It was a generic."

"That's industrial," said Ygo. "Construction, excavation, and mining companies load their own."

"Huh," said Cuss to both of them. Ygo's comment sparked a different thought. "The doers used a high-powered laser with a beam cutoff. Does that say military or industrial to you?"

"Probably both," said Juan.

"Agreed," said Ygo.

"Not a lot to go on." Cuss filled his dainty cup for the third time and watched the presentation. After a few moments of quiet, he asked his favorite question. "Who are you liking for it?" Then he interrupted himself. "Any theories on why they killed the pilot?"

"As I understand it, their MO is to use the hull breach to trap the pilots in their quarters. Most of the pilots involved say they were warned to stay there. Maybe your guy did something that spooked them. Maybe it was a new crew who was easily spooked. Maybe they murdered him." Juan shook his head. "All I have are guesses." He looked up at the stage. "Let's talk later. I need to be seen helping with the discussion."

As Juan returned to his seat, Cuss stayed at his perch near the coffee urn. It was a new twist on an old trick he'd learned in his twenties. At crowded parties, hang out in the kitchen near the refrigerator. It keeps you close to the beer and it pretty much guarantees that you'll see everyone else before the end of the night.

The next presenter was a captain from Space Watch who began with an interesting topic: scanning ships for stolen goods. They had agreements with Lagrange and Nova Terra that allowed them to scan craft on approach to those worlds. While Space Watch's motivation was to recover goods for member nations on Earth, they passed on leads to the locals in exchange for the access.

"Our scanners read ID tags and compare them to a database of stolen goods," said the Space Watch captain. "Tags are embedded in pretty much everything and are hard to mask if we can get close enough, say half a kilometer or less."

The big display behind the captain showed a simulation of a Space Watch ship scanning a freighter in orbit above the Moon. "The challenge is maintaining the quality of the database itself, mostly because of human misbehavior. Items reported stolen are sometimes recovered but never removed from the list. There are items on the list that were never stolen, simply misplaced and later found. And then there's malicious actions, like deliberately adding stock items to the list to degrade its value."

He went on to say that if they detained a ship, searched it, and didn't find stolen goods, repercussions came back hard on the crew and the service. "Newer data has the most value," he concluded. "We used to remove items from the list when they reached four weeks past the theft. To combat the surge in piracy, we extended that to six weeks, and false positives are climbing. It's a problem."

He also discussed the pirates' modus operandi, echoing Juan's story that the doers trapped the pilots in their quarters using rapid decompression from a seeker explosive loop. Pilots not already in their rooms were given a warning to shelter before the hull was breached. Based on pilot reports, the doers dressed in industry-standard pressure suits, and cut comms within seconds of boarding, isolating the pilots. They took the feed archive hardware and the cargo, leaving the ship and pilot unharmed.

Except once.

"Of the twenty-eight assaults using this MO in the past two years," said the Space Watch captain, "there has been just one fatality."

"That would be Santiago 'Moby' Navarro," said Ygo.

Julie joined the captain on the stage and called for questions and discussion. That's when Mia rose from her seat and headed toward Cuss and the food table.

Cuss watched her approach, trying not to smile as he thought of his "hang out and see everyone" strategy.

"Mind if I squeeze in?" she asked as she picked up a cup.

His perch against the wall was a good three paces from the coffee urn. "By all means," he said without moving.

She filled her cup.

Cuss waited.

She turned to him. "I have an idea that's a little out there. Mind if I bounce it off you?"

"Of course." He kept his attention on the stage. Looking at her would only raise his blood pressure.

She stood next to him against the wall. "Suppose we analyze the thefts and figure out the perfect shipment, one the pirates will definitely want. For that flight, I take the pilot's place, remain vigilant, and when they attack, I take them down."

"Oh, lord," said Ygo.

Cuss couldn't decide whether to laugh, sigh, or play along. "Isn't the piracy rate something like one in every hundred-some flights? Are you prepared to ride a flight every day for however long, waiting for it to happen?"

"More like one in every two hundred," said Ygo.

Mia shook her head. "If we analyze the goods they target, really learn their market, we can tempt them with a sweet load. We let the manifest leak in a believable fashion. Make the flight be on one of the ships they prefer, on a route and time and destination they prefer. A proper analysis lets us change the odds."

"She's not wrong," said Ygo. "It could shift the odds to *maybe* one in twenty. Still a lot of trips, though."

"If we know the loads and ships and times they'll hijack," said Cuss, "maybe we should use that knowledge to lower their success rate. Shuffle the ships. Scramble the loads. Like that."

Mia folded her arms defensively. "That's a bureaucratic answer. Temporary at best. I need to find a permanent solution soon or Royale becomes my boss."

Chapter 6

O utside the Orini Hotel, Cuss followed the pedestrian thoroughfare away from the hustle and bustle of the town center, heading toward the quieter setting of the Baylight Suites. The food at the task force dinner had been tasty, the setting pleasant. But Julie hadn't been great company, spending most of the meal stressing about the group and her agenda.

He'd given her moral support throughout the meal, chatted with a few attendees, had a slice of pie for dessert. After agreeing to meet her the next evening, he'd cut out, heading for bed so he could chip away at his growing sleep deficit.

He'd walked two blocks, his meal just starting to settle, when Ygo said with some urgency, "I think you have a tail. Test at the grocery mart?"

Up ahead, Cuss saw a sign for GG's Market, a greengrocer at the end of the next block. "Got it."

Keeping a brisk pace, he walked past GG's main entrance and continued for the length of the store, studying the inside layout through the big front windows. After turning the corner at the intersection, he entered the market through a second door on that side, hidden from his suspected tail. He walked to the back of the store, traversed its length, and then worked his way forward, putting himself near the main entrance.

He turned away from the front windows and pretended to inspect lettuce in a display bin. "Show me," he said to Ygo.

The woman next to him thought he was talking to her and held up the head of lettuce she'd been examining. He looked at it, smiled as he gave her a nod of thanks, and moved over to a bin of onions and leeks.

His lens came alive with a scene from outside the store, a view looking back the way he'd come. It was dark, typical for this time of night. Foot traffic was light.

Ygo zoomed in on a man dressed in a black shirt and black pants. He stood on the sidewalk, hands in his pockets, feigning interest in a shop window display. While Cuss watched, the man looked up the street toward the grocery mart, stared for a couple of seconds, and then returned his attention to the shop display. After a wait, he looked again. And then again.

"He stopped walking the moment you turned the corner. I can't see that he has a partner. Don't know what tech he has."

"Who is he?"

"Georgio Navarro from Chiva, Spain. Arrived in Hermes yesterday. Coincidentally employed at Valencia Catering on Deck 9."

"Navarro and Valencia."

"That's right. Moby is a Navarro, and Chiva is a small town in the foothills of Spain just outside of Valencia. I'm suddenly curious if that place has something to do with the thefts and murder."

"Me, too." Cuss pretended to shop while he waited for Georgio to approach, frustrated because the man should have followed.

Patience was a virtue when stalking intelligent creatures. Cuss knew he should continue to wait and, eventually, Georgio would act. But he was too tired to be patient, and he feared the man would turn and leave before they had a chance to talk.

"How far to the next ute?" he asked Ygo, pronouncing it as "yoot." Utes were the city's utility tunnels, the below-deck shafts that carried air, water, waste, comms, and power throughout the city. There were ute entryways every few blocks, each with a restricted-access door, making them his go-to choice when he wanted to confront someone out of the public eye.

"Three blocks on this side." Ygo paused. "But you've lost him. Why not just go to bed?"

"He's following for a reason. I want to know why."

Before Ygo could continue the debate, Cuss left the market by the front door. Outside, he stood on the sidewalk and pretended to look for something in his pockets, the improvisation designed to give Georgio plenty of time to react. Then he started down the street, away from the man and toward the ute, keeping a modest pace.

The ute door was crafted to look like decorative molding on the exterior of the building. Vines hanging from the wall covered the top portion. So even though Ygo gave Cuss a heads-up as he neared the door, he still missed it and walked past. Ygo had to back him up and direct him step-by-step across a flower bed to reach it.

Ygo unlatched the door and Cuss pushed it open. The door swung in. Lights clicked on inside, casting a white glow through the door crack and across the flower bed.

"I want to be sure he sees it," said Cuss. He stepped inside but held the door so it would stay open, the light a beacon in the dark for his tail.

"Okay, he's seen it," said Ygo.

Cuss let go of the door, but as it swung shut, it caught on a vine and wouldn't close all the way. He began to clear the blockage but then decided to leave it. The light spilling out through the crack would guide Georgio to the door.

Like the other utes he'd used, the door led into a stark, cement-like bunker. He scanned the small chamber for a weapon. To his left was a gray slab wall. Straight ahead was a tunnel big enough for him to walk through. It was packed with different-size ducts carrying the utility network for the city.

The wall to his right held a field-station display for maintenance workers. And just like the other utes he'd been in, below the display were shallow shelves holding an assortment of tools, items left for the techs.

Squatting, he considered a longish piece of pipe sitting across the back of the top shelf, but decided the bunker was too small to wield it effectively. There was a hammer on that same shelf, but hammers were short and had an awkward weight distribution. His gaze fell to a pipe wrench on the middle shelf. Picking it up, he swung it back and forth, approving its length and heft.

"Hurry," said Ygo.

With the pipe wrench in hand, Cuss tucked in behind the door and waited for his stalker's entry. He didn't want to hurt the guy, someone who hadn't done anything wrong, yet. But a stranger tailing an Interworld Marshal did so for a reason. If Cuss wasn't prepared for violence, if he wasn't ready to react instantly in self-defense, he wouldn't survive the job.

"Here he is," said Ygo.

The door wiggled. When Cuss saw Georgio's fingers curl around its edge, his heart rate spiked. His lens came alive with a feed sent by Ygo. He could see himself standing there, staring at the edge of the door, pipe wrench cocked like he was preparing to swing a baseball bat.

The door opened farther. A foot and leg moved inside. Georgio's head peeked around and pulled back. His other hand came forward, leading the way. It held a knife. Not a hunter's knife or tactical knife or switchblade. It was a small paring knife like you'd find in a cook's kitchen.

When Cuss saw the knife, his attitude hardened. The man was playing for keeps, leaving him no choice but to respond in kind.

Ygo dropped the lights just as Georgio committed to his entry. Cuss, his lens adjusting on the fly so he could see in the dark, swung the pipe wrench at the man's head. But Georgio lifted his arm when the lights went out, perhaps by reflex, maybe in response to the swish of the tool moving through the air. Whatever the reason, his action placed his forearm in the path of the wrench.

The blow was solid. Cuss could feel it through the handle of the tool, could hear the sickening crack of breaking bone. Georgio dropped the knife and howled.

The lights came on. Cuss kicked the knife away, his wrench drawn back for a finishing blow. But he hesitated when he saw Georgio on his knees, bent forward, moaning, cradling his damaged arm with his good hand.

"What the fuck, man," Georgio wailed, looking up at Cuss from the ground. "You broke my arm!"

"You started it. Why are you following me?"

"I didn't start anything," he cried. "Jesus, it hurts."

Cuss grabbed a handful of hair and pulled Georgio's head up.

The man screamed.

"You threatened me with a knife. Remember?"

"I didn't know what this place was." His crying made him choke on his words. "I was scared."

"You always carry a blade?"

"No! I grabbed it from the kitchen on my way out the door."

The kitchen comment confused Cuss. While he believed the man had fight left in him, he let go of his hair. "What do you want?"

"To help you find my grandpa's killer."

"What?" Now Cuss was completely confused.

"Santiago Navarro," said Georgio. Wincing, he looked down at his damaged arm before returning his gaze to Cuss. "Moby Navarro."

"Checking," said Ygo. "He is the grandson. Interesting." Then, "I've paged a med cart. It will be here in one minute."

Cuss mentally kicked himself. Not because he'd broken the guy's arm. That was an appropriate penalty for threatening an Interworld Marshal with a knife. He was annoyed because he couldn't interrogate the guy while he received medical attention, and that meant delay.

"Speak," said Cuss. He'd use every second until the med cart arrived.

"Can I sit? I feel weak."

"Oh, for Christ's sake, sit and speak. Be fast."

Georgio lowered himself to his butt, whimpering quietly. It took him a moment to get comfortable. Cuss was fast approaching the limit of his patience.

"My cousin Aurora owns Valencia Catering on Deck 9 here in Hermes. She called me when she saw a catering job posted for a cop's antipirate meeting. We decided she should offer a generous spread at a cheap price so she'd win the bid, and then we could be there to listen in and learn how to get more attention for grandpa's murder."

"You're serious?" It sounded too crazy to be made up.

"Completely. She won the job, so I flew here to help. She was stocking the food table earlier today when she heard the lady say that you were doing Moby's murder.

You're Marshal Abbott, right? So when you left the meeting early, I chased after you so we could talk."

"You chased me with a knife."

"Sorry, man. I've never been to Lagrange before. I don't know anything about this place. Where I live in Chiva, there are areas you never go without protection."

"What do you want to tell me about Moby?"

"That he was murdered."

"He died during a robbery," replied Cuss. "Why do you call it murder? What proof do you have?"

"The med cart is here," Ygo told him.

"I don't have proof. But grandpa told me before his last trip that he'd said the wrong thing to the wrong person. He was sad. Worried. I could see it in his face."

"That's it?"

"There are other bits and pieces. Aurora has more. My arm hurts so much I can hardly think."

"Stand up," Cuss told him. He hooked a hand under Georgio's good arm and helped him to his feet, but since the man was using his good arm to support the injured one, he groaned and whimpered during the process.

"I have a med cart for you outside. The pain will be gone very soon." Cuss paused, knowing the wait was torture for the guy, but he needed Georgio to hear the next part. "You can tell the doctor that you fell and that Marshal Abbott will corroborate. Or you can tell them you attacked me with a knife and I broke your arm. That one lands you in jail and hands me a ton of report work. I'd like to have you free so you can help with your grandpa. It's your choice, but I strongly suggest you go with the first story."

Cuss supported Georgio as they walked out the door, across the flower bed, and to the automated medical cart waiting at the edge of the pedestrian thoroughfare. As he helped Georgio into the seat, he said, "It will take you to the nearest clinic. You'll get the fastest relief by answering its questions and submitting to its tests. I'll see you and Aurora tomorrow morning. Arrange it with her. I'll call you at seven thirty for a meeting at eight."

"Where?"

"At Valencia Catering on Deck 9. I want both of you there. I'll call at seven thirty for a meeting at eight."

"You said that."

"And you heard it." Cuss patted the top of the med cart and he stepped back. It purred away, cruising down the pedestrian thoroughfare, weaving to avoid walkers. Cuss watched until it turned a corner at the next block. Then he looked back at the ute door hung up on the vine. Walking to it, he pulled the problem plant to the side and held it until the door clicked shut.

Starting up the thoroughfare, he walked in the same direction as the med cart, traveling the last few blocks to his room at the Baylight Suites.

. . .

Cuss stepped through the door. As it closed behind him, he scanned the room, confirming what he'd come to expect from the Baylight chain: clean and comfortable suites. He emptied the contents of his pockets onto the side table in the foyer, then he took off his sport coat, shirt, and pants and let them fall in a pile on the floor.

Walking into the kitchen in socks and boxers, he grabbed a beer from the refrigerator, downed half of it, and belched. Then he turned his attention to the brightly colored delivery box on the counter next to the sink. Opening it, he reveled in the smell of chicken fried to crispy deliciousness. Drumstick, thigh, and breast. His mouth started to water.

He reached for the drumstick, mentally praising Ygo for his foresight. The normal-size portions at the task force dinner just weren't enough for a big guy like him. And he slept better on a full stomach.

He leaned over the sink and started eating. "What are you listening to?" he asked Ygo between bites.

The room filled with sounds of a jazz quartet playing an engaging progression. Not his thing, but it fit the mood well enough. He nodded his approval.

After devouring the chicken, he grabbed a fresh beer from the refrigerator and moved into the bedroom. He looked in the closet to see what Ygo had readied for the next day. Blue button-down shirt, sturdy black pants, and gray blazer. His uniform. The clothes he'd dropped by the door would be cleaned and returned to the *Nelly Marie*.

The bed had eight pillows leaning against the headboard. Cuss shoved all but two onto the floor, and positioned those two behind his back and head. Taking a sip of beer, he sighed, happy to be spending the night on Terra Deck. It meant he could sleep, wash, eat, dress, and everything else in a familiar gravity. The lifestyle he preferred. Something he couldn't experience more often because of his job.

The Marshals Service provided the *Nelly Marie* as a mobile home of sorts, one he shared with Ygo. The ship was new and well-appointed, with room enough for both of them. And to the envy of many in the service, Lagrange was their home port. They were free to park in Hermes, Athena, Demeter, or Apollo. They could rotate daily if they wished. But no matter which spaceport they chose, it meant they would be living in a weightless environment.

After a few years of living in zero gee, Cuss finally tired of the hassle. There were more steps to every task. Pulling on pants and socks had him floating in circles in the middle of the room. Showering meant being in a closed cubical, splashed with a barely adequate soapy mist, and surrounded by a whooshing suction that pulled moisture out of the air. And eating from pouches and covered cups wasn't nearly as satisfying as a tasty meal over a sink.

So he'd gamed the system, finding reasons to be temporarily docked on Earth or the Moon, or to at least be underway where acceleration gave him weight. But then he'd learned that Ygo preferred weightlessness, even needed it to some extent. Otherwise, the man had to rely on his special capsule-bed-chair device that alternately floated him in liquid, suspended him on dry netting, and levitated him on jets of air to ensure his skin remained healthy.

The solution they converged on was to dock in the various ports of Lagrange as the Interworld Marshals Service expected of them, providing Ygo the weightless world he sought. Several times a week in return, Ygo provided Cuss very nice accommodations on a gravity deck near wherever he was engaged that night.

Cuss never asked how Ygo pulled it off. The expense. Marshals Service approval. The gruesome details. He'd learned long ago to trust his partner.

"How is it going with Georgio?" he asked Ygo.

Ygo sent him a feed of Georgio at the clinic. He was sitting in a chair with his right arm inside a small rejuv machine, a silver box with black leads attached to the outside.

Cuss looked at Georgio dispassionately for the first time. The notes in the display said he was twenty-six years old, younger than Cuss would have guessed. He was bulky in the chest. Thin waist. Hair trimmed short. Mustache that connected down to a goatee. His eyes were closed, his relaxed state likely the result of medication.

"His right ulna had a bad fracture," said Ygo. "They've repaired it and are giving him regenerative therapy. He'll be sore for a week and in a brace for three."

"Which story did he go with?"

"He fell."

"Good." Cuss took a sip of beer. "So Moby's been murdered, and out of the woodwork come his grandchildren, Georgio and Aurora. By definition there has to be a generation in between."

"I've only started digging. So far, I've learned that Moby worked for the Gastrow Group's propulsion division outside Valencia. He spent his career in maintenance, directing projects for about fifteen years and then managing a small subdivision for the last decade before retirement."

"And then he went on to ride delivery ships."

"It appears so," said Ygo. "Anyway, he had two sons."

"How old was he again?"

"Moby? Eighty-two. His sons are Oliver and Nick. Oliver is Georgio's father. He died nine years ago. Nick is Aurora's father. He's alive and well. Here's an archive clip."

Cuss's feed changed to show a man at a workbench. The notes said it was Nicholas "Nick" Navarro, fifty-seven years old. He was working on a complex device the size of a bale of hay, a tubular framework containing canisters and pumps and manifolds and nozzles.

He had a pleasant face. Bright eyes. Square chin. Hair slicked back. Smudge on one cheek. Cuss's gaze was drawn to his hands, the calloused mitts of someone who made his living gripping and twisting and pulling things.

"He owns a small company in Nova Terra. Thrust Tech. They make small rocket engines for niche users."

"What does that mean?"

"Small rockets like you see him working on. You strap them onto things to move them around in space. Think researchers using them to position equipment on the cheap, or hobbyists making racing rigs, or end-of-worlders and their home-brewed emergency habitats."

"He must be a smart man." Cuss drained his beer and set the bottle on the side table. "What have we learned about Aurora?"

His feed switched again, this time showing a woman unloading a tray of food onto the serving table. She was working hard, her expression one of concentration. The notes said she was thirty-one years old.

"This is from earlier today. She's asleep right now."

Cuss watched her for a bit, finding it hypnotic. She had black hair pulled into a ponytail. A delicate oval face. Soft features. Brown eyes. Smooth skin. Trim figure. Pretty. Her eyebrows were a little bushier than most women kept them. For some reason he found them mesmerizing. His mind began to wander.

"She started Valencia Catering two years ago," said Ygo. "The company paperwork has Moby's name all over it, so I'm guessing he either gave or loaned her the funds. She's been successful in growing the business. Getting the task force catering job is proof of that."

Cuss continued to watch her work until Ygo interrupted. "And then there's the task force."

"What about it?" Cuss's sharp response reflected his annoyance. He wanted to watch Aurora.

"When dinner was over, Mia presented her idea to the group."

Cuss sat up on the bed, now engaged. "The perfect load? How did they react?"

"The meeting came alive when she suggested the idea," said Ygo. "They argued about the nature of the doers. Who they are, how they behaved, what they wanted. They argued about whether the doers might have more than one MO. And they argued about what they'd want next based on what they'd taken so far."

"Does anyone know who they are?"

"No one is admitting it. Different agencies have their eyes on this or that player. But they mostly agreed there's one group responsible for the organized piracy. The raids have a distinct MO."

"Did they agree on the perfect load?"

"They eventually converged on the idea of shipping motors to run the pumps and compressors the pirates already stole. It adds big value to them."

"Who suggested that?"

"Royale, of all people."

"And Mia went along with it?"

"There were so many people talking, with ideas being introduced, then modified, then discarded, then brought back by someone else, I don't think she associated it with him after a while."

"Do you think she'll actually follow through?"

"She's already organized three loads of motors to be shipped from Earth to Nova Terra, spaced far enough apart that she can get back from the Moon to ride the next one.

After that, the decision will be out about the next LOCU director."

"How did Royale respond when she agreed to the final plan?"

"He cheered her on. Stood and applauded."

"Because it's making him look good? Or because it's making her look desperate?"

"Maybe both?"

Chapter 7

Feeling refreshed after a good night's sleep, Cuss stepped into the shower, put the stream on full blast, and reveled as gravity sent cascades of hot water spilling over him. He used the small bar of soap provided by the Baylight Suites to lather up, then he rinsed and repeated.

He was dressing when Ygo said, "It's seven thirty. Ready for Georgio?"

Cuss went into the kitchen and poured a cup of coffee while Ygo placed the call. He'd opened a breakfast pastry and was heating it up when Georgio finally responded.

"Sorry, man. The pain meds are making me groggy. I'm up, though."

"Are we good for eight?" asked Cuss.

"We are. Deck 9. Valencia Catering."

"Aurora will be there?"

"She will." Georgio paused, but not long enough for Cuss to speak. "Have you eaten, Marshal? We'd love to serve you breakfast. We can talk while we eat."

"I could eat." That statement was pretty much always true.

"Aurora will make her famous tortilla Española. It's a traditional Spanish breakfast. See you at eight?"

Cuss's mouth watered as he nodded. "I'm on my way."

. . .

Valencia Catering was in a commercial building located a block from the interdeck shaft, giving the company convenient access to other decks and their hungry customers. As Cuss approached the building entrance, Ygo said, "They're on the second floor. No need to pay ground-floor rent when you don't offer eat-in service."

Cuss bypassed the lift and made for the stairwell. At the first landing, he stepped into the hall, a stark passageway with gray unfinished surfaces and no adornment of any kind. Though it looked like a basement tunnel, it smelled more like grandma's kitchen back in the day, a wonderful mélange of baked, fried, and savory aromas.

"To your right," said Ygo.

As he started in that direction, a door opened and Georgio leaned out, motioning to him. "This way, Marshal."

Cuss saw the brace on Georgio's arm when he waved, and his cheeks flushed. He'd never shared a meal with someone he'd just bludgeoned.

He fist-bumped Georgio's uninjured hand and followed him into Valencia Catering. The front room was a small, homey space. Pictures on the wall showed plates of food, perhaps dishes clients could order. There were plants around the perimeter with enough dust on the leaves to tell

Cuss they were fake. A dining table in the center of the room had eight chairs tucked beneath.

"This is the tasting room," said Georgio. "Corporate clients tend to order from the menu and trust the company's reputation. But private parties, people planning weddings, birthdays, and whatnot, like to come in and sample everything." He walked through the room to the back wall and paused at a second door. "We'll be eating on the patio."

The door at the back of the room led into a small commercial kitchen: stovetop heating elements, ceramic grill, flame broiler, deep-fat fryer. Fist-size knobs in a row along the front. Silver exhaust hoods overhead. Ovens below.

Cuss followed Georgio through the back of the kitchen and out to the patio.

As they passed through the kitchen, Aurora was staring intently into an open oven. She was bent at the waist, her back to them, her attractive bottom up in the air. Cuss looked for longer than was polite. Stared, actually.

On the patio, Georgio motioned to a small table. "Have a seat. Can I get you coffee?"

Cuss nodded. "Black, please."

Georgio went inside.

Before Cuss sat, he viewed the patio and concluded it was a fancy name for a standard building balcony. This one overlooked the pedestrian thoroughfare. While it was just wide enough for the table and chairs, it felt comfortable, with paper lanterns, strings of lights, and flowering plants adding to the ambiance.

Leaning over the railing, he looked to his left and saw a long row of commercial buildings covered by flowering vines cascading in layers from above like the ruffles of an old-time dress.

He looked to the right and his heart jumped. Royale was standing on the corner across and down the street, looking up at him. Cuss zoomed his lens for a closer look, but the LOCU agent ducked out of sight behind the building.

Ygo found him in seconds on a public monitoring feed. It was Royale, no question. He was hurrying down a side street, head lowered, hands in his pockets, cheeks bulging from clenching his jaw. All pointing to intense frustration. Or aggravation. Or anger.

"What's his game?" asked Cuss.

"Mia wanted to follow you, too. Maybe it's all they know how to do."

"That's twice he's run away. Next time I'm gonna chase him down." Cuss shook his head as he sat. "I can see why Mia finds him annoying."

"Maybe annoying is a LOCU hiring requirement."

Cuss smiled. "How's her project going?"

"She rides her first shipment tomorrow. The idea has taken on a life of its own. Victory has a thousand fathers, as they say. People are clamoring to join her, to share the credit, to be part of the success. So far, she's turned them all away."

"She's going without backup? That's dumb." Cuss crossed his arms. "It's not leadership."

Georgio stepped out from the doorway, interrupting their conversation. He was using his good hand to carry a small tray holding a carafe of coffee and three cups, balancing the load from underneath with his braced hand. He set the tray on the table, placed a cup in front of Cuss, and poured.

Cuss took a sip. Hot, flavorful, strong: the trifecta. He nodded. "Hits the spot."

He was sipping again when Aurora appeared. He grinned when she smiled at him. She was even more attractive in person. Her gaze was electric.

She continued to smile as she reached a hand across the table. "Hello Marshal, I'm Aurora. Thank you for coming."

He stood and took her hand. "Cuss, please." She squeezed rather than shook. But it was a firm squeeze with good eye contact.

Still holding his hand, she looked at Georgio, her face shifting from happy to stony. "We're not set." She turned back to Cuss, her face smiling again. "Excuse us. Back in a flash."

They both stepped inside and Georgio returned in seconds with silverware and napkins. He set the table, went inside, and returned with glasses of ice water. He went inside again, and after most of a minute, he returned with Aurora. She was carrying three heaping plates in one hand, a skill likely developed in a past life as a waitress. She placed them at each setting and sat. Georgio had a platter with breakfast meats and a selection of breads. He plopped it in the center of the table and sat as well.

The food was presented beautifully. Tortilla Española turned out to be eggs mixed with potatoes and onions and herbs, cooked on a stovetop. There were no tortillas anywhere, which confused him. He thought about asking, but they appeared to be waiting for him to start eating, so he took a bite.

"It's wonderful," he told Aurora. "Delicious." It was.

She rewarded him with a wink, and then she and Georgio joined him in eating.

He found himself rushing through the meal, wanting to talk business, but knowing that polite people wait until the end of a meal before discussing weighty topics.

Aurora slowed him down. "Cuss, do you mind if we talk while we eat? They're releasing Moby's body at noon and we need to worry about getting him home."

"Of course." Cuss put his fork down, picked up his coffee, and sat back in his chair. "You call him Moby?"

She nodded. "Everyone does. Even my dad. He was quite the character."

"Where's home?"

"Valencia," said Georgio. He said it with pride in his voice, almost a swagger. He left the country unsaid, as if anyone would know.

"When do you leave?"

"Today," said Aurora. "We're still finalizing details." She looked at Georgio. "Let's see. We plan on having him cremated here in Hermes and bringing his ashes to Earth on a flight that leaves at nineteen thirty tonight. We land in Albacete and should be in Valencia tomorrow late." She toyed with her necklace for a moment and then shook her head. "There's a crazy lot to do in a short amount of time."

"The reservations check out," said Ygo.

"How long will you be gone?" asked Cuss.

She opened a personal display and chewed her lower lip as she studied it. "Today's Wednesday. We'll get there Thursday late. Georgio's mom lives in town so she's already there. My mom and dad get there Friday morning. We'll celebrate his life, say, Friday and Saturday." She looked at Georgio. "Probably have the open house on Saturday, don't you think?" Then to Cuss. "I need to be back here by midday Monday because I cater a lunch on Tuesday."

"Are you coming back with her?" Cuss asked Georgio.

Georgio shook his head. "I came here to help get your attention. I have to get back to my real job or I lose it."

"What do you do?"

"I work for a company called Gastrow. I'm a waste man coordinator."

"Their waste management unit," said Ygo.

"Isn't that the same company where Moby worked?" asked Cuss.

Georgio slid a clean butter knife into the top of his arm brace and moved it back and forth to scratch an itch. "That's right. They're the biggest employer in the Valencia area."

Cuss nodded as if he understood. "You told me yesterday that Moby had said the wrong thing to the wrong person and it worried him. Tell me more about that conversation. When did this happen, and where?"

"Wait," interrupted Aurora, her lush eyebrows raised in surprise. She turned in her seat and faced Georgio. "Moby said this?"

Georgio stopped scratching. "He did. I saw him Sunday for lunch at his house after his last trip, so that would be ten days ago. Or eleven." He began counting fingers.

Aurora looked from Georgio to Cuss, her eyes wide. "Dad said something similar when I talked to him on Monday. Well, equally dramatic. Let's see, it was like, 'My mouth keeps getting me in trouble.' I asked him several times what he meant. He sulked but wouldn't elaborate. Whatever happened, it clearly bothered him."

She sat back and pushed her plate toward the center of the table. "When Moby got killed, Dad freaked out. I'd expect him to be upset, but this was different. He seemed more angry than sad. Outraged. Gripping his hands into fists. Grinding his teeth."

"So Moby and Nick had an argument," said Cuss. "Father and son, but we don't know what it was about."

"A disagreement, anyway," said Georgio.

"Do you think the disagreement had something to do with why Moby was killed?"

Aurora shook her head. "I don't see how." Then her eyebrows scrunched in a frown and her voice took on an edge. "Like, did my dad kill Moby? You better not even be hinting at that."

Cuss held up both hands, palms forward, like he was surrendering. "Of course not." He wanted to keep them talking and scrambled for the save. "My brain thinks in tangents." He tilted his head and then shrugged, hoping they wouldn't ask what that meant, because he didn't know.

"Moby was well off," said Ygo. "Why did he ride cargo ships?"

Cuss asked and Georgio answered. "He rode to Nova Terra every Thursday, spent a day and a half with Uncle Nick, and rode another cargo ship home on Saturday. He did it for years and loved it. Why? Because it gave him the chance to visit his son every week. He'd stay at Patsy and Nick's house…"

"That's my mom and dad," said Aurora.

"…so the visits were cost-free." Georgio laughed and looked at Aurora. "He built his wealth by being cheap as hell. He'd brag that they were paying him to nap, something he'd be doing anyway. He thought it was the perfect arrangement."

"My dad loved it, too," said Aurora, "because Moby spent all day Friday helping in the shop. It was a pair of hands he trusted. Even depended on."

Cuss forked a sausage patty onto his plate, took a bite, and made his "that's delicious" face. Then he asked one of his favorite open-ended questions. "Tell me about that?"

"My dad builds small multiuse rocket engines," began Aurora. Her pride in her father was as evident as Georgio's pride in Valencia. "He started the company with his brother about the time I was born. Moby had planted the idea in their heads that a line of small, adaptable engines was a growth sector the majors were ignoring."

She turned to Georgio and rested a hand on his shoulder. "His brother is Oliver, Georgio's dad, who tragically passed away almost ten years ago."

"Drowned while boating on the Mediterranean," said Ygo.

Aurora was wearing a short-sleeved blouse, and when she turned and reached out to Georgio, the sleeve on her left arm lifted enough to expose most of a tattoo. It was a smaller version of the one on Moby: a Christian cross inside a triangle inside a circle, drawn with simple lines.

Cuss pointed. "Moby has one just like that. What does it mean?"

Aurora pulled up her sleeve and turned to show him. "It's crazy you would ask about this at the exact moment that we're talking about him." She nudged Georgio, who pulled up his own shirt sleeve, revealing the same tattoo, a big version like Moby's

"The O is for Oliver," said Aurora. "The triangle is a sail. He loved boating and died doing something he loved. The cross is because he's with Jesus until we meet again."

She spent a moment looking at Georgio before continuing. "Georgio and I are going to get tats in honor of Moby, but we're stuck on ideas. Any thoughts?"

Ygo suggested, "How about an M riding through space?"

"Maybe an *M* riding in a spaceship," said Cuss. "It was his career and his hobby."

"Nice. I like that it's dynamic," said Aurora. "Dad has an Oliver and will probably get a Moby, so we'll need his input before we finalize anything."

"You were telling me about your dad's rocket engines," said Cuss, hoping to get her back on track.

Aurora sipped her coffee before continuing. "When Oliver died, my dad moved the shop to Nova Terra. He said it was because that's where most of his business came from. But I sensed that it was also about changing scenery so he wasn't constantly reminded of his brother. He worked long hours after that growing the business, and it seems to have paid off. The past couple of years have been lucrative."

"How long will he be in Valencia?" Cuss wanted to meet Nick face-to-face, preferably on his home turf. He'd wait until after Moby's memorial.

"We never talked about his return. But he's busier than me, so I'd guess he'll leave Sunday to be at work on Monday. Like father, like daughter."

Cuss held up the coffee carafe and offered to pour. They both declined, so he filled his own cup. "Could you find out and let me know?"

"Is this so you can question him?" She said it with attitude but didn't wait for him to respond. "I'll let you know when I find out." Then she shook her head and removed some of the edge. "Dad didn't do it, Marshal. I say that with absolute certainty. Clear him from your checklist quickly so you can chase the real killers."

Chapter 8

Cuss gripped the ball in his right hand and took a bead on his target, exhaling slowly through pursed lips. The ball looked like a standard baseball. Same size. Same horseshoe-shaped seam. But this was a few grams lighter than standard. And it had a small weight buried inside, offset from center to cause the ball to wobble and drift from its expected course when thrown.

He'd learned from past experience that if he threw the ball in a way that gave it spin, typical for a fastball and especially so for a curveball, the weight inside would cause the ball to swerve in unexpected ways. But if he threw a knuckleball, a throw designed to keep the ball from rotating, then the path would stay true.

He gauged the target, counted the timing in his head, and wound up in anticipation. At just the right moment, he let the ball fly. It zipped about ten meters, staying level with the ground, and hit the target square-on with a satisfying *smack*. A tower of bottles on an oscillating platform tumbled to the ground.

"Winner, winner, chicken dinner," crowed the carny.

"Hooray," said Julie. "My hero."

The carny reached for a pink stuffed bear hanging on the wall.

"No." She pointed to the one next to it. "A brown one."

The man pulled down the brown bear and gave it to her. "Everyone's a winner."

She thanked him and hugged it, grinning at Cuss. "It's exciting that you won this for me using your manly skills."

Cuss laughed. "Wanna ride the boat coaster?"

"Sure do."

Starting away from the carnival game, they passed a young boy, maybe six or seven years old, who'd been watching Cuss throw. Julie stooped and held out the bear, offering it to the boy while eyeing his mother to see if she approved.

"His name is Theodore," she told the child. "But he goes by Teddy. He told me he likes you."

The boy took Teddy and hugged him.

Cuss put an arm around Julie, gave her a squeeze, and together they walked down the row of carnival booths, making their way to the boat coaster ride. He let Julie take the lead as they moved through the crowds, the music and shouting and laughter creating a happy cacophony. While they walked, he mulled over his visit with detective Juan Luisa earlier in the day.

After breakfast with Georgio and Aurora, Cuss had stopped by the Community Patrol station to meet with his friend. Juan had confided that he and his colleagues were boxed in on the case. Their mission portfolio didn't include chasing criminals off world, or monitoring space traffic, or launching investigations in foreign lands. So they were left trying to solve a puzzle where they could see only a portion of the pieces, and a small portion at that.

Juan had looked him in the eye and confided, "If you got a plan, I'm ready to help."

They'd spent an hour in the detective's bullpen bullshitting while they exchanged ideas. Cuss told him about Georgio and Aurora, and about how Moby and son Nick had apparently squabbled.

But as they talked it through, neither of them could imagine how Nick, who ran a small, busy shop in Nova Terra, could be controlling pirates who boarded spaceships and stole industrial equipment. Because it was the pirates who'd killed Moby. The MO was too perfect.

Juan then shared what he'd learned about Space Watch and the policy for rescuing pilots and their craft. By interworld treaty, it applied to just three cases: any flight that originated from Earth, any Earth-flagged vessel, or any flight whose pilot was a citizen of Earth. Juan laughed at the silliness of it all. "The list is so broad, it includes every known case of piracy. So far, anyway."

Ygo added context for Cuss. "Senator Cumins' family controls the Gastrow Group, the shipping company where Georgio works and Moby retired. The senator sponsored the pilot rescue amendment, adding it to a trade agreement years ago, doing so to save his family a pile of money. What's interesting is that the amendment had broad support from his colleagues then, and it still does now. Not because it helps Gastrow, but because it gives Space Watch permission to patrol near Lagrange and Nova Terra without raising territorial sensitivities."

"Here," said Julie, pointing to the entrance of the boat coaster carnival ride. They queued up in line.

The line moved reasonably quickly, everyone shuffling forward every few seconds. Cuss kept smelling food and started thinking they should have stopped at a concession before getting in line. He took his mind off his stomach by making small talk with Julie. "How are you feeling about your task force meeting? It seemed pretty successful."

Her face went slack as she shifted from the excitement of the carnival world around them to one of thoughtful reflection. "You could tell at dinner that I was feeling angsty. All afternoon, people had shared facts. Talked of procedure. Described observations. But there hadn't been any spark. No debate. No back-and-forth. I was sweating bullets, hoping people wouldn't cut out after dinner." She elbowed him in the ribs, he presumed because he had cut out after dinner.

Julie's eyes lit up. "And then that LOCU agent proposed an idea that *everyone* had an opinion on. Holy smokes, the arguments were exactly what I'd hoped for. People offering insights. Highlighting nuances. Suggesting things not seen in any data but that they believed anyway." She put a hand on his arm. "This morning, I ran a study using a company algorithm, this analyzer we call a situation sieve. It suggested a profile of the pirates, their cargo preferences, and their methods." She nodded. "It looks really good. I can use it to craft solutions to pitch to the client."

"The Gastrow Group, right?"

She wrinkled her nose. "I probably shouldn't have told you that."

"I can keep a secret." He took her hand and held it in his. "Can you share that sieve thing? It sounds like stuff I could use."

Julie nodded. "There are insights I can share, but I can't share the analysis itself. Give me some time to sort it out." They shuffled forward in line, still hand-in-hand. "I did find something for Mia."

"Do tell."

"It's about her perfect load."

"You mean drive motors that power the equipment the doers already stole?" Cuss spoke authoritatively to let Julie know that in spite of his early departure, he'd followed along with the meeting. Ignoring the part, of course, where it had been Ygo who'd actually done the following.

"That's right," she said. "It's a great idea, made even better when I learned that the pirates have taken eight Flo-AV pumps, a model whose drive motor is on *long* back order. Like, ten months. If Mia were to let out that she was carrying a load of those motors, she'd have their attention."

"Nice," said Ygo, admiration clear in his tone. "Good work, Julie."

"It's perfect," Cuss told her. "Except for the part where Mia's plan is reckless as hell. I've defended a ship being boarded, and I've boarded one being defended. It's incredibly dangerous from either side. Anyone who appreciates what's involved would never go it alone." He shook his head. "Without a trained team helping her, it's probably best if she doesn't know."

"Oops."

He looked at her.

"I may have already told her." She shrugged and feigned a grin. "Sorry."

Cuss thought it was bad news for Mia. The doers were capable people with advanced tactical gear. Repelling them—stopping them from boarding but letting them escape—would require a skilled defensive team. Arresting them—capturing them with no loss of life—would require additional ships. Going it alone would be suicide.

He hoped to talk sense into her. But based on their past interactions, he didn't think she'd listen. "I said probably. Which means there's a chance it will all work out."

"You don't believe that."

"Not a huge chance," he admitted as they shuffled forward in line. "Is she still planning on three trips? Or is she just going for the one perfect load?"

"Still three as far as I know. The Flo-AV motors will be on the third flight, and even that will be a scramble. Her agency is working to buy equipment back from customers who've taken recent deliveries. I guess an earthquake took out the plant, and the manufacturer literally has nothing to sell."

They made it to the front of the line.

The boat coaster was a modern version of an old-style flume ride. They climbed into the seat of what looked like a small rowboat floating on a rushing stream of water. But beneath the surface, a complex mechanical system with actuators and rollers and guides would move them through the course in a fast, safe, and medium-wet manner.

"The thing I like about boat coasters," Cuss told Julie as safety straps wrapped around them, "is that it's a real ride where you get splashed by real water. The sim rides are fun and all, but you don't need to be at a park to ride one."

He also liked that the seating on physical rides allowed him to put an arm around Julie and pull her hip-to-hip.

As their boat began the initial hill climb, Ygo said, "Aurora just sent a message saying her dad will be back in Nova Terra late Sunday."

Cuss nodded, and then the boat crested the rise and started careening downhill on a rush of water. Julie screamed and laughed and waved her arms overhead as they banked around a corner and dove through a splash pool, curtains of water billowing on either side, a cool mist blowing over them.

The ride continued for a series of ups and downs and twists and turns, with more splashes along the way. Just as they were settling into their groove, the ride ended. At the exit, Julie detoured them into the optional drying tunnel, which was something like the drying station at the end of a carwash. She put the safety goggles on upside down and acted silly as they walked through it, making faces and cavorting about as a whirlwind of warm air blew at them from all directions.

From there they made for the more sedate Ferris wheel, where they enjoyed a bird's-eye view of the fairgrounds each time the ride carried them up over the top. Julie used the high vantage point to search for the carnival game where Cuss had won the bear for her. It took her three rounds before she spotted it. "There!" she called in triumph, leaning forward against the safety bar and pointing.

After a few more rounds, they reached the point in the ride where the wheel made frequent stops so the operator could switch passengers in and out of seats. While they waited their turn, Julie shared some insights from her company's situation sieve.

"It's easy to identify their work," she said. "They warn the pilot to get in their quarters and then use a seeker tool to blast their way onto the ship. Two people enter, one with a laser on his hip."

She turned to him and, as if to emphasize a point, rested a hand on his thigh. "Most pilots identify the shooter as a male." She left her hand there when she returned to her story. "Anyway, the pirates cut the comms, isolating the pilots, who sit in their rooms and listen to thumps and bumps and try to guess what's happening. When Space Watch arrives, they find the ship's drives shut down, the bay door open, and the cargo gone."

Her summary was consistent with his own understanding, but his version had another piece. "The archiving hardware is taken."

"That's right. Anyway, the seeker explosives and laser gun are industrial tools." She paused. "These aren't my observations, by the way. This is what the sieve spit out from all the stuff presented at the meeting."

"What do you mean by industrial?"

"I'm getting to that," she said with a pat to his thigh. "So, the sieve suggests that the pirates take four or five loads that fit together into a common theme. Then they take something random that doesn't fit with anything."

"Can I ask about that?"

She nodded. "Most of the loads can be combined to construct complex facilities."

"That's pretty vague. Like an office complex?"

She shook her head. "More like a mining or manufacturing facility. Or maybe food production. Waste processing. Or an air or water project, since that's where some of the parts were destined for here on Hermes. All of them use equipment like the pirates stole. And those industries all use seeker tools and commercial lasers somewhere in their operations."

He paused to digest her words.

"The beginnings of a profile," said Ygo. "I can see why you copied off her."

But Cuss couldn't see past a practical hurdle. "The parts are tagged. How do they get around that?"

Her brow scrunched. "I don't know what you mean."

"They have identifiers embedded during manufacturing that detectors can read. Remember when the Space Watch captain talked about them? Anyway, the first thing a tech does when performing maintenance on a machine is to run its tags to learn its history. All those parts will show as stolen."

"Maybe the company is big enough to have their own in-house staff who don't ask questions?"

"Maybe." Except that one disgruntled employee could expose the thieves, making the scheme risky for the doers.

Ygo asked, "What's in the odd loads?"

Cuss relayed the question.

"Things like kitchen appliances, sports equipment. Let's see…" She rubbed her neck. "Designer lamps. Ladies shoes. Random stuff."

"Could they be using those to throw off the scent?" asked Cuss.

Julie nodded. "The sieve thought they were using those to mask their bigger goal. It also suggested with a lower certainty that they were upgrading their personal lifestyle."

Their Ferris wheel car stopped at the loading platform. They stepped out and exited the ride through a roped aisle.

"You hungry?" Cuss asked as he led her out into pedestrian traffic. He kept going straight, cutting across the flow of people in a beeline to a cluster of food vendors on the other side.

"Maybe an iced tea. Unsweetened."

He got in line at a booth that was selling Philly cheesesteak sandwiches and ordered a double double—twice the filling on a bun that was twice the regular length. The vendor made the sandwich in a series of practiced moves and handed it to Cuss through the counter window along with Julie's drink.

They walked to a spot away from the flow of traffic, one where they could watch the crowds while he ate. He unwrapped his sandwich and took a bite. It tasted amazing.

While he devoured his food, Julie said, "Did you hear? The pirates struck earlier today, putting the tally at twenty-nine events in total. Space Watch has reached the ship and reports that the pilot is safe."

"Checking on it," said Ygo. "She's right. That news is forty minutes old. She must have been so annoying in school."

Cuss took a bite of his sandwich to hide his snicker.

"I'm curious about your work," she said, her demeanor earnest. "Does the fact that Moby Navarro is now a one-off, that the pattern is back to normal, heighten the odds that he wasn't random. That he was murdered?"

Cuss looked at her like she was Wonder Woman. "It's my turn to share something private. Yes, I believe he was murdered. I thought so before today, and this strengthens that conclusion. How and when and where he died are clear. I'm still working on who and why." He had a brainstorm. "Any chance your company algorithms could suggest likely candidates?"

She looked down as she thought about it and then lifted her head. "If we suggested names, would Capit be free from legal peril? Held harmless from lawsuits if we're wrong?" She returned focus to him. "I don't know that we can do it. I'll give it a try. But I do know our lawyers won't let me expose the company just to be a good citizen."

"Fair enough. I'll have my people contact your people." His people was Ygo, the thought creating pangs of guilt because of his partner's ever-growing to-do list. But the guilt was fleeting, gone when he had another thought. "Do you know if Gastrow's feed archive got corrupted during this attack?"

"What?"

"Their ships send feeds to a home repository. Gastrow reports that the segments showing the doers in action are missing. Snipped out and gone. This is for all twenty-eight previous cases."

"Really? I hadn't heard that." Her surprise seemed real, and she returned to her thoughtful gaze. "I wonder if that information will change the sieve results."

"Ask if she can guide us to the right person in Gastrow," said Ygo.

"I'd like to talk with Gastrow about it," said Cuss. "Would you be able to connect me with the person supervising their archiving system?"

She didn't respond for several seconds. "I don't know how to do that without revealing that I confided in you." She pressed her lips together. "I guess I can say that I'm helping a task force participant move toward a solution. But be prepared for them to tell me, 'Thanks, but no thanks.'"

"Any help would be appreciated." He tossed his sandwich wrapper into a waste bin, wiped his face and hands with a wad of napkins, and tossed those as well.

"Ready?" he asked, even though he'd been the one holding them up.

She nodded.

"Can I have some of your drink?"

She held it out for him.

He took it, drained it, and tossed the cup.

He took her hand, and they explored a few more exhibits before calling it a night. Then they made for Julie's hotel.

Chapter 9

Ygo used the quantum link embedded in his brain to access POTS, the population tracking system used by Community Patrol to monitor public spaces. Through it, he watched as Cuss walked Julie down the third-floor hallway of the Arborvue Hotel. It was a nice place. Upscale. Just a few blocks from where Cuss had stayed the night before.

This hotel chain hyped the wood theme. Overdid it, in Ygo's opinion. Floors of tiger maple. Arches and moldings of hewn timber. Oak doors stained to highlight the woodgrain. All of it condensate material that had been formed to look the part.

Throughout the evening, Ygo had monitored Cuss and Julie, keeping an eye on things, watching for danger. Since his physical limitations kept him from the field, Ygo compensated by supporting his partner with technology: assessing, anticipating, and—where he could—acting.

So he couldn't miss the clear signs that Julie was smitten. She touched Cuss, bumped against him, leaned into him. Teased him. Complimented him. Confided in him. Ygo expected her to invite Cuss to spend the night.

And while Cuss had laughed with her, held her hand, and hugged her close, he'd never crossed that final hurdle.

He'd never kissed her. So Ygo felt certain Cuss would say no.

When Cuss and Julie reached her door, they stopped and faced each other. Cuss held both of her hands in his. "It was so great to see you."

"You're welcome to come in. To stay if you want." She looked at her feet and toed the floor. "But I sense you won't."

"You are so tempting, Julie. I wish I could. But I can't."

"I figured. You would have kissed me by now otherwise."

Cuss used an index finger to move a lock of Julie's hair behind an ear. Ygo knew it was a move he normally made behind closed doors. He kissed her forehead. "When do you head home?"

"My flight is tomorrow afternoon."

"Where do you land?"

"Stagecoach." It was the spaceport in Nevada that served the Reno, Sacramento, San Francisco corridor.

Ygo said with urgency, "We're going to Gastrow's tech center in Denver, and Mia is launching from the Chicago hub. We aren't going anywhere near Nevada."

"I'm headed there tomorrow," Cuss told her with a smile. "You can ride with me and we can talk about the case on the way."

"To Stagecoach? Really? What time are you leaving?"

"That's the beauty of having your own ride. Whenever we want."

They agreed to meet at eight thirty the next morning in the shuttle station of the passenger spaceport. From there, Cuss would escort her to the *Nelly Marie*.

He gave her a hug, and after she entered her room, he started down the hall. "It's weird. Back in school, I thought of her more like a sister than anything else. Now she's this smart hottie and my brain hasn't caught up to my libido."

"You like her?"

"She's turning my head, no question."

While the two chatted, Ygo scanned ahead along Cuss's path. He saw a bank of elevators in a side alcove at the end of the hallway. The alcove was empty, and one of the lift doors was open, available if Cuss chose to ride. Across the hall from the elevators was the stairwell door.

Checking the stairwell monitors, Ygo found two men rounding the second-floor landing and marching up the steps. Big men. Men on a mission. Wearing one-piece coveralls with hoods over their heads.

POTS identified both as Rodney Beckers. While theoretically possible that they were identical twins and the system was confused, Ygo suspected that someone had learned a new trick for spoofing the tech.

"Danger ahead," Ygo called with urgency. "Two toughs coming up the stairwell. Seven seconds to the door."

Cuss launched down the hallway like a sprinter, leaning forward and taking short steps to build speed, and then lifting his head and lengthening his stride as he transitioned into a run. "Time?" he called.

Ygo counted down the seconds. "Five, four…"

When Cuss reached the door, he rolled on the floor to stay beneath the window. As he stood up on the other side, he pasted his body against the wall, his only cover a narrow support abutment at the edge of the door.

Ygo spotted a third man coming up the stairwell at the far end of the hallway, this one also wearing coveralls, also identified as Rodney Beckers. "Third man in the far stairwell."

"*Don't* call Julie," Cuss hissed.

"…one."

The door next to Cuss opened, the hinges set so the tough was looking down the hall away from him. Rodney One stepped through the door and held it open for his partner, his attention on Rodney Three, who was yelling and pointing from the far end of the hallway, "He's right there!"

Any doubts Ygo may have had about the thugs was erased. "They're here for you," he told Cuss.

"What?" called Rodney One, pulling back his hood so he could hear better. Rodney One figured it out an instant later and turned to look for Cuss. But Rodney Two had crowded him out the door and they bumped into each other, creating a moment of confusion.

Cuss took advantage of the opportunity. Stepping away from the wall, he spun at the waist, his shoulders following in a matching rotation. The movement accelerated his elbow in a short arc, which he planted into the back of Rodney Two's neck. The fragile bones and ligaments of the man's cervical spine flexed in response, the blunt trauma popping his head back in a dramatic whiplash.

Ygo cringed at the sickening *crunch*, audible above everything else.

Rodney Two spasmed as his body arched. Cuss used a leg sweep to bring him to the ground and then stomped on his head, removing him from battle.

Now it was two against one. Two enormous men. Rodney One and Rodney Three crouching shoulder to shoulder in the hallway, looking like linebackers ready to tear Cuss apart.

Cuss faced them. Ygo thought he looked confident. Unconcerned, anyway. Rodney Two was stretched out on the floor, a mountain of human flesh between the two parties. The elevator alcove was to Cuss's right, the door to the stairwell to his left, and behind him, the wall at the end of the corridor.

In a weird choreography, the toughs limbered up in a synchronized ritual. They tilted their heads left and right, producing a *critch* sound each time. They rotated their shoulders forward and back. They opened and closed their fat fingers, forming and unforming brick-size fists.

Their swollen physiques suggested pharma fitness. Muscles from a bottle, the kind that were more show than go. It meant that Cuss stood an excellent chance of making short work of them.

Still, anything could happen in a fight. And it did when Rodney Three reached into his pocket, pulled out a knife, and opened it with a *snick*.

Ygo held his breath, remaining silent so Cuss could focus on the battle. He expected Cuss to fake an advance. Maybe take off his jacket and use it defensively. Perhaps wave his arms and yell. But he surprised Ygo by pushing open the door to the stairwell and diving through.

Cuss was moving so fast that Ygo felt certain he would tumble down the steps. But in a spectacular maneuver, he held on to the door handle with a death grip, stopping his forward progress like a dog reaching the end of its leash. Instead of dropping down the stairs, he swung back with the door.

Rodney Three, head down and snorting as he charged into the stairwell, was close behind, his knife out in front. But he'd gone a step too far before he realized that Cuss was next to him, not in front. Cuss stuck out a leg and tripped the man before he could change course. The tough stumbled, lurched, and when Cuss shoved him from behind, he flew out over the steps.

That should have been the end of it. But in a remarkably athletic move, Rodney Three turned, stretched, and slashed at Cuss with the blade as he took flight, cutting him on the left upper arm. The thug paid a steep price for his heroic effort, landing hard, cracking the back of his head on the edge of a step most of the way down the flight. He crumpled into a heap at the bottom of the stairs and remained still.

While Ygo eyed the wound with concern, Cuss ignored it, turning to face Rodney One. The blade had sliced through his jacket, through his shirt, and into the flesh at the top of the arm. How deep, Ygo couldn't tell. But he fretted as a bloodstain grew down Cuss's coat sleeve.

Fearing for his partner's safety, Ygo paged a med cart, coding it with "officer injured" to give it high priority. That coding had the attendant effect of triggering an alert to Community Patrol, who confirmed that two nearby teams were en route to provide assistance.

"Hurry," Ygo willed them.

Rodney One, who'd followed his partner into the stairwell, backed away from Cuss, edging slowly through the door and into the hall. The door closed on its own, and the tough held his hands in front of the window, wiggling his fingers, challenging Cuss to come out and join him.

Cuss obliged, pulling the door wide and stepping through.

Down the hall, a door opened. A hotel guest leaned out, looked in their direction, yelled, "Quiet, please," and shut the door.

Rodney One ignored the guest. Staring at Cuss through lifeless eyes, he continued his backward retreat as Cuss advanced.

Without looking, the thug stepped over Rodney Two and kept going, making space so Cuss could follow. Cuss obliged again, following him over the fallen man.

Rodney One stopped backing up.

Cuss faced him square on, feet planted a bit wider than shoulder-width apart, fists raised in front like he was a prizefighter preparing to box.

Ygo knew immediately that he was pretending to give Rodney One an opening to kick him in the balls. The thug took the bait.

Like a bull pawing the ground before charging, the big man shifted his weight to his left foot and then pulled back his right foot to deliver the killer blow. The moves were slow and deliberate. He may as well have marched into the town square, unfurled a scroll, and read a public proclamation of his intentions.

Cuss waited until the thug's foot had begun its forward swing. When the man was committed to the kick, Cuss pivoted sideways so the foot hit his thigh. He accepted the blow and the bruise it would create.

And then, in a lightning response, he delivered a thrust-kick into the side of Rodney One's left knee, the one holding the man up. Cuss extended fully on the follow-through, multiplying the damage to the fragile structure.

With a bloodcurdling howl, the man toppled like a sequoia, holding the knee with both hands.

Cuss quieted him by dropping a knee onto his throat. He leaned into it enough to cause breathing distress. "What do you want?"

The man writhed and whimpered but didn't respond.

Another door opened down the hall.

Cuss added more weight and Rodney One's choking became real. But the thug's face didn't redden, instead remaining the same fleshy white.

Ygo suspected a mask. Cuss must have noticed as well because he began scraping beneath the man's chin, working loose the edge of a thin film that covered the thug's face.

When Ygo saw the film, an overlay surely packed with tech to confuse sensors, he understood how POTS could see multiple Rodneys.

"Who sent you?" Cuss demanded.

"Fuck off," mouthed the thug through chokes and gasps.

Cuss lifted weight off his knee and let the man take a breath. "Last chance."

"You got lucky, asshole. Won't happen next time."

Cuss stood upright, and with the full weight of his two hundred twenty pounds, dropped his knee onto the side of the man's head.

"Cuss Abbott, what in God's name are you doing!?" Julie stood in the hallway wearing a white terrycloth robe, hands on her hips, scowling.

Breathing hard, Cuss stood and faced her, blushing the way a schoolboy might when caught in the act by his teacher. Cuss strove to keep the details of his craft away from the public in general, and away from friends in particular. Ygo knew he'd berate himself for this lapse for some time to come.

"Oh my God." Ignoring Rodney One's limp body at her feet, Julie took Cuss's injured arm in her hands. "You're bleeding."

Cuss looked down at the wound, scrunched his brow as though he was just becoming aware of it, and took off his jacket. The shirt sleeve underneath was bloody down to the cuff. He unbuttoned the front of his shirt and pulled that arm out of the sleeve.

When Julie lifted the arm to examine it, Ygo could see that the slice was clean, the benefit of a sharp blade. The wound itself was about as long as one of Julie's fingers.

"There's a med cart outside the lobby downstairs," Ygo told him, having received confirmation of its arrival moments earlier.

Julie helped Cuss remove his shirt completely, shuffled it to find the clean right sleeve, and tore it off in a decisive display of strength and technique. She lay the cuff end of the sleeve over the wound and wrapped the length around his arm. When a short piece remained, she used her teeth to split the cloth and then tied the end strips together. "Let's get you to a clinic."

"It's nothing sanitizer, glue, and a clean bandage won't cure," said Cuss, adding, "Impressive field technique, by the way."

"The med cart has all three," said Ygo. "Please, ride it to a clinic."

"A med cart is downstairs," Cuss said to Julie. "I'll go tend to it."

"Hold on. Let me put on some clothes and I'll go with you." She waved a hand toward the two men on the floor, both of whom had begun showing signs of awakening. "Maybe you can tell me about them on the way."

As Julie opened the door to her room, Cuss called, "Will you look for something to tie these guys up with?"

"No need," said Ygo. "Two officers are on their way up."

Hearing they were on a short clock, Cuss hustled down the stairs to where Rodney Three lay. The guy wasn't moving. He found the knife that had cut his arm on the landing near the wall. Without touching it, he used his lens to take a surface scan of the handle and blade.

While Cuss climbed back up the stairs, Ygo analyzed the data, looking for anything of concern.

The scan found Cuss's blood along the length of the blade. It found microscopic traces of his flesh. And it found specks of fabric that matched Cuss's coat and shirt. The rest of the blade and handle were clean except for a trace coating of Disolv, a cleansing product that obliterated all biological matter.

Certain criminals made a habit of rinsing their weapons with Disolv because it eliminated evidence that could link them to a crime. The upside of the cleansing was that Cuss didn't need to worry about any sort of exotic infection from his wound.

Julie, now dressed in jeans and a blouse, met him in the hallway. She held a T-shirt in one hand and a family-sized package of dental floss in the other. She handed him the shirt. "You should probably cover up."

Indeed, Cuss was standing in the hallway naked from the waist up. Having been his partner for years, Ygo knew that many people responded to him positively because they found him attractive, and that's when he was fully dressed. With his muscled physique now exposed, he was an outright spectacle. And with two Community Patrol officers due out of the stairwell at any moment, it was a good idea for him to get his spectacle covered.

"Will it fit?" he asked as he pulled it over his head.

"It's my nightshirt," said Julie. "It's a men's extra-large."

The shirt was tight on Cuss, a formfitting cover of red with a Stanford Law logo on his chest.

Pointing to the dental floss in her hand, he said, "Great idea. But it turns out that Community Patrol is almost here."

Ygo checked on the officers' progress. They were paused in the stairwell, bent over Rodney Three, discussing their observations. He'd wondered why the two hadn't taken the lift, a practice he'd come to expect of Community Patrol. As he listened to them talk, it became apparent that they had known about the thug in the stairwell before their arrival.

"Damn it," he said privately, berating himself from his capsule bed in the hold of the *Nelly Marie*.

If Community Patrol knew that Rodney Three was injured in the stairwell, it meant someone had taken the time to watch the incident involving Cuss and the thugs, probably from start to finish, probably with several other people. Maybe even with someone from the municipal attorney's office. He cursed himself because his habit was to always review the feed of Cuss in action before letting it become part of the record. That way he could smooth the occasional incident, if need be, leaving Cuss free to do his job.

But he'd been so worried about Cuss's injury that his priority had shifted to getting him medical assistance. The price of that decision had been an unedited record.

In a "better late than never" review, he sped through the feed of Cuss and the three Rodneys. He saw a problem right away. A big one. Huge. Not just the elephant in the room. This was a blue whale.

Cuss had struck the first blow. Not only that, at the time Cuss hit the guy, he wasn't being threatened. No weapons were visible. No punches were taken and missed. In fact, Cuss hit the guy from behind without ever being confronted.

That meant the thugs' lawyer would be screaming self-defense. That Cuss was a bad actor. A madman gone rogue. A menace to society.

What made it worse for Ygo was that Cuss had been responding to his encouragement. He was the one who'd told Cuss, "They're here for you."

His partner would prevail. Ygo would make certain of that. But it would be an unnecessary disruption for both of them. It would take time away from the case. And going forward, their files would include the gory details of a fight in a hotel hallway on this unfortunate day.

Chapter 10

Standing beside Julie in the hallway, Cuss rubbed has hands up and down his chest to create friction, the action causing Julie's shirt to release a spicy floral scent that wafted up to tickle his nose. He was enjoying the diversion, waiting for the officers to emerge from the stairwell, when Ygo spoiled his fun. "Community Patrol saw the feed before I could massage it. Sorry, pal. You hit first. You assaulted three guys without provocation."

"What?" Cuss said aloud, astounded by Ygo's words.

"I know. I encouraged you and I'd do it again. They were here for you. But my words aren't in the feed."

"What's going on?" asked Julie.

"I just received notice that I'm being investigated for protecting myself."

"Beating these guys up?"

Both hallway Rodneys were moaning and rolling on the ground at this point. Cuss eyed them, trying to decide if he needed to tie them up after all. "Damn right. They were here to hurt me."

Two Community Patrol officers entered the hallway from the stairwell.

"Accept me as your lawyer," Julie hissed.

"What?"

"Accept me as your lawyer. Hurry."

"Do it," urged Ygo.

"I accept you as my lawyer," he whispered back.

While one officer knelt next to Rodney Two and began checking his vitals, the other, a woman with blonde streaks and a solid build, squared up in front of them. "Marshal Cuss Abbott? I'm Officer Macbride." Her name tag gave her first name as Hannah. "May I see your ID?"

"It's in my coat." He bent slowly and picked up his jacket, retrieved his badge wallet, and held it open for Hannah to scan.

"My client is injured," said Julie. "He needs medical attention."

"Your client?" Hannah glanced back at her partner and then looked at Cuss. "Why would an Interworld Marshal need a lawyer?"

"Please address all questions to me," said Julie in a voice that would freeze the sun.

"Understood. Would you please provide your name and practitioner's ID, Counselor?"

Julie opened a personal display, found her credentials, and shared them with Hannah, who collected them on her own display and ran them through the system.

Hannah nodded. "Thank you, Attorney Kapoeta." She showed the display to Cuss. "I need you to approve."

He did so while looking at Julie, marveling at this person who just kept surprising him.

But Julie was glaring at Hannah. "For the second time, the marshal is in urgent need of medical attention."

The elevator doors chimed open and two med techs emerged. One was pushing two upright towers that unfolded into mobile gurneys. The other was pushing a third gurney tower with one hand, and pulling a wheeled medical case with the other.

"It's a knife wound, right?" Hannah lifted Cuss's arm and examined the makeshift bandage. "Let's get you to the hospital. Can you make it downstairs on your own?"

Cuss had no intention of traveling with the Rodneys, nor did he want to share the emergency room with them. "It's a clean slice. Not too deep." He looked halfway between the women as he spoke. "Can we do it here?"

Hannah turned and took in the scene. One of her crew had disappeared down the stairwell to help Rodney Three. The other two were struggling to put a neck brace on Rodney Two. Rodney One was rocking on the floor, holding his knee and groaning.

She shook her head. "Their injuries are more serious. You'll have to wait."

Cuss looked at Julie. "You want to give it a go?"

Before Julie could answer, Hannah said, "I was a med tech before I switched to patrol. If you're in a hurry and don't mind a small scar, I can clean and glue it for you."

"Works for me," said Cuss, happy for a solution.

Hannah retrieved a medical kit the size of a shoebox from the wheeled case, looked up and down the busy corridor, and said, "Someplace quiet where we can sit would be good. With light. Maybe down in the lobby?"

"We can use my room." Julie pointed down the hall.

Both women looked at Cuss, who shrugged and nodded. They followed Julie to the door.

The size and décor of her room were typical for a business-class traveler. There was a bathroom and closet near the door, a combination desk-credenza-dresser at the foot of two queen-size beds in the middle, and a table and chairs arranged at the far end.

Above the table hung a light fixture that Hannah pointed to. "That'll work."

Julie lit the hanging lamp while Cuss arranged himself at the table, resting his arm on top so his shoulder was easily accessible. Hannah turned a chair and sat facing Cuss.

Opening the medical kit, Hannah unpacked an assortment of packets and vials and containers. Viewing the collection, she picked out a dispenser of sterile wet cloths and positioned it for easy access. She pulled on disposable gloves and started the process of removing the makeshift bandage that Julie had applied.

With the bandage off, Hannah used a sterile cloth to clean the wound. "He got you good." The cut was oozing blood and she picked up a squirt bottle. "It's gonna sting." She spritzed the wound, and his skin burned, the sting lasting for several seconds before fading. The bleeding stopped and Hannah examined the cut. "We'll be able to fix this here."

She pulled another sterile cloth from the packet and cleaned down his arm. As she wiped, she glanced over at Julie, who was watching from the edge of the nearest bed.

"Assistant Municipal Attorney Hayes asks that Marshal Abbott come by the office tomorrow morning."

"Why?" asked Julie.

"You can call me Cuss," said Cuss.

"I'm Hannah," replied Hannah with a shy grin. Then looking at Julie, she said, "I'm just the messenger. Patrol doesn't get explanations, and we don't ask for them."

Picking up a bioglue applicator, Hannah gently opened the wound and pressed the plunger with her thumb, laying a bead down the groove the way she might if she were caulking a sink. She squeezed the wound closed and held it shut while the glue set, using a cloth to wipe away the blood and excess glue. "They asked for a confirmation of compliance."

Cuss looked at Julie, unsure if he should speak.

"We'll be there," said Julie. She stood, moved to the far side of the far bed, and sat with her back to them. "I'm going to call Jeremiah and find out what's going on."

"I think she means Jeremiah Routh," said Ygo. "Chief MA for Hermes."

"Jeremiah?" Julie said in a warm voice. "Thanks, I'm doing fine. How about you?" She fiddled her fingers, and a privacy shield blurred her image and muffled the sound of her voice.

"How does she know the MA?" Ygo asked Cuss.

Cuss was wondering the same thing.

Hannah pulled a thin, clear bandage off a sheet of backing, placed it over the wound, and rubbed it to seal the edges. "The glue and bandage will dissolve over the next week or so. Try to keep everything dry for a good hour."

She collected the trash in a small waste bag and stuffed the unused supplies back into the medical kit. "Just so you know, we're all on your side. Face-film tech is a new thing, and the crews using it are bad people. Dangerous." She glanced over at Julie, who was still in her privacy shroud. "I shouldn't say it, but we all cheered watching you take down those assholes. A thing of beauty. I watched it four times." She tilted her head toward the door to the hallway. "One of the guys with me added your whole sequence to his training sim. Says he's gonna practice until he can do the thing clean."

Reappearing from the blur, Julie stood and faced them. "Shit. The men have an attorney and are filing charges. Jeremiah wants us to come in and help his office understand what happened. I agreed. We'll miss tomorrow's departure, but he thinks we can be out by Friday. Saturday at the latest."

Hannah stood, tucked the medical kit under her arm, and picked up the waste bag. "Okay, so your injury is sorted and the message from the assistant MA has been delivered and confirmed. I'm going to check on my crew now." She paused at the door. "Good luck fighting the bullshit." She waved a hand behind her head on the way out. The door shut behind her.

Julie looked at him and then at his arm. "You okay? What do you need?"

"I need a burger. Two beers. A hot shower. A warm bed."

Julie motioned to the bathroom. "Help yourself to the shower. I'll call room service."

Ygo said, "There's nice suite down the hall. Big tub. Big bed. Want it?"

Cuss gave a slow blink for Ygo while saying to Julie, "I just remembered that I can't get this thing wet, so I should probably take a bath, and your tub is too small for me. But there's one down the hall that's perfect. Maybe you could keep me company while I clean up? There's more space for us to eat down there, too."

She motioned to his arm. "I could cover that if you want to shower."

Cuss smiled. "Or you could keep me company down the hall."

"You really have another room?"

"Just a couple of doors away. My assistant arranged it. Join me."

She bit her lip and looked around the room. "Let me grab a few things." As her arms began to fill, she said, "I can come back if I forget anything?"

"You can."

"Then I'm ready. Let's go." She sounded excited. Almost giddy.

The hallway was empty, with Community Patrol and the Rodneys nowhere in sight. As they walked, Julie said, "Jeremiah said the attorney is repping *three* guys. Do you know what that's about? I saw two."

"The third guy fell down the stairs," said Cuss. He stopped in front of the door Ygo indicated. It opened, and he led the way inside.

The room was a more generous version of Julie's. More floor space. More furniture. More bathroom. A kitchen nook. Privacy wall shielding the bed. Same overall vibe.

In the bathroom, Cuss saw double sinks in front of a huge mirror. Showy light fixtures with dimmers. Floor tiles in warm colors. And a big tub on its own platform, with towels and gels and bowls of whatnot placed artistically around it.

He bent over the tub, a spa-sized item with seats molded into the sides and a dozen jets that swirled the water. After taking a moment to decipher the controls, he selected the "deep fill with medium-hot water" option and started the cycle.

"I'm targeting the food to arrive in an hour," said Ygo. "Could we get her order?"

Julie was standing at the bathroom door, looking in from the room atrium, arms still full.

"My food will be here in an hour," Cuss told her. "Please don't make me eat alone. Something to eat? Drink?"

"You're having a burger?"

Cuss nodded.

"I'll have the same. I can't drink tonight, though. I need to work on documenting everything for Jeremiah. He says we need to help him help you."

"Then I have good news for you. The Marshals Service is working on it already. You'll have a complete report tomorrow morning. We can review it together over breakfast."

She twisted her mouth as she thought, then shook her head. "I learned the hard way to do my own work. I've been burned before."

"Fair enough." He blushed, something which seemed to happen often with Julie. He was pretty sure she was referring to a time in high school when she'd wanted to attend a special dinner, an event hosted by a civic organization that was presenting her with an award. Cuss had promised to do their homework that night and hadn't, letting them both down.

The flow stopped when the water neared the lip of the tub, the lack of sound drawing his attention. He swirled a hand in the liquid. The temperature was perfect.

As he shook water from his hand, he vowed to make it up to her. Well, for Ygo to, anyway. "Tell me four things you'd include in your brief. I'll have them detailed in writing for you by the time we're finished with dinner. Say, two hours from now."

"I wasn't going to start until then, so this is a sure bet from my view." Her brow creased. "Let's see, we need your timeline from the start of the day through when Community Patrol arrived on the scene. Time, place, activity." She shifted the bundle in her arms, improving her grip before continuing. "And we need to know everything behind your decision to attack them. What you knew. How. When."

She chewed on her lower lip for a moment, staring into the distance. "We need to know everything we can about the attackers. Who they are, who they're working for, why they were following you." She returned focus to him. "I guess a fourth thing would be about the face tech. Where did they get it. How rare is it. Does it associate them with anyone. What crimes have been committed by other face-film users."

"That's all?" said Cuss.

"That was my line," said Ygo.

She smiled. "You offered. If you can get it done, I get to sleep tonight." Then her forehead wrinkled and she shook her head. "Your job is crazy dangerous."

Cuss watched her expressions change from curiosity to confusion to alarm as she considered the idea of confronting brutal criminals for a living.

He gave a small shrug. "It can be."

She shifted the load in her arms yet again. "Am I in danger?"

"Before the attack, I would have said no. But if you'd been in the hall with me, you could have been hurt."

She nodded slowly and then disappeared from the doorway, moving into the bedroom. He heard a thump that sounded like she'd plopped her armload onto the bed. She reappeared empty-handed.

Crossing her arms, she leaned a shoulder against the bathroom doorframe and spoke in a whisper, "Will you protect me if I stay?"

"Do you want to?"

"I do. The experience will bolster my image at Capit, and that can only be good for business. And being at your side is a thrill, I won't deny it."

"Then I won't let anyone harm you."

When he said it, he meant it. But then he thought of the men and women he cared about who'd died because of his work. Colleagues, friends. His wife, Becca. A flood of guilt washed over him.

She studied him and then compounded his guilt by nodding slowly. "I believe you."

Before he could speak, her face fell and she said, "Goddamn, Cuss Abbott. The way you mess with my head isn't fair."

Flummoxed, Cuss stepped in her direction. "Tell me."

"I spent years imagining being with you. Romping with you." She gestured toward the tub. "Taking a bath together." She looked at the ground. "It just makes me sad that for you it's the wrong chemistry."

"Ah, geez, Julie." He decided to be honest. "Truth is, you intimidate me. The macho in me doesn't know where to start with a woman like you."

"Same place you start with any woman." After a pause, she continued. "At least you didn't say I was like a sister to you. Anyway, I'm old enough to know that chemistry is chemistry. It's not a thing that can be cured with logic or reason. Take your bath. I'll be out here on this massive bed, daydreaming."

He watched her leave. He looked at the tub. And then he followed her out into the room.

She was on the bed, flopped on her back, her legs dangling over the edge.

He sat next to her. "The thing is, I don't take baths. I'm a shower guy. I picked this as something that I thought would work for both of us. Something low pressure. I guess I hadn't thought it through. Sorry."

She lifted her head. "Really?"

He nodded.

She propped herself up on her elbows. "I wonder if there's a way we could make it work this one time?"

He leaned over and kissed her. A lingering peck. "The water is warm. I could dim the lights way down so it's more mysterious. Less intimidating."

"Hell no. I want to see. That is, if you don't mind."

He laughed. Standing, he took her by the hand and led her to the tub.

. . .

When Cuss began to remove Julie's blouse, Ygo cut the vid feed from the bathroom, though he continued monitoring Cuss's audio and biometric signals. Not out of prurient interest, but because broad, continuous surveillance was foundational to his partner's safety.

In the past, Ygo watched everything. But then he'd been called out for invading the privacy of Cuss's intimate guests, the embarrassing charge leaving him to make difficult choices.

Losing video was a huge penalty in a business where seconds mattered. And that was no exaggeration. An hour earlier, he'd been able to give Cuss just seven seconds to prepare for an attack by the Rodneys. Seven seconds with full video.

Still raw from that encounter, Ygo heightened his vigilance. He reviewed the backgrounds of the other guests on the floor. Used the public-spaces monitors to patrol the hallways, the stairwells, the lobby. Watched the sidewalks outside. Checked in on the hotel's kitchen to ensure that food preparation was on schedule and without concern.

While he was scouting the food service area, he spotted a row of delivery carts, automated boxes on wheels that carried food and tableware to the different rooms. He had an inspiration.

Hacking into the hotel hospitality system, he took control of two large carts, drove them onto the service elevator, and sent them up to the third floor. There, he guided them down the hall to Cuss's room, where he parked them in tight formation to form a barrier in front of the door. The carts were substantial items, heavy and awkward in a way that would add seconds of delay to anyone trying to force their way past them.

And while he was doing that, he started on Julie's list. Four big complicated questions. He spawned four AI agents, assigned one to each issue, and gave them the authority to create subordinates to pursue the bits and pieces.

He monitored the feed as information rolled in, paying special attention to information that would absolve Cuss of the charge of unprovoked aggression. He didn't have to wait long. One of the agents found what he needed in the POTS record, the population tracking system archive.

The Rodneys had staged their operation from a bar three blocks from the Arborvue Hotel. While seated at the bar, they were careful not to discuss specifics of their assignment. But outside, as they walked up the pedestrian thoroughfare toward the hotel, one of the group made their intentions clear.

Ygo clipped fragments for the summary: "He's a big guy...an Interworld Marshal...put his head through a wall...help him fall down the steps." The "help him fall" part was met with laughter from the other two.

As Ygo reviewed the legal briefs, his mind drifted to fundamental questions about the incident. Why was Cuss attacked? Who ordered it? What did they expect to achieve?

The Rodneys had admitted nothing, and now with a lawyer at their side, they certainly never would.

He would talk about it later with Cuss, though he was all but certain of his response: "It's proof we're on the right track."

It was easy to believe that the attack was confirmation that the pirates were worried, so much so that they took the huge risk of sending muscle to slow Cuss down. Perhaps to stop him. But there was an outside chance that this was about something else, and Ygo wanted to remain vigilant to that possibility.

The conversation between Cuss and Julie changed. He could tell they were up and about, so he expedited their food. He had three of Julie's four report items in good shape by the time they were done eating. He sent the last one before they finished coffee.

Chapter 11

The *Nelly Marie* launched from Hermes' spaceport, the start of a ten-hour flight to Stagecoach, Nevada. Once underway, Cuss released his seat restraints and waited while Julie did the same. Ygo was accelerating the craft at just over one gee, creating Earthlike gravity for them during the trip.

Julie rose and strolled around the command deck, looking out the two big viewports, giving the different ops panels a once-over. Beneath her feet, Ygo lived in his den, a fact she'd likely never know.

"The Marshals Service treats you well," she said after completing a circuit.

"They do indeed." He chose not to talk about the hassles of weightless living, instead leading her up to the middeck. Ygo had used Peanut, the *Nelly Marie*'s utility bot, to set up a table and two comfortable chairs.

"Have a seat." He motioned to the chairs and made for the kitchenette, where he poured two coffees from a carafe before joining her at the table.

"You gave up a day for me," he began. "I appreciate it. I'm going to say something that I hope doesn't insult you, but I want to make the offer. If you would like to submit an invoice for your legal counsel, the Marshals Service will happily pay it."

"I am so glad you said that." She put a hand over her heart. "Capit Legal has been after me to submit an invoice, not for the money, but to document our interaction. Something about protecting the position of the company and its good name." She gave a cute frown. "It will be for a nominal amount, but the delivery of services will include details of my involvement and, more to the point from Legal's view, what I didn't promise or suggest or imply or any of that. Is that okay?"

Cuss laughed. "Absolutely, happy to push it through."

Julie had done an outstanding job orchestrating the dynamic between Jeremiah Routh, Hermes' chief municipal attorney, and the thugs' attorney, a gruff older man. Using the briefs Ygo had prepared, she proved to be a master of pacing, detail, and theater, guiding the discussion to position the chief MA against the thugs, and then aligning Cuss with the chief MA, deftly putting their lawyer on the defensive.

Still, the Rodneys' attorney presented a persuasive argument that painted Cuss as a rogue cop, a perspective with enough selective facts to potentially create trouble for him with the Interworld Marshals Service, and if presented to a jury, perhaps enough to create doubt.

At Cuss's encouragement, Julie negotiated an expedient compromise. The thugs would drop the assault charges against Cuss if the city would drop the assault charges against them. They would still be charged with using unlicensed camo technology, a less serious offense.

Cuss tasted his coffee. "Did the day cost you anything in your personal life?"

"Glen is my only concern there, and he's with his dad in Los Angeles this week." Julie checked the time. "Our daily is coming up in a few minutes, by the way. I don't want you to think I'm ducking out on you. But he's my high point. The reason I do anything." She got a faraway look in her eyes and shook her head. "I keep worrying that he'll grow out of them, decide that daily chats with Mom are too childish or something."

"I'm sure you've done an amazing job raising him."

She gave a small shrug. "I'm doing my best. That's all anyone can do."

Then she shifted in her seat to face him, her eyebrows leveling, her tone becoming serious. "I fed the information about the Gastrow Group into the company's situation sieve. The observation it spat back is glaringly obvious, but I hadn't reduced it in my head that way. The pirates only hit Gastrow ships. The vids logs are missing in Gastrow's archives. The man killed was a Gastrow retiree."

Her voice took on a sharp edge, the features of her face hardening. "If they hired me because they think I'll screw it up, in the process somehow giving them cover for whatever they have going on, I will be so livid." Her hands formed into small fists. "I mean dangerously angry."

Cuss patted her shoulder. "I would be too. But I doubt the doer is the big boss who hired you. If anything, it's some midlevel employee taking advantage of the company."

"It would have to be a few employees, not just one." Her nod of agreement transitioned into a headshake. "Ned wouldn't be setting me up. He's executive VP for Operations at Gastrow. Ned Nisseki. When he hired me, he seemed sincerely interested in stopping the raids."

"And my instincts tell me it's not Gastrow driving this. Not directly, anyway. They are being used, no doubt. But there are other, bigger pieces."

"That sounds so mysterious."

"Don't get me wrong," said Cuss. "I plan on questioning the tech lead in their archiving area. We'll see if I feel the same afterward."

"I have the name of a guy at the Denver tech center, a supervisor in the comms department. Swindel Hasegawa. But I'm not sure if he's the person you're looking for."

"I'll follow up," said Ygo.

"He sounds like a good place to start," said Cuss. "If it's not him, hopefully he can point the way."

"I can't approach him for you," said Julie. "Ned made it clear to keep him in the loop, so I would have to start with him, explain the need, and get his permission. And if I start down the road of investigating the company that hired me and come up empty, then I can say goodbye to any future contracts."

"I'll reach out to him, no problem," said Cuss.

She averted her eyes and bit her lip. "Would you mind if I tagged along when you talk to him? That way I'm keeping an eye on things, something I could defend to Ned if he asks about it."

Cuss stepped over to her, helped her to her feet, wrapped his arms around her, and rocked her slowly back and forth. "Julie, I have a hundred favors lined up to give you. Happily." He stepped back, holding her hands, linking eyes. "Well, maybe not a hundred. But a lot."

"Well, thank you, Marshal. I do declare." She waved her hand in front of her face like it was a fan.

Cuss laughed. "So change course from Stagecoach to Denver?"

"Is it possible?"

"Piece of cake. Love having you along." Both statements were true.

Julie lifted her head in a way that made Cuss think she'd received a private comm. She glanced over at the ladder down to the command deck. "I need someplace to talk with Glen. Is downstairs okay?"

"It is. Or you can stay here. I'm going up to my room to catch a nap. When you're done, feel free to join me, or give a shout and I'll join you."

. . .

Cuss surfaced with his face buried in the pillow. His internal clock said he'd been asleep for forty minutes. Turning his head, he peeked at the clock. Forty-two. *It took two minutes to fall asleep,* he thought, explaining the difference to himself.

Looking across the bed, he confirmed he was alone. Standing, he put his hands on his lower back and leaned into a stretch, continuing until he heard a *crick*.

Then he called Aurora. When she didn't answer, he left a message. "I'll be stopping by your dad's place on Monday and I'd like to talk with you in advance. I'd appreciate a callback when you're free."

After closing the call, he climbed down to the middeck. Julie was sitting in a chair.

"You didn't wake me up," he said.

"I just now finished with Glen."

"How is he doing?"

"School is boring. His friends never want to do anything fun. Oh, and he's playing his dad against me to fund a new sim game." She smirked. "Otherwise, just fine."

"What kinds of games does he play?"

"War. Fighting. Shoot 'em up." She looked up at him. "What is it with males and mayhem?"

Cuss shrugged. "What kind of games do you play?"

"PingPing is my go-to."

"Really?" It was a popular sim version of ping-pong. "Want to plink some balls? Get our bodies moving?"

"Is there enough room?" She scanned the middeck.

"It's tight, but the system makes it work."

"If you're ready for defeat, I'll play."

Cuss moved to the middle of the deck and pointed to a spot three steps away. "You stand there."

She moved into position and Cuss engaged the sim. As it came alive, Julie appeared to move away from him. They were now separated by a simulated but very realistic ping-pong table.

Cuss formed a grip like he was holding a paddle, and the sim projected one in his hand. "Let's keep this fair and square." He was talking to Ygo, telling him to stay out of it.

"Always," said Julie.

He picked up the ball from the table and plunked it across the net. Julie plunked it back.

As they felt each other out, Julie asked, "Why do you think someone hired the Rodneys to attack you?"

"Because I'm on the right track." He hit the ball into the net and it bounced off the table. A new ball appeared in front of him, one of the great conveniences of a modern sim. He restarted the volley.

"What track are you on?" She was a competent player, returning the ball down the center.

"In truth, I don't know. But the fact that I'm making them nervous tells me to keep at it. That wherever I'm digging, there's something to find."

He sent the ball to her left corner with a bit of topspin. She snapped it back, just catching the corner on his backhand side, the ball sailing past him.

He switched the paddle from his left hand to his right.

"Oh my God, I did *not* just see that." Fists on her hips, lips pressed together, she shook her head. "Tell me you didn't do that."

He feigned innocence. "What? I was feeling you out."

"So I've been felt. Let's play." She pointed at the ball in his hand. "I'll give you the serve. Long game to twenty-one. Win by two."

Wishing he hadn't offended her, he served the ball with a modest backspin, expecting the reverse rotation to drive her return down into the net.

She snapped the ball across the table to his backhand, again just catching the corner.

Cuss's hand shot out, his reflexes driving the paddle behind the ball as it flew past, catching it, lobbing it back over the net.

Julie smashed it this time, the ball hitting the flat of the table and rebounding into his chin.

"Now you've made *me* mad," he teased with a grin. He began playing in earnest, relying on his hand-eye coordination and fast reaction time to carry the day. And in the end, it did. But they had to play to twenty-four before he had the requisite two-point lead.

They called a truce after that and switched to a downhill snow-surfing sim where points were earned through cooperation and teamwork. They were laughing in no time as they repeatedly attempted to ride an avalanche down a mountain face, failing in spectacular crashes made dramatic by the sim projector.

Then it was Cuss's turn to keep an appointment. "I've got a call with Mia coming up. Care to join in? Help me convince her to take appropriate precautions when she rides along with her perfect load?"

"If I'm welcome, I'd love to."

They sat in their chairs, and a large hoverview opened in front of them.

Ygo told Cuss, "Just learned she's running late."

"Mia needs a few minutes," Cuss said to Julie. "Have you been keeping up with her flights?"

"I know her first trip was uneventful. She completed delivery to Nova Terra, and last we spoke, which was a day and a half ago, she was about to travel back to Earth."

"Here she is," said Ygo.

The hoverview came alive, showing Mia sitting at a park bench, the Chicago Hub Spaceport logo visible on the backrest behind her. Over her shoulder in the distance, the brilliant trail of a ship descending to Earth made the scene dramatic. She wore her trademark sunglasses, a quirk Cuss still found annoying.

After an exchange of greetings, Cuss asked, "I hear your first trip was uneventful. Are you making any changes for your second flight?"

Mia nodded. "A big one. My team was able to secure eight Flo-AV motors in record time. I'm scrapping the second trip and moving on to the perfect load."

"Didn't you spread the word that that would be your third trip?"

"Yeah." She tilted her head in a shrug. "Now the pirates won't think it's a setup. What we did was advertise for a tech to do an emergency repair on one of the Flo-AV motors, including that it had to be completed prior to an upcoming launch. We put ads everywhere, and they included the launch date as well as the motor needing work.

In the picture you could see all eight drives. I'm certain the message got out."

"So you're prepared to be boarded by pirates, people who've killed." He spoke in a grave tone. "Would you mind walking me through how you're going to do this alone? What do you see happening?"

"When they blow the ship's hatch, they will be greeted by a Tefnik 316 pulser. It will be mounted securely to the deck, barrel pointed right at them, me operating from the pilot's quarters." She flashed a careless grin. "Let 'em come. It'll be fun to watch."

"Tech can fail," said Julie. "And what if they change their boarding tactics?"

"It won't and they won't. They've done it the same way almost thirty times. And pulsers don't fail."

"So you kill the boarding party," said Cuss. "How do you stop their ship?"

She crossed her arms in front of her. "I don't. But if I have bodies, I have identities. I'm pretty confident my team can track them back to the vipers' nest."

"This is incredibly risky, Mia," said Cuss. "Is a promotion worth it?"

"I don't see the danger the way you do. That pulser beam will stop them from boarding. I'm a hundred percent on that. The hatch will be damaged, but there are four places on the ship that I can close off and have life support until help arrives. I'm prepared to be bored waiting for rescue, but that will be the worst of it." She bit her lip. "Can you get here by tomorrow morning? I could wait until then. We'd be a formidable team."

He shook his head. "Sorry. Other commitments."

She nodded like she understood. "Well, wish me luck."

"I wish you safe passage," said Cuss. "I really do."

"Godspeed, Mia," said Julie.

They closed the call.

"If they go for the bait," said Cuss, "I don't see her surviving."

"Can't space patrol park a few ships along the route?" said Julie. "Be at the ready to provide backup?"

Cuss looked at her and smiled. "So there is something you don't know."

"What?"

"You know the Moon moves around the Earth, which is moving around the Sun, which is traveling through our galaxy."

She nodded. "I see it now."

He explained it anyway. Holding out his fists, one near his waist and the other at head level, he wiggled them. "This is the Earth and this is the Moon. When a ship launches, it will travel through the space between my fists." He turned sideways, his fists moving with him. "A ship that launches later will be traveling through space over here. The point being, the early ones can't park and wait, because they'll be left behind. Sort of like drifting away on a current."

"And…" said Ygo.

Figuring Julie was enough of a nerd that she'd appreciate the detail, he kept going. "And nothing can park in space anyway. Gravity from the Sun, Earth, and Moon will pull on a ship, dragging it in one direction or another."

"Finish it," said Ygo.

She seemed to be listening, so Cuss gave her a thumbnail of the speech tour guides use when showing off one of the cities of Lagrange. "Back in the seventeen hundreds, mathematician Joseph-Louis Lagrange studied how gravitational forces interact in space. He recognized that all planets pull, and objects naturally move toward the strongest gravity. Near Earth, things fall toward Earth. Near the Sun, they drift sunward. Same with the Moon. Lagrange calculated a sweet spot in the Moon-Earth-Sun system where the combined gravitational pulls create a stable balance, which means that things placed there essentially hover forever. Lagrange is named after him because the tube cities sit at the exact spot he predicted."

Her face brightened. "On my trip up, I watched a show that explained all that, but it didn't register. Nice job, Professor."

"There will be a quiz later." He looked her up and down. "You don't even want to know the penalty for a wrong answer."

"If it's what I'm hoping, I'm going to deliberately flunk."

Chapter 12

They walked through the lush courtyard, Cuss feeling energized by his surroundings. He loved being on Earth. Loved the outdoorsy culture of Colorado. Enjoyed Denver as a city. Loved looking across open vistas at the foothills, the snow-covered mountains rising behind, the cool spring breeze tingling his face.

Julie seemed less enthralled, but she lived on Earth, so perhaps that was to be expected.

The tech center was located just south of Denver in a small municipality called Lone Tree. Officially named the Gastrow Research & Technology Park, the tech center was housed in a sprawling three-story glass-and-brick complex placed at the rear of an attractive campus.

They approached the building, and Julie led them through a door that opened to a glass box, a gateway to the larger atrium. A holo-greeter asked their business, confirmed their appointment and identities, and summoned Swindel Hasegawa.

After testing the door out to the atrium and finding it locked, Cuss viewed the space inside the box. There were three chairs, a couch, and an end table holding a wood carving of a horse. Neither he nor Julie sat. It took Swindel

Hasegawa four and a half minutes to appear. Cuss was timing him.

As Swindel approached, Cuss saw a disheveled man pushing forty. His hair was uncombed, and his beard looked scraggly. Cuss assumed it was in its first weeks of growth. But as the man got closer, he realized that scraggle was all there'd ever be.

Swindel entered the glass box and reached out to shake hands, looking down instead of meeting Cuss's gaze. He shook with a flaccid grip, one that felt to Cuss like holding a warm, dead fish.

Cuss sighed quietly, his way of telling Ygo, "I'm not optimistic."

After exchanging greetings with Julie, Swindel led them out of the cubicle, across the atrium's terracotta-tiled floor, and down the right side of a double-wide stairway. The terracotta gave way to blue carpet at the bottom, which they followed down a hallway, passing several doors before entering a conference room.

Seated inside were three men, who turned out to be Swindel's subordinates. He introduced them by name, but Cuss remembered them as the guy who supervised human comms, the guy who supervised ships comms, and the guy who managed the record archives for the other two.

Cuss and Julie sat across from the three men. Swindel took the seat at the head of the table and began the meeting. "I understand you're interested in learning about the lost archive segments from the ships that have been raided."

Cuss nodded. "That and any other bits you can add about the events."

"Like what?"

"Let's start by reviewing the basics. So, of the twenty-eight raids…"

"Twenty-nine," corrected Julie. "There was one a few days ago."

"…Of the twenty-nine raids," continued Cuss, "all of them were Gastrow ships. Any ideas why you're being singled out?"

"None," replied Swindel, shaking his head. "Gastrow is one of three majors, so we compete for business in that group. Then add the half-dozen midsize players fighting us for market share. That's a lot of competition, and we all carry the same cargo, just for different clients."

"I understand the raids have focused on two of your shipping companies?"

Swindel nodded. "I haven't been updated on the event from the other day. But of the twenty-eight raids the company has processed so far, twenty-five have been Dependable Delivery hits, and four have been hits on Affordable Delivery. Dependable has a fleet of midsize ships. Affordable hauls larger loads on bigger, slower vessels."

"And Gastrow self-insures?" asked Cuss. "You've been absorbing all the losses yourselves?"

Swindel sat back in his seat. "We're discouraged from discussing business outside our areas of responsibility."

The three subordinates nodded their heads in support. "But off the record, I believe we do self-insure."

"So of the twenty-eight ships you know of that have been disabled by explosions, how much of your fleet is that?"

"For Dependable Delivery's twenty-five hits, that's a huge part of their fleet. But that's over a twenty-month period, which puts it at just over one attack per month."

"How long does it take to repair a ship?" asked Julie.

"Again not our field. But off the record, I've heard repairs take two or three months, meaning they'll have maybe three or four ships out of action at any one time."

"And the repair time isn't a complete loss," said Ships Comms Guy. "Every ship has a maintenance punch list. Things that need fixing but aren't bad enough to take the ship out of service. Items could range from a cabinet door that won't stay closed to a buzzing noise that's driving someone nuts. Those all get handled while the hatch is being replaced and the hull repaired."

"Let me add," said Swindel, "given that you're a marshal investigating piracy and all, punch lists aren't a reason for Gastrow to be involved with the criminals. Hatch repairs and loss of use of a ship are fantastically expensive."

Cuss had been intrigued by the idea that Gastrow might somehow benefit from the raids. But after hearing Swindel's comments, he agreed that it didn't make sense as a motive. He also chose not to correct the man's assumption that he was investigating piracy. "Where do they do the repairs?"

"Gastrow has a dedicated facility on the Drome," said Swindel, referring to a city-size platform circling in low Earth orbit. The Drome served as a staging gateway for ships outbound and inbound from the other worlds.

Cuss glanced at Julie. He was toying with the idea of stopping by the Drome on his way to see Aurora's dad in Nova Terra and wondered if she'd be interested in tagging along. Then he faced the group. "For the missing data, where is the archive equipment physically located?"

"That's not how it works," said Archives Guy, shaking his head. "The information is everywhere. The important point is that it's only accessible to us."

"But it's transmitted from a ship," said Cuss. "So initially, anyway, it's one signal. There must be a place where that transmission is received and then distributed across the datasphere?"

Archives Guy shook his head again. "No. The transmission is picked up by, shit, millions of receivers. Tens of millions, all the way out to Utopia. But it's encrypted, so it's gibberish to everyone who isn't authorized. And we don't have any leaks."

Ships Comms Guy elbowed Archives Guy and pointed into the air. It was clear to Cuss they were looking at something he couldn't see.

Ygo noticed and said, "Checking." Then, "They're watching Mia as she pilots her perfect load."

Archives Guy's mouth opened in astonishment. He began moving his hands rapidly on the tabletop.

Cuss was anxious to see. "You're watching LOCU agent Mia Moreau as she pilots one of your ships. May we watch as well?"

"What?" asked Julie, looking around the room, trying to understand.

Ships Comms Guy looked at Swindel, who said to Cuss with a tilted head, "Nice trick." He nodded approval to his subordinate.

"She's being boarded," said Ygo.

A large hoverview opened at the far end of the table, the display sectioned into four separate camera views. The window in the upper left showed Mia in her cabin, sitting in front of an ops panel for the pulser gun. The window in the upper right showed a side view of the Tefnik 316 pulser as it sat bolted to the deck outside her room. The lower two windows showed a closeup of the main hatch from inside and outside Mia's ship.

As they watched, someone in a heavy-gauge pressure suit pulled themselves along a line, approaching the hatch from outside the ship. The person spent several minutes positioning a seeker loop around the edge of the oval doorway. When the job was complete, they pushed off, following the line back until they moved off the display.

"Can you show us their ship?" asked Cuss. "Maybe pull back on the gun and show it and the hatch together. That'll free up a window."

Archives Guy moved his fingers, and the hoverview display changed as Cuss had suggested.

The new window showed the pirate craft. It was a smaller vessel, its exterior reflecting age and utility. Its hull was octagonal, and the eight flat surfaces had patches and weld lines and rivets, the battle scars of an old warrior. Some patches looked fresh, but most were not. Everything was lathered with battleship-gray paint, a color often chosen for price and availability rather than aesthetics.

The ship's utilitarian appearance made Cuss think of a beat-up shop truck, the kind that Earth businesses use for local chores. Only this workhorse was for space chores, which apparently included accosting other craft.

Ygo confirmed that it was a Bendolin Sprint. "Seven hundred were built starting forty years ago in a fourteen-year production run. Of the craft still in service, most are unregistered rescues from the scrapyards. Literally crates cobbled together. Makes it impossible to know who owns what."

Cuss couldn't see any logos or registration tags or service numbers or anything else that might help them identify an owner. He hoped Ygo had better luck.

A ring of light appeared around the edge of the pirate ship's main hatchway, and then the hatch swung open. Archives Guy zoomed the camera view closer. A construction bot moved into the opening.

Using four of its arms, the bot gripped around the edge of the hatch frame and held tight, securing itself into position. With the four arms as leverage points, it shifted its body outside the craft, projecting like a figurehead jutting from the bow of an old sailing ship, except here it stuck out awkwardly from the side of the vessel.

The presence of such a bot near Mia's ship would be threatening enough, but the menace was compounded by the laser rifle the automaton held in its last two arms. The rifle stock was a black rectangular box with silver ribs. Its barrel was a small-diameter tube with rings spaced up its length.

Julie moved a hand below the table and rested it on Cuss's leg. He took it in his, and as the bot leveled the gun at Mia's ship, he gave it a squeeze.

The bot pulled the trigger. First, a tiny red light no bigger than a fine thread, one invisible to those not wearing a lens, flashed out from the barrel. This was the depth sensor that would tell the gun when to cut the beam.

At the same moment, the internals of the laser stirred into action, electromagnets accelerating a stream of photons down the rifle's bore. Mirrored surfaces guided the packets of light back and forth in a dance of reflection and return, each cycle adding energy, building intensity. In less than a microsecond, the stream became so energetic that it breached the barriers of its confinement. Out flashed a beam from the rifle bore, an unstoppable torrent of light projecting through space.

In the blink of an eye, the brilliant column of energy pierced the hull of the craft, crossed an open passageway, pierced the wall into the pilot's quarters, crossed to the chair, and hit Mia in the right temple. Cauterizing the wound as it traveled, the beam continued through her skull, through her brain, exiting out her left ear.

The job complete, the depth sensor cut the beam.

Mia slumped back, held in the chair by her harness. The beam and her movements had dislodged her sunglasses, sending them spinning across the room. For the briefest of moments, Cuss saw the vitality of the woman reflected in her eyes. A fierce defiance. And then they became lifeless, staring without seeing, her head lolling to the side.

"Oh my God!" wailed Julie. "We have to help her!"

Cuss didn't reply, giving Julie time to process her shock and grief.

In the display, he watched as air spewed out from the laser hole in the ship's hull, the humidity in the air crystalizing to form a growing ice fog trailing behind the ship. As the cloud grew larger, Ygo said, "That model of bot can see through walls no problem. It could target her like she was just sitting there."

Cuss felt sad about Mia. But his grief was not deep, probably because he'd been so annoyed by her bullheaded rejection of his concerns. To minimize his aggravation, he'd acknowledged that her situation was beyond his control and put it out of his mind. This was just one of a dozen obvious ways it could have gone wrong.

And then the charges on the seeker ring began to move. They traveled slowly around the loop, small cones on a wire track. One by one, they stopped over the next pinion, cylinders of alloy that locked the hatch to the hull. The last cone stopped.

A ring of silent flashes signaled detonation, and then a much bigger ice cloud rushed out through the opening, obscuring their view. When it thinned, Cuss could see that the oval hatch was free from the hull, its center distended, fist-size pockmarks around the perimeter.

Two people in pressure suits floated up to the hatch. Cuss figured the bigger one was male based on his size and shape. Plus he had a laser rifle hanging at his side, an affectation Cuss felt was more consistent with male bravado.

Big Man grabbed the edge of the hatch, put a foot against the ship's exterior, and muscled the damaged door away from the hull. When the opening was wide enough, he led the way into the living area of the craft.

Inside, Big Man fixated on the pulser, studying it from different angles, gripping the stock, running a gloved hand up the barrel. After carrying on for a bit, he stopped and looked at the hatch. This seemingly odd behavior was soon explained when the construction bot arrived.

Talking to it, Big Man pointed to different parts of the gun. Cuss couldn't hear what he was saying, but the message became clear when the bot disassembled the weapon and carried the pieces back to the pirate ship.

While that was happening, the smaller pirate moved through the ship to the cargo hold. Stopping at the operator's station at the front of the bay, the pirate opened the cabinet below the display, pulled out a rolling shelf, and waved a small silver box above the equipment.

The hoverview they were watching in the Gastrow conference room blinked a bright white static and went dark.

"What the hell?" said Archives Guy, who began tapping and swiping in the space in front of him. Human Comms Guy and Ships Comms Guy leaned in to watch him work.

"What *was* that?" asked Swindel.

"No way," said Archives Guy, shaking his head and pointing at whatever the three were studying.

Cuss, Julie, and Swindel watched their growing agitation, waiting to hear.

With a "Fuck me," Ships Comms Guy grabbed control of the invisible workstation. He spent most of a minute tapping and swiping, his frown deepening. He looked at his partners, shrugged, and said to Swindel, "The record's been modified."

"Corrupted, more accurately," said Archives Guy. "The last thirty minutes are white noise on all channels from the ship."

"How is that even possible?" asked Swindel.

"It's not," said Archives Guy.

The three subordinates continued to investigate, arguing quietly among themselves.

"Best guess," said Ygo, "is they piggybacked an exploit onto the feed from the ship."

"C'mon, guys," Swindel said to his team. "We all saw it happen. Enlighten me."

"We'll need some time to understand it," said Archives Guy. The other two nodded in agreement. "For the record, I think they're inside our system. There's something they can trigger to start the data corruption."

"Allen and I agree that's one of two ideas," said Ships Comms Guy. "The other being that they somehow attached a payload to the feed from the ship."

Human Comms Guy nodded in support, but Archives Guy said, "They'd still need something on our end to catch it."

Julie leaned close to Cuss, put her lips near his ear, and whispered, "Now we know why they target Gastrow."

"So," said Swindel, looking at Cuss and Julie. "You'd asked why they target Gastrow. I think this is the answer. They can hide their tracks with us. I'm embarrassed to admit it, but we all saw it happen, so there's no point in pretending."

Ygo asked, "Do they have the original feeds from what we were watching?"

Cuss asked. The answer was no. They were watching from a feed that was supposedly sent everywhere and yet somehow every copy was corrupted.

"At least I recorded the holodisplay itself," said Ygo. "It's a low-quality source, but it's something."

After several minutes of awkward interaction, the three subordinates excused themselves so they could argue in private. Swindel stood and said he needed to call his boss. Cuss and Julie said their goodbyes and departed.

Outside, as they walked away from the building, Ygo told Cuss, "The hoverview record was good enough for me to see that the beam cut out after killing Mia. It didn't penetrate the back wall."

Cuss had expected as much. "It's been confirmed as a murder," he told Julie.

She remained quiet, shaken from watching Mia die.

Chapter 13

Cuss sat with Julie on the *Nelly Marie*'s command deck, chatting about nothing, marking time. They'd shown up at the Eastern Plains Regional Spaceport on short notice with plans to fly to the Drome, only to learn that the launch schedule was full until late afternoon.

Since he had time, he chose not to pull the "I'm an Interworld Marshal on official business" card and ruin everyone's morning. After a modest wait, flight control found him a slot in the next hour, which he gladly accepted.

It turned out that the wait came at a fortuitous time, because Royale called with a request to talk. Cuss asked him if Julie could join the call. Royale hesitated, perhaps caught by surprise by what seemed like an odd request, and then agreed.

"Hello Cuss. Hello Julie," he began. "I'm glad I was able to catch up with you."

"Congrats on your new role, Mr. Director of the Lunar Organized Crime Unit," said Cuss, still hating the sunglasses. "I'm so sorry about Mia. I'm sure you didn't want to win this way."

"There is no universe where I would consider this a win, Marshal," said Royale in an icy tone. "The LOCU family has taken the loss hard, and finding Mia's killers is *the* top priority for our agency." He paused to rub his neck. "You're probably aware that I've submitted a file to the Interworld Marshals Service requesting interagency cooperation while we take the lead on her case. All resources are on the table from our end."

Cuss nodded. Yesterday afternoon, maybe two hours after Mia's murder, Cuss's boss, Girish Mannan, had assigned him the case, explaining his reasoning with a brief message that noted the similarities in Moby's and Mia's murders.

Girish received Royale's request a few hours after that, and he'd called Cuss to ask his opinion. Cuss explained that he had no problems letting LOCU conduct an investigation as they saw fit, that he was happy to help them where he could, that he would not get in their way. But he wasn't about to sit around waiting for them to finish, either.

Girish agreed, so they decided to slow walk the matter. The Interworld Marshals Service would send LOCU an acknowledgement that the request had been received. A day later, they'd report that it was being processed. A day after that, that it had been forwarded to the director. And next, that the director was meeting with his advisors to discuss it. A question would arise about one issue or another, and the request would be returned to LOCU for clarification. And then the cycle would begin anew.

"I assume I can get updates at any time?" Cuss asked Royale.

"Absolutely. We're on the same team." Royale gave a thin smile, and then he shook his head. "Look, Cuss. I appreciate your support on this. I'm anxious to deliver one for the team. They're all looking to me to make it right. When we bring the killers to justice, it will rally the troops. Jump-start the healing process." He pressed his lips together for a moment before continuing. "How about this. If we don't close it in a week, we'll step back and let everyone in. I'm that confident."

"And we'll keep you in the loop as well," replied Cuss. Something about the guy annoyed him. Lots of somethings, actually. He decided to mark his territory. "Julie and I are on our way to the Drome to check in with the Gastrow maintenance team. Hear what they've learned from working on the damaged ships."

Royale's brow furrowed. "But we just agreed that LOCU would take the lead."

"For Mia's case. Don't forget I'm still investigating Moby Navarro's murder."

"Right." He hit the side of his head with the palm of a hand, a big lug needing to wake up. "Happy hunting, Marshal. If you learn anything that would help us, please let me know."

"Likewise," replied Cuss.

They closed the call.

"It sounds to me like he'll be solving this case in no time," said Julie. "Maybe I should hang out with him for a while."

Cuss shook his head. "He sounds off. Like maybe he still needs to prove himself to the hiring committee. Or to his troops." He made air quotes when he said that last word. "All I know is that his 'teams and troops' talk is bullshit."

"Agreed," said Ygo privately.

Julie stared into the distance for a moment before nodding. "I don't think I'd enjoy spending time with him anyway. I guess I'll stay here with you."

Her impish grin made him laugh. He leaned over and kissed her cheek.

They received launch verification soon after and readied for liftoff. A short, thrilling ride and they were in orbit above Earth. Ygo guided their approach to the Drome, a dance through traffic that would take about forty minutes.

"I haven't been here in more than four years," said Cuss as the enormous space platform loomed ahead. "I think then it was to question a suspect."

"That's right," said Ygo. "Luke Friedens for the Florida Central case."

Julie said, "I was here earlier this week on my outbound trip to Hermes. I've spent *a lot* of hours in the passenger concourse over the years, but I've never been outside its confines. Never explored the city."

Easily visible in daylight from Earth, the Drome started life forty years earlier as an interworld gateway. Brawny transports, ships designed for launching and landing in strong gravity, ferried people and goods between Earth and the Drome. Craft designed for fast spaceflight then moved everything from there out to the other worlds.

From those humble beginnings, the Drome had grown into a cramped city, with four busy flight decks, massive staging areas, and row upon row of docking piers. Below deck, three pressurized levels held hotels, restaurants, food markets, repair shops, warehouses, support services, vendor stores, fuel depots, and a cramped housing block for resident workers.

Ygo guided the *Nelly Marie* into their assigned space along a pier filled with midsize ships. As the craft nosed into its mooring slot, clamps gripped catches on the hull, securing the vessel in place. Hoses and conduits rose from the pier and attached to the ship. A flexible tunnel latched over the *Nelly Marie*'s main hatch, providing a passageway into the Drome.

When the safety light inside the *Nelly Marie* turned green, Cuss pulled open the hatch. He and Julie floated through the tunnel to an airlock door. They entered the bustling habitat and moved to an alcove near the main corridor.

It was weightless living on the Drome, and grav suits were common. Ygo directed Cuss to a cabinet where there were two suits, both blue and white, the colors of law enforcement. He passed the small one to Julie and slid into the big one.

"I have Julie listed as a provisional assistant deputy marshal," said Ygo. It was the lowest possible rank and the shortest possible term available in the Interworld Marshals Service employment catalog.

Since Cuss was visiting in his professional capacity, Drome law required that he wear cop colors. He hated being on display. It changed how people reacted to him, making it harder to do his job. But the Drome council was particular about the issue, and the Marshals Service expected him to cooperate. Listing Julie as a provisional assistant deputy qualified her for the colors, barely, with the benefit that she could follow Cuss into restricted spaces.

"You wear the colors well," he told her. The sleek outfit flattered her figure, and he found his gaze lingering.

"Where's my gun?" She smirked as she patted her hips, making a show of looking in the cabinet where the suits had been stored.

Cuss laughed. "Keep dreaming."

He looked up and down the broad corridor, a rectangular conduit tall enough for two-way traffic. From their current orientation, people traveling right moved along the ceiling. People going left used the floor. Most were walking with exaggerated knee lifts, the result of grav suit mechanics. The occasional free floater zoomed by, rogues shunning conformity by zipping down the center of the tall corridor.

"Our first stop is Bethel Tools," Cuss said aloud, an announcement for Julie, a request for directions from Ygo.

"Go right," said Ygo.

Cuss looked overhead at the traffic moving right, turned to Julie so she could see what he was doing, and powered down his suit. Now weightless, he pushed gently with his toes and rose toward the ceiling. Halfway along, he flipped in the air, and as he approached the ceiling, he reactivated his suit. Cuss settled onto what was now his floor, the orientation again normal to his senses. Julie settled in next to him.

He started walking, Julie at his side. Pedestrian traffic thinned near them, a reaction to their cop suits.

"Why Bethel Tools?" asked Julie. "Do they do lasers?"

"That's right. Good for you." Her insight continued to amaze him.

"Turn left," said Ygo.

Cuss continued the conversation as he followed Ygo's direction. "Francine Bethel worked as a laser specialist at the same agency where my boss started his career. About the time he left to work for the Marshals Service, Francine quit to start an industrial tools business with her mom. I guess she and Girish are still friends. Anyway, Girish has arranged for us to talk with Francine about the weapons used in Mia's attack. See if she can offer any insights."

Ygo said, "Up ahead. It's the second hatch on the right."

Hatches were in the middle of the tall corridors, halfway between the two traffic streams. Cuss and Julie deactivated their grav suits and floated up to it. A red Bethel Tools emblem on the wall next to the tall hatch confirmed they were at the right place. They announced themselves to an automated greeter, who told them it would be a moment.

The hatch opened.

"C'mon in, Marshals," said a woman in a well-worn red-and-white grav suit. She was somewhere in her sixties or seventies, close-cropped gray hair, lined face, stern demeanor.

Cuss and Julie introduced themselves. The woman shook hands and was pleasant enough but never said her name. Cuss used his lens to identify her as Lana Herskowitz, seventy-seven years old.

Lana tilted a head toward a woman across the room talking with two men. "She'll be with you when she's done with them." With that, Lana marched away, returning to her work.

They engaged their grav suits and walked a few steps into the large space, which proved to be a combination workshop and warehouse. On the left was a floor-to-ceiling array of storage bins. Ahead were workbenches, one with a partially assembled laser on the benchtop, a bot leaning over it, attaching more parts. To the right was a row of three large display booths, each with a different laser on a stand, accessories mounted on the wall behind.

A woman was conversing with two men in front of the middle display, pointing to different places on the laser as she spoke.

Cuss used his lens to confirm she was Francine Bethel. She sported a red cap that said Bethel Tools on the front and wore the same style grav suit as Lana. Her expression jumped from serious to cheerful and back again, nodding every time one of the men spoke, working hard on what Cuss presumed was a big sale.

They waited their turn, entertaining themselves by watching Lana do her thing. Which seemed to be directing the actions of two bots, sending them zipping here and there, gathering items from the different bins and strapping them onto pallets, fulfilling customer orders. She directed them by wiggling her fingers, sometimes pointing for emphasis, occasionally clapping her hands in a sharp *smack* if the bots weren't responding as she desired.

"Those look much bigger than the ones used on Mia," Julie said of the lasers on display.

Cuss nodded. Bethel's lasers looked more like cannons compared to the rifles used in the assault. Ygo had briefed him earlier about the technology, but Cuss had listened with only one ear, figuring Francine would go through it again anyway.

She finally came over and introduced herself. "How's Girish doing?" she asked with a friendly smile.

"He's doing well. Sends his regards."

After a bit of back-and-forth, Cuss got to it. "I wonder if you could look at a couple of lasers used in recent assaults and let us know your thoughts?"

"Lasers come in all sizes. I know the big stuff best." She gestured toward the display cases. "We joke about how these are for turning the asteroid belt into the great dust belt." She pointed down the row. "That one's used for slicing asteroids into sections. That one's for drilling and hollowing. That's for facing and chiseling."

"Does a miner really need all three to work the asteroids?" asked Julie.

Francine shook her head. "My recommendation is to make sure you buy enough firepower for the job at hand. If you buy a chisel and try to slice open an asteroid, you're going to be unhappy. Maybe even injure yourself in the process."

There was a pause in the conversation, and Cuss used the opening to launch a viewer. He showed Francine a holo of the laser held by the bot, and another of the one on the man's hip.

She pointed to the bot's laser. "That's old tech. Those rings up the barrel and the length of the bore are a dead giveaway." She studied it for a minute. "What's the hole diameter?"

"The hole the laser makes?"

"That's right. There are five major players in the mid tool game, and they each have unique beam diameters. Tell me a size and I can tell you the source."

Ygo said privately, "I have raw feeds from when we toured Moby's ship. Let's see. The holes are two point six centimeters. That's likely from the hip gun."

"Two point six centimeters," Cuss repeated. "That's likely from the hip gun."

Julie looked at him, eyebrows raised, her turn to be impressed.

Francine checked a private display and nodded. "That's Brace Harde of Harde Hardware. What time is it?" She checked. "We might be able to catch him."

She initiated a call, and while waiting for a response, she explained, "Brace provides specialized solutions for surface customers. Not excavation. But midscale stuff. Drilling, etchings, abrading. Like that."

"What are surface customers?" asked Julie.

Francine shrugged. "There are probably twenty big projects underway on the surface of the Moon within two kilometers of the Nova Terra canyon. Ore, water, food, waste processing, manufacturing. Most have laser tools for the odd job. Companies that have been in business for a while will have multiple generations of equipment, old stuff falling off inventory but still around. Think about how people accumulate old lawn tools over time in their shed or garage on Earth. Same thing only on an industrial scale."

Cuss was intrigued by the idea of an employee "borrowing" a laser gun without anyone at the company knowing.

A chime told Francine that Brace Harde was answering her call. When she spoke to him, her excited tone told Cuss that the two were at least good friends. Francine asked Brace if Cuss and Julie could join the call, identifying them as Interworld Marshals. He agreed.

Francine put Brace up on a big hoverview display: a lean fifty-year-old with longish brown hair tied back, piercing gray eyes, and a square jaw. He smiled when he saw them.

"I should start by clarifying that I'm no laser expert," said Brace. "Not like this one." He gestured to Francine, who beamed. "My business is selling supplies and hardware for lunar-based projects. Lasers are a small part of our catalog, and those we sell are made from parts we import from Earth and assemble here."

"I understand," said Cuss. He showed Brace the feed of the bot's laser rifle and the doer's hip laser.

Brace pointed to the rings up the barrel of the bot's rifle. "We haven't used heat dissipation like that in a decade."

"Would you have records of who might have purchased this particular model?"

"Probably. Hold a sec." His image faded, and a few moments later, he was back. "I was right. We sold this model for about six years with the last sale nine years ago. The tally is five lasers to Mars, nine to Earth, and twenty-eight sales here on the Moon. I'll send the list."

"Thanks. It turns out I'm going to be in Nova Terra tomorrow. Any chance I could swing by and pick your brain?"

"You're standing next to the expert. You should ask her."

"She's been extremely helpful." Cuss acknowledged Francine with a nod. "This would be about the companies on your list. Who they are. What they do. Local gossip and all."

Brace scratched the back of his head as he thought. Cuss understood that there wasn't any upside for him to cooperate. There was even a small chance that it could cost him business if word got out that he was a snitch. Finally he spoke. "Julie, are you coming?"

She nodded and grinned. "I will if I'm welcome."

"Okay. Drinks tomorrow afternoon at my house. I'm in Armstrong on Lansing Street. It's near the North Gate. I'll send the address when I send the list."

Ygo said, "Nick Navarro's rocket engine company is not far from there."

"See you then," said Cuss.

Chapter 14

Ygo heard the perimeter alarm and accessed the exterior cameras. Two people in lightweight pressure suits were floating across open space toward the *Nelly Marie*. He traced back from their angle of approach and determined that they'd pushed off from the neighboring pier. It was an unusual way to approach a ship in port. So unusual that Ygo was certain their intentions were nefarious.

Switching through different camera views, he found one that let him capture their faces through their helmet visors. A man and a woman. Paval Backus and Danika Lanka. They'd arrived at the Drome three hours earlier. According to their criminal records, Danika was skilled at gaining entry into space-borne vessels. Paval was an expert in violence and mayhem.

The *Nelly Marie* detected the threat, readied a paralyzing electric discharge, and sought Ygo's approval to fire. Ygo put a hold on the action, instead choosing to call on Peanut, the *Nelly Marie*'s utility bot, a droid that resembled an upside-down trash can fashioned with a short, thick arm out the side and long spindly arm on the top.

Peanut awoke in its charging closet at Ygo's command. Its tool carousel currently held a selection of hand tools, and on the way out of its closet, Ygo had the bot add a spool of medium-gauge wire to the mix. He directed Peanut to the hold at the bottom of the ship.

The hold was a place packed with tech. The top of the Paulson drives poked up in the center. Around the circumference were fuel pods, stores of air and water, the life support system, waste-processing and recycling units, power generation, multiple electronics racks. And, of course, Ygo's private room.

After Peanut reached the hold, Ygo directed the bot around the perimeter, past his den, and to a stop at a trapdoor in the deck, an accessway down into a maintenance compartment used for servicing the Paulson drives. Inside was a place that glowed and throbbed when the ship was underway. Now it was dark and quiet.

Peanut opened the trapdoor, floated down into the compartment, and sealed the door shut. As the bot drifted in the compartment, Ygo assessed his options. The front wall was the containment for the Paulson drives themselves. The walls on either side were covered with the piping and electronics that gave the drives life. The back wall held a largish utility hatch that led out into space, an accessway big enough to clear the equipment used to service the drives. This was the hatch that Paval and Danika had just reached.

Ygo decided to have Peanut squeeze into an opening on a side wall between a run of pipe and a breaker box. He positioned the bot and the angle of its arms to look vaguely like another piece of equipment on the wall, at least to the peripheral vision of someone paying attention to other things.

While Peanut got into position, Paval, floating outside the utility hatch, was wrestling with a work tent. In a brazen move, he attached it to the side of the *Nelly Marie*, positioning it so it shielded the hatch. When he opened it, the broad side of the tent showed the Drome Port Authority logo, a display that gave their presence legitimacy to outside observers.

Drome Port Authority tents were a safety requirement for all space work performed along the piers. Their function was to corral loose scraps and lost tools from a project for easy retrieval at the end of the day. If not contained, these bits and pieces would drift into the void. Since the Drome was moving in orbit around Earth at ten times the speed of a medium-caliber bullet, lost items would be moving that fast as well, becoming dangerous projectiles threatening everything in their paths for centuries to come.

But Paval wasn't unfurling a tent to comply with Drome port regulations. Nor was he concerned about errant space junk. As Ygo had guessed, he was using the tent to hide his and Danika's criminal mischief. Specifically, their attempt to break into the *Nelly Marie*.

With the tent in place, the two ducked under its cover and Danika began fidgeting with a device strapped to her left forearm. She tapped and swiped, and a malware agent popped open inside the *Nelly Marie*'s central computer system.

Ygo had helped design the ship's defensive capabilities and knew Danika's attack didn't stand a chance. He studied the malware long enough to understand that its goal was to open the utility hatch. Then he freed the *Nelly Marie* to corner and kill it.

With the ship secure, he pondered the situation for a moment more. He wanted to question the intruders, which meant he needed to capture them. So he opened the utility hatch anyway and let them in.

When the door released, Danika looked at Paval, who pumped a fist in the air. Ygo couldn't hear their words, but imagined it was something like, "Holy shit, it worked!"

Danika led the way into the *Nelly Marie*'s maintenance compartment with Paval following close behind. Ygo powered a single light inside as they entered, one that pointed up at the trapdoor, the next stage in their advance. Paval signaled for Danika to wait while he pulled the utility hatch shut. He tapped a button next to the hatch, and the compartment flooded with air. They started for the trapdoor.

While their focus was upward, Ygo had Peanut push off from the wall and approach Paval from behind. The bot had prepared a wire lasso, and in a fluid move, dropped it over the man's head, pulled it down over his arms, and cinched it tight.

Paval reacted violently when the wire bit, struggling, bucking, yelling. But Peanut was able to control him enough to twirl him in the air. As the man spun, wire wrapped around him, immobilizing him from shoulder to knee.

With Paval incapacitated, Ygo turned his attention to Danika, who was reaching for a gun in a leg pocket of her pressure suit. Before the gun cleared the suit, Peanut grabbed her wrist, disarmed her, and stashed the weapon in its tool carousel. The two wrestled for a moment before Peanut got control of her, and then the bot bound her in wire.

When she was immobilized, Ygo saw that Paval was trying to worm a hand down his leg. Peanut searched him, and confiscated a gun and a knife.

With the prisoners controlled and disarmed, Ygo had Peanut crush the comms circuits in their pressure suits to isolate them from the world, then anchor the intruders to opposite walls.

And then he called Cuss.

. . .

Cuss hurried through the *Nelly Marie*'s main hatch and down into the ship's hold, Julie following close behind. From what he could tell, Ygo had the prisoners secured. He led the way around the hold to the trapdoor, thinking about what to do next.

He was anxious to learn their who, what, and whys. But to get those answers, he'd have to use an agency interrogator, which meant sending them to Seattle.

Ygo seemed to read his mind. "Drome laws require that we work through them. If we skip the locals and take them to Earth ourselves, the boss will be seriously unhappy."

"He'd only know if the locals complained."

Girish Mannan was indeed a stickler for rules, but Cuss thought it might be worth a scolding to speed things along. Then he thought of an issue he didn't want to discuss in front of Julie.

Ygo had registered them both as Interworld Marshals with the Drome police. But he had never actually completed Julie's registration as a provisional assistant deputy with the Marshals Service. Which meant that, technically, she'd been impersonating an officer when she'd been wearing the blue-and-white grav suit.

What made the issue stickier was that Julie was unaware this could possibly become an issue for her. The good news was that they were back in street clothing, so she was no longer in violation.

As he hovered above the trapdoor, Cuss toyed with the idea of questioning the assholes himself before calling the locals. According to Ygo, the prisoners were a couple, and that gave him options in an interrogation, though the theory kept flip-flopping about the best approach. Whether to use threats or rewards. If it was threats, whether to start with the man or woman. Whether to make it perverse or violent. Whether to make the other watch.

Cuss had been taught the techniques. But each stage of pressure became more gruesome or depraved, methods that conflicted with his basic nature and moral compass. He'd have to be feeling visceral rage to go down that road.

He lifted the trapdoor, studied the pair of wire-wrapped bodies floating in the compartment, and decided he was more annoyed than enraged.

Ygo weighed in, "They have the resources to hire excellent legal representation. Top-tier firms. And so far, they've never given up a client."

Cuss didn't need to hear any more. He turned to Julie but was really speaking to Ygo. "Let's call the locals."

. . .

Drome Enforcement Officer Ryan Jagoda, early fifties, dressed in black with a gold badge on his chest and matching epaulets on his shoulders, arrived at the *Nelly Marie*'s main hatch twenty minutes later. When Cuss told him that Julie was up on the middeck in a chat session with her son and would contact him later to answer any questions, Officer Jagoda responded with a shrug.

Cuss went on to explain that the ship's bot had confronted and subdued the intruders, and that he'd reported the incident as soon as he'd learned of it.

Officer Jagoda inspected the offenders. They were still wrapped in wire, Paval tied to the pilot's seat, Danika to the copilot's seat. And their suit helmets were still up over their heads, ensuring their isolation.

"You can't handle it?" asked Officer Jagoda.

"Aren't I required to call you?"

"Civilians, yeah. But I don't think that applies to marshals. Let me check." He hooked a foot under the pilot's seat to keep from drifting, then used his helmet tech to contact base. After a private exchange, he said, "It'll take a minute for an answer. They're asking the captain."

While he waited to hear back, he looked around the command deck, and then at the prisoners. "Must be awesome chasing real criminals. You guys hiring?"

"You don't do that here?"

Officer Jagoda tilted his head in a mix of a shake and a shrug. "Our job is to keep the ships on schedule, so it's all small stuff. Unruly passengers. Luggage theft. Break-ins. And we're so shorthanded, we're constantly in reaction mode. No planning whatsoever."

He held up an index finger and looked away. After a pause, he nodded and turned back to Cuss. "I'm supposed to bring the prisoners in for processing, get samples and whatnot so we can identify them should they ever return in whatever form. You can have them after. Maybe three hours?"

Cuss nodded. "Deal."

A second officer arrived a few minutes later, and the two floated the prisoners away, pulling them on wire leads like parade balloons.

"Check their oxygen supply," Cuss called as they disappeared down the tunnel. "They've been in those suits awhile."

As Cuss closed the main hatch, he said to Ygo, "That played out different from what I expected."

"Me too. I expected them to care. Sorry for the bad intel. I'm going to leave a snooper behind to observe operations and update my procedures. Make sure I have the facts for next time."

"Don't be hard on yourself. It worked out okay." Cuss pressed his lips together as he thought. "What do you think about letting Pina have a go?"

"The Mistress of Pain interrogating a couple of nobodies? She's in heavy demand. You'd have to defend it."

"Someone is spooked by our investigation. But since we don't have a target yet, it's our reputation they're reacting to, not our actual progress. Fear based on perception. That's a huge clue and I want to know where it leads. Who are we scaring?"

He heard Julie's voice become louder as she closed her call. "Love you, hon. Be good. See you tomorrow."

He looked up the stairway and she appeared at the top. "The prisoners are gone?"

"For a few hours. They're going to let us take them later." He floated up and joined her on the middeck. "I'm going to run them down to Seattle for questioning. See what a pro can learn."

"Let me guess." She smirked. "That you're on the right track?"

"I've got someone worried. That's pretty clear."

Ygo interrupted their exchange. "Georgio is calling. He's panicked about Aurora."

Cuss turned to Julie, squaring up to get her attention. "I'm getting an urgent call from Georgio Navarro. He's Moby Navarro's grandson."

Ygo launched a hoverview with Georgio in the display. Cuss was surprised by his appearance. Face drawn. Hair disheveled. Bags under bloodshot eyes.

"Hi Georgio. I'm here with Julie Kapoeta. She's the one who hired Aurora to cater the pirate conference. What's up?"

"I can't get hold of Aurora."

"Tell me."

"She left for Lagrange yesterday afternoon. She should've arrived in Hermes seven hours ago. She doesn't answer, no one has seen her, no one has talked to her."

"When did you last talk to her?"

"Right before she left Valencia for the spaceport."

"Which one?"

"Which spaceport? Albacete. It's closest to Valencia."

"Did she board the craft?"

"How would I know?" Georgio's sharpened tone reflected his frustration. "That's why I'm calling. Did she board? Did she make her connection on the Drome? Did she arrive in Hermes? If not, where is she now?"

"On it," said Ygo.

"Georgio." Cuss locked eyes with him to focus his attention. "A colleague has just confirmed that he's started the search for Aurora. He's working on it as we speak. You've achieved your goal. Us talking isn't delaying anything. Now take a deep breath and let's piece through it. Have you contacted her folks? What do they say?"

"Her folks can't get hold of her either."

"Are they back in Nova Terra?"

"That's right. Her mom is really worried. Crying and everything. Says Aurora would never just disappear like this."

"What about her father?"

"Between Moby and this, Nick is barely keeping it together."

"Does he have any ideas?"

"He won't talk. He's out in his shop working on rocket engines."

"How about her friends and neighbors? Or employees at her catering company?"

"I don't know any of her friends or neighbors in Hermes. She has a catering assistant named Jenna who says she can't reach her either. She's worried because they have a job they need to get going. Says Aurora would never skip out on it."

Julie asked, "What do you think happened to her?"

"No idea," said Georgio, desperation in his voice. "She's a cook, for God's sake."

"I fear she's been taken," said Ygo. "I'll know soon."

The words sent a chill down Cuss's spine. Every minute counted in a kidnapping. "Thank you, Georgio," he said. "I'm going to get started myself. An agent will be contacting you soon to ask more questions. It's part of our process. Please cooperate."

Georgio gave him a blank stare.

"Contact me immediately if you hear from her. I'll be in touch." Cuss closed the call, hoping Ygo would soon report that it was all a mistake.

Chapter 15

Ygo accessed the Albacete Spaceport public monitoring system and located the ID trail for Aurora Navarro. She'd arrived on a tram two hours before launch. The playback showed her walking up the sidewalk toward the passenger pavilion, a suitcase trailing behind her and a daypack over her shoulder. She was moving along with the crowd.

The pavilion was a visual feast from the inside, the main concourse constructed in a style suggestive of Albacete's own Cathedral of San Juan Bautista. But like most of the other passengers in the crowded pavilion, Aurora wasn't paying attention to the architecture. She was following a guide, a dot of light hovering out in front of her, leading her through the labyrinthine building to her launch gate.

And like most of the crowd, she was following the guide using her peripheral senses, her attention centered on a private display, the contents of which Ygo couldn't see. She was mostly listening but occasionally talking. When he had an angle that let him read her lips, she spoke in short sentences: "That would work," and "I've done those," and "That's a good choice."

She was maintaining a brisk pace, her guide dot weaving her through the swarm of travelers. But her path wasn't symmetrical. She was moving more to the right than to the left. Soon she was on the edge of the crowd along the far wall. Perhaps it made sense to her because it moved her out of the throng.

A door opened on her right, and she followed the guide dot inside. When the door closed, Ygo saw it had a small *Employees Only* sign.

He searched for active sensors in the room, anxious to learn what was happening. But inexplicably, the room was offline. No active devices available.

He sped forward in the record.

Eleven minutes after Aurora disappeared, an attendant entered the room. The door remained open and Ygo found a camera across the way that gave him a glimpse inside. He saw a row of shelves with clear boxes holding random items. His best guess was a lost-and-found room.

The attendant stepped out again, empty-handed, neutral expression, as if nothing were amiss. The door shut.

Racing through the next several hours of playback, Ygo counted six people and three bots visiting the room. A few carried small items in or out. But Aurora never came out, nor did any crate or package or bundle large enough to conceal her. He contacted port security and made an urgent request to have the room searched.

Then he restarted the record at the point where Aurora disappeared, this time casting a wide net, working systematically, checking everywhere. But the spaceport complex was huge, with seemingly endless waiting areas, corridors, bathrooms, equipment rooms, storage spaces, shops, and restaurants, with travelers milling about, luggage and bags and boxes moving this way and that, workers and bots accompanied by carts and trollies.

She could be anywhere.

Ygo started an AI agent on a parsing task, having it check each of the eight hundred cameras in the spaceport. He directed it to move through the record starting when Aurora disappeared, stepping forward in millisecond increments, scouring each image from each camera for hints of her.

While that was working, he located a building schematic. It confirmed there weren't any doors in the lost-and-found room that led to other places. But to his dismay, he saw that the room had a common wall with the spaceport luggage sorting center, a huge room filled with spinning carousels, conveyor belts, and mechanical arms that directed a torrent of luggage and containers to locations all over the spaceport.

Port security reached the lost-and-found room forty seconds after Ygo's initial call. Their search confirmed his fears.

They found a panel in the back wall that was loose, its location allowing a container to be slipped onto the conveyor system without being seen by a camera. Another loose panel farther along provided a pathway for the doers to escape.

Concluding that Aurora was likely kidnapped, Ygo switched his attention outside to the launchpads, speeding through the record yet again, this time watching the different ships launch. Three hours after she had disappeared, an ancient gray Bendolin Sprint took flight, the same ship that had attacked Mia.

Ygo accessed the Spaceport Customs and Immigration Office archives and retrieved the documents for the ship. The Bendolin Sprint was owned by a company with a contact address in Antigua in the Caribbean. The address was for a lonely mailbox on the outskirts of the town of Yorks. When Ygo learned that a hundred other companies were also hiding their identities behind that sham address, he concluded the worst.

Three minutes after Ygo had told Cuss, "I'll know soon," he delivered his report. "She's been taken."

. . .

Georgio's holo-image on the hoverview was replaced by that of an unfamiliar man. Angular face, gawky demeanor, maybe forty years old. He had a neural cap on his bald dome, an optical stim hanging over one eye, an aural lift hooked to an ear, and aug gloves on his hands.

Cuss knew immediately that it was Ygo. His partner took great joy in creating inventive personas when other people were present, doing so to relieve Cuss of the burden of explaining that his partner was actually a bedridden soul holed up in a den just a few meters away.

"Hi, Ygo." He'd considered the idea of giving him a fun name to add to the spectacle, maybe something like Synchro or Techneek, but knew from past experience that it would become a hassle to remember the name in later conversations. "This is Julie. She's consulting on the case. Julie, Ygo is a fellow marshal."

Ygo greeted Julie and then briefed them. He told them about Aurora's guide dot leading her to the lost-and-found room, the panels missing in the room's back wall, the luggage sorting center on the other side, and the Bendolin Sprint that looked like the one involved in Mia's murder.

"How could they gain control of her dot like that?" asked Julie.

"Guide dots are a feature provided by the spaceport, so the doers could manipulate it if they had access to the port's central systems. And since they were able to take the sensors in the lost-and-found room offline at a critical moment, it's apparent they had access."

"Any idea who she was talking to?" asked Cuss.

"Best guess is a catering prospect," said Ygo.

Julie's brows leveled. "Probably a phony customer whose job was to distract her."

Cuss liked the idea. "Given the tight timing on the abduction sequence, they'd want to start the con before she entered the pavilion." Then to Ygo, "Do we know where the ship was headed?"

"They were accelerating out of Earth orbit when they cut their transponder and disappeared into background traffic. That ship couldn't make it to Mars. And it'd stand out like a sore thumb in Lagrange. Same with Port Collins. Best guess is they landed somewhere on the surface of the Moon. If not that, then they circled back and landed here on Earth."

"Brace Harde knows the companies working the Moon's surface," said Julie. "He might recognize the ship."

"Can you follow up on that?" Cuss asked Ygo, beginning to accept Julie as a valued partner. "What a break that would be." He rubbed his neck while he brainstormed, the thrill of the hunt stirring his blood. "My brain keeps bringing me back to Nick Navarro. His dad is murdered and his daughter is taken, and he has nothing to say? He should be screaming to the authorities. Pounding the table and demanding action."

The Moon held answers. But Cuss feared burning up precious hours to get there, only to learn that he needed to turn around and race back to Earth. Kidnapping was a time-sensitive crime, where lost minutes could lead to lost lives.

In the end, though, he couldn't see an alternative. "I'm going to sprint to Terra Nova," he told Julie. "You're welcome to join me, or I can leave you here to catch a flight home." He held up a finger before she could respond. "I need to get there fast, so the ship will be moving at two gees. It'll feel like a big dog is sitting on your chest for several hours."

The ship rumbled as the Paulson drives came to life.

"Are we talking a Lab or a mastiff?" asked Julie.

Cuss grinned. "I take a palliative, so it feels more like a dachshund."

She bit her lip and looked into the distance.

Cuss imagined her working through the adjustments she'd need to make in her life if she were to accompany him.

She shrugged and then nodded. "I like dachshunds. And Brace invited us to drinks. I'm in."

. . .

Ygo had hoped to get lucky. That finding the Bendolin Sprint would be as easy as contacting Lagrange or Port Collins on the Moon to confirm the ship had landed there.

It hadn't. Which meant either it had returned to Earth or, more likely, it had landed somewhere on the surface of the Moon. To answer that question, he sought to track the ship to its landing spot.

Space Watch had followed the Bendolin Sprint through launch and up into orbit. After looping once around the globe, the ship had headed away from Earth, disabling its drives and transponder soon after. The VICO flight monitoring system used transponder signals for tracking. Without it, the Bendolin Sprint became just another piece of detritus in the cloud of stuff near Earth.

Since the craft was coasting, it was straightforward for Ygo to predict its flight path. He computed where it should be after one hour and used Space Watch archive data to look there, finding dozens of objects that could be the missing craft. He sorted through them one by one until he found the Bendolin Sprint. Then he repeated the process, stepping forward another hour in time.

The method worked well enough, for a while. Then a cycle came where the ship wasn't where he predicted. He backed up in the record and made a tweak, trying again and again without success.

Perhaps the ship had disintegrated in an explosion. Maybe a second ship had been following behind with an active transponder, and they had swapped identities as they passed in flight. More likely, the Bendolin Sprint had fired its engines and changed course. Whatever the reason, he'd lost track of the ship.

Accepting the fact, he turned to basic detective work. His gut told him to start on the surface of the Moon. Given that space piracy was driving the whole mess, Earth didn't make sense as a home base. If the doers lived there, why wouldn't they make their lives easy by stealing from trucks or boats or warehouses?

And he had solid leads on the Moon. Brace Harde had provided a list of companies that had purchased a laser similar to the one used to kill Mia.

But as he read the message Brace had included with the list, his early optimism faded. Brace reiterated that the purchases had taken place nine to fifteen years ago. That the Moon was a dynamic commercial environment with companies routinely being bought and sold in a merry-go-round of mergers and acquisitions. And in the process, inventory was often liquidated and distributed to other shops. Brace hadn't tracked any of it and said he didn't want to try.

"No worries," Ygo said aloud, speaking as if Brace could hear him. "I've got it."

Contemplating where to start, he sipped stim soda from a straw, swished it in his mouth the way he might for a fine wine, and swallowed, savoring the rush of energy as the drink stirred his system.

He was submerged in liquid at the moment, one of the configurations of his capsule bed. The fluid surrounding him diffused the pressure of the ship's acceleration, relieving him of the "dog sitting on your chest" heaviness that Cuss and Julie were experiencing. So while they were resting with the help of a calming gas, he was fully alert, his goal to use the next hours generating solid leads to share with Cuss when he resurfaced.

His knees wiggling in nervous excitement, Ygo decided to start with a scan of the ships in lunar orbit. If the Bendolin Sprint had landed there, it would have been recorded on approach to the Moon prior to descent.

Working through the record, he found three Bendolin Sprints passing through lunar orbit within the time span of interest. All three were painted battleship gray, and all three had patch repairs that, to Ygo's dismay, did not match the patches on "their" Bendolin Sprint.

So he moved a layer inward, identifying and profiling the companies working the Moon's surface around the Nova Terra canyon. He was able to locate thirty-seven operating plants, most of them commercial, though some were controlled by the Nova Terra government. As he scanned the names, he subconsciously sorted the plants into industry categories: mining operations, power generation, air and water resources, waste recovery, food factories, and commercial manufacturing.

He noted that the mining operations did not serve Nova Terra, but were owned by conglomerates that moved the minerals to Earth for final processing. On the flip side, the plants for power generation, air and water resources, and waste recovery were government entities that existed solely to serve the residents. The Nova Terra government owned and operated five solar power installations, the nuclear backup station, and two waste recovery and recycle plants.

It also owned the two air and water resources plants. These were operations that mined and melted water from underground deposits and pumped it to the cities, where a portion was electrolyzed to create oxygen for air. A third plant was under construction by an outside company on speculation, the investors believing that the residents would happily breathe and drink their product if they could succeed in getting it to them.

On the commercial side, there were more than a dozen food factories, all owned by off-world outfits. The government had offered lavish incentives to the early food pioneers to ensure basic nutrition for the populace. As the companies grew profitable on their own, more players joined the ranks. There was now enough activity to provide a broad and varied diet for the residents, and the subsidies had shrunk over time from lavish to large, and were reportedly trending toward meager.

Manufacturing was a sector bigger than food, and it was still growing even though it received the least generous financial incentives from the government. Manufacturing didn't produce vital necessities like food or air or water or power. Factories made stuff. And companies would produce it locally if that was cheaper than importing the items from Lagrange or Earth. The number of plants was growing, the government welcoming all comers. To ease the pain of relocation, the Nova Terra government provided building plots with power, air, comms, and water preinstalled.

Thirty-seven operating plants was too many to concentrate on. He needed to cull the list to around five.

He yawned, realized he was tired, and decided to take a nap. He'd work through the list with Cuss and Julie in a couple of hours.

Before he could rest, though, he spawned an AI agent to follow up with the officers watching Paval and Danika, the prisoners they'd left behind on the Drome. He tasked the agent with delivering the two doers to their appointment with the Mistress of Pain in Seattle.

He spawned a second AI agent to scour Earth for any signs of Aurora, or the pirates, or the Bendolin Sprint, or the stolen goods. He gave this agent permission to create AI swarms as needed, and the authority to draw additional resources if a lead proved promising.

He spawned a third AI agent to gather details about the different companies around the Nova Terra canyon. Where was each plant located? Who were their human employees? Did they have warehouse space to store multiple shiploads of stolen pumps and pipes and pylons? Did they have a Bendolin Sprint parked near their building or a hangar to hide one? Were they on Brace Harde's list of laser purchasers? Did they buy liquidation inventory from a company that was? Did they use laser guns in any part of their operation?

And then he skimmed through the responses that an AI agent had gathered from questioning Georgio, the detailed interrogation that Cuss had promised him. Nothing about Georgio's answers or behavior during the interview drew suspicion, nor did the man offer information or insights that would move them closer to finding Aurora.

With his chore list complete, Ygo goosed the drives so they'd move even faster while everyone was sleeping. He checked in on Cuss and Julie to make sure they were handling the pressure from the acceleration. And then he closed his eyes and slept.

Chapter 16

When Cuss surfaced, his tongue felt like dry rubber, his lips crusty plastic. He grabbed the water bottle from its holder next to the pilot's seat and downed half of it in one go.

Dry mouth was a side effect of the palliative, what Ygo called calming gas. The mix included additional oxygen to allow for shallower breathing, a stimulant that supported the muscles of the diaphragm, and a mood enhancer to ease the mental stress of the physical punishment. Cuss used it during extended periods of acceleration when he wanted to catch up on sleep.

As his awareness returned, the lightness in his chest told him they were no longer pushing two gees. Ygo had slowed them down.

"ETA?" he asked.

"Two hours," replied Ygo. "Same schedule as before. I ran hot while we were sleeping so we could back off now and relax while we plan. How are you doing?"

"Good. Is Julie up?"

"Not yet. Do we have anything confidential to discuss?"

Sitting forward, Cuss looked at Julie in the seat next to him. She looked peaceful. Cute, even with a drop of saliva drooling from the corner of her mouth. He thought of a few juvenile replies before shaking his head. "Not unless you do."

"Nope. Give her ten minutes."

Cuss sat back, closed his eyes, and rested, enjoying the twilight zone between half-asleep and half-awake. Before long he heard Julie stir.

"Water," she croaked.

He leaned over and guided her hand to her bottle. She drank a series of small sips, belched, snickered, and took a long pull.

While he waited for her to fully awaken, he thought about Aurora. Every minute counted, and at this point it had been most of a day. He wanted to know what Dad—Nick Navarro—had learned. Had there been a ransom demand? Any other contact? Who would do this and why?

The large display at the front of the command deck came alive. On it was Ygo, reprising his quirky marshal character. "Rise and shine, you two. We're still on schedule, landing in Port Collins at thirteen hundred hours. Now might be a good time to plan."

Cuss interrupted. "I want to talk with Nick Navarro. Has there been a ransom demand? Has he had contact with them?"

"I have Nick's private link courtesy of Georgio," said Ygo. "Let's see if he has answers."

While they waited, Ygo said, "I reviewed Georgio's interview while you were sleeping. I read him as clean. He doesn't know who, what, or why."

"When Moby was killed," said Julie, "it felt like the pirates were making a statement. Maybe a warning or a threat. But now that Moby's granddaughter's been taken, it feels completely different. Like it's personal." Then she connected the dots. "And Nick is in the middle. His dad. His daughter."

Ygo's holo was replaced by that of a haggard-looking middle-aged man. Stringy hair. Bleary eyes. Frown lines all over his face. Jaw set in defiance.

Nick Navarro spoke to them through clenched teeth. "State your business."

"Hello, Mr. Navarro. I'm Interworld Marshal Cuss Abbott. This is Julie Kapoeta, working with me as a consultant. We're investigating your father's murder and need to talk with you about it."

"I don't know anything more than's in the report."

"I understand. But part of our process is to sit with the relatives when there's been a murder. Hear about it ourselves. Ask questions. We need time with you and your wife to talk it through."

"I'm busy as hell, and Priscilla isn't feeling well." He glared at them through the display. "It's not a good time for either of us. Ask your questions now and I'll see what I can do."

"Can you tell us anything that might help with the investigation? People your father might have argued with, maybe offended in some way, or he did something they didn't like. Anything along those lines?" Cuss could feel Julie staring at him.

"If I knew I'd tell you. But no, nothing like that. He was in the wrong place at the wrong time, that's all." Nick glanced to the side at something off camera. "Look, I've got orders to fill even while I'm grieving. My body hurts. My heart hurts. Is there anything else?"

"I do have more questions, but I can tell that now's not a good time. Would you call me back as soon as you can break free?"

Nick nodded. "I can do that."

"Include Priscilla. We'll need to talk with the both of you."

"Sure thing."

The display went dark. Nick had closed the call.

Quirky Ygo returned to the display. "That was interesting."

Julie was incredulous. "You didn't even ask about Aurora."

Cuss looked at her with a blank expression, waiting for her to catch up.

She returned his gaze for a good three heartbeats and then her face relaxed. She nodded. "And he didn't either, putting him squarely in the middle."

"The lady got it in one," said Ygo.

"What are you going to do?" she asked.

"Make some calls."

"You said 'calls,'" said Ygo. "You're including Royale?"

"Absolutely. I'm sure he's distracted with Mia's case. But LOCU exists to fight lunar organized crime. It's in their name, for Christ's sake. If this isn't it, what is? His people have insider knowledge. The question is, will they share it?"

"Toni shows as available. Wanna start with him? If you learn anything juicy, you can use it as leverage with Royale."

Cuss nodded. "Agreed."

Toni Carrabelle was Armstrong's chief of detectives. He and Cuss were longtime friends. After a brief delay, the front display came alive with his holo, a man with soft features backed by a personality that Cuss knew was tough as nails. Typical of the Nova Terran custom, he was dressed in an outfit swirling with color.

They exchanged greetings, Cuss introduced Julie, and then he got down to business. "We're chasing kidnappers."

He briefed Toni on the saga, finishing with, "We think one of the companies up on the rim is involved, maybe acting as home base. Early leads are sending us that way, anyway."

"My jurisdiction ends at the canyon walls." Toni tugged on an earlobe as he thought. "I'd need a court order to work up there. Not to mention the budget."

"Understood. Still, though, I could use some help with background. The kind of insider information you get from the streets. And who knows. If we root them out, they may run your way."

Toni nodded slowly. "We can help there." He checked something Cuss couldn't see. "Henderson and Rinaldi are next on rotation. They work for you?"

Cuss didn't know either of them.

"They're okay," Ygo told him privately.

"Happy to have them," Cuss said to Toni.

"Ah, damn. Henderson is going on leave in two days. Any chance you'll be wrapped by then?"

"I wish. I hope. But not likely."

Toni nodded. "Let me see who's next. Washington and Bronson? They're solid."

Cuss knew them both. He liked working with Darlena Washington. She was good at her job, supportive of the Marshals Service, and committed to catching bad guys. Hobby Bronson was an asshole. The kind of guy who'd be a criminal if he weren't a cop.

"Even better," said Cuss.

"Good. Give me a few hours to track them down and brief them. If you don't hear from them by fifteen hundred, here's their link." Toni sent it to Cuss and then caught his eye. "If you're in a bind, reach out. I can probably shake resources loose for a small operation." He paused. "Let's have a beer or three after it's over."

Cuss grinned. "Sold."

Toni winked and gave a mock salute. The display went dark.

Ygo replaced him. "I've prepared a briefing on the different surface companies. Should we work through it before calling Royale?"

Cuss shook his head. "We won't be talking specifics. And I want to get it over with. The guy gives me the creeps."

"He's an odd one, no doubt." Ygo paused. "I've called and we're on a six-minute hold. Want to wait?"

Cuss would normally assume that Royale was on another call, or perhaps busy with a colleague. But his gut told him that the guy was just being a jerk with a childish "make 'em wait" power play.

"Yeah," he grumbled. "Let's get it over with."

He grabbed his water bottle and drained it. His stomach growled when the liquid reached his gut, but rather than think about food, his thoughts shifted back to Nick. The guy hadn't been behaving the way most people do when dealing with the authorities. Most people try to please. To cooperate. A smaller fraction demand lawyers. Fewer still rant about their rights. Nick seemed to be cooperating in an uncooperative fashion.

"Did Nick Navarro seem right to you?" he asked aloud.

"I was wondering that myself," said Julie. "He was nervous as hell, and his whole energy was about having us go away and leave him alone. But was it because he was hiding something? Or was it because he's being forced to perform?"

Julie's insights matched his own. "Like maybe someone was standing offscreen, telling him to get rid of us?" Then he sat up, his brain swerving in a completely different thought. "I'm pretty sure Aurora said her mother's name is Patsy. What did Nick call her?"

"Priscilla," said Ygo from the front display.

Inside Cuss's head, Ygo said, "Nice one."

"Is Patsy a nickname for Priscilla?" Cuss asked aloud.

"Not that I ever heard," said Julie.

"I believe it's short for Patricia," said Ygo from the front display.

Goosebumps prickled up Cuss's forearms as his concern morphed into alarm. "How long before we get to his place?"

"We land in Port Collins in seventy minutes," said Ygo. "Then thirty minutes to get towed and secured in our berth. Two hours more from there to his place."

"Let's call him," said Cuss.

"Done. All his links show him as unavailable."

"Any chance you'd have links for Patsy?"

"I can get them." A pause. "Calling. She's unavailable as well."

"Well, shit," said Cuss. "I can't spend my one free pass on a look-see. I need to save it for Aurora's rescue. Maybe to save myself." He looked at Julie and explained. "The first time I call Darlena and Hobby for help, they'll respond immediately and professionally. The second time, not so much."

"Good news," said Ygo from the front display. "It looks like my credentials will let me link to the monitors for his business. Not the house, though. Give me a few minutes and your look-see may be free." Then, "Heads-up. Here's Royale."

Royale appeared in the display. Cuss viewed him with the same assessment as before, a compact man in his mid- to late-forties, likely of East Asian heritage, the details hard to judge because of his damn sunglasses.

"Hello Marshal," said Royale. "Are you calling with news of Moby's killer?"

"Not yet. At the moment I'm chasing an abduction."

"We haven't closed Mia's case either, though we're making good progress. But remember, we started *after* you by several days."

"I'll remember," replied Cuss, wishing he could reach through the display and slap the glasses off the man. "Back to the kidnapping. It's Moby's granddaughter of all people. Early indications are that one of the companies up on the canyon rim is acting as a home base for the doers."

Royale interrupted. "How is it that *you* caught the case? Doesn't the service have something like fifty or sixty marshals?"

"My boss felt bad for me when you took charge of Mia's case. I guess this was the consolation prize." He'd given up talking to the man like he was a normal person.

"Huh." Royale folded his arms in front of him. "I assume you're calling because you want something?"

"I suppose that's true. I was hoping you had information to share." Cuss found himself wishing he'd taken Ygo's briefing. "There are quite a few companies operating up on the surface, and LOCU surely has insider intelligence on them. Would you or one of your staff be available to help us think it through? Suggest which companies match our profile?"

"I've heard that's how you do it. You get other people to do your work and then you take all the credit." His cheeks bulged as he clenched his teeth. "Tell you what.

Give us the kidnapping case and we'll solve it for you. Plus Mia. Plus the pirates. We'll wrap them up and tie it in a bow for you. Let your boss see how real detectives work."

"If you can solve them, I'd be grateful for the help, and I'll happily tell the worlds that it was you."

"You're giving us the kidnapping?"

"No. But if you solve it, you'll get the credit."

"Yeah, well, it turns out that we're looking up on the rim ourselves, and it won't work if there are two agencies poking around, tripping over each other without discretion."

"We could coordinate."

Royale shook his head. "That's code for, 'We'll hang on your coattails.'"

Cuss sat back, struggling to control his temper. "What the holy fuck. How did someone with your attitude get appointed director?"

"Pride of ownership, Marshal. This is our land. We decide how to run it. Not some off-world agency. Not some off-world cop. I'm not afraid to stand up for Nova Terra. I think the board likes that. Please, though, go to them and whine that I hurt your fragile feelings."

Angry beyond words, Cuss reached to close the call. But before he could complete the act, Julie said, "Gosh. We'd planned on including you in our submission for the prestigious Hoskinson Award."

"The what?" It was Royale's first response not delivered with a sneer.

"The Hoskinson Award. It's new, sponsored by a host of companies, endorsed by the senate, named after the late great Senator Blaine Hoskinson. Big ceremony. Big cash award. Big plaque. Human interest stories. But it's a team award for outstanding investigative work leading to an interworld outcome. We thought the team bringing down the pirates would be a sure winner."

"I'm honored." Royale looked flustered. "But my focus is on finding Mia's killer. If I can help you without slowing that objective, I will. Unfortunately, our current investigations have us running at a hundred and ten percent. I wish I had the resources to worry about missing women or prestigious awards."

Royale looked at them for a long moment. "When we find the doers, I'll let you know." He closed the call.

Cuss exhaled forcefully, trying to expel his fury with his breath. After a moment, he reached over and touched Julie's arm. "Nice effort. You had him thinking."

She was as angry as he was. "That is the biggest asshole I've ever tried to engage. I mean, screw him. I don't understand how his attitude helps his cause, though I don't doubt his board would support him once he began accusing us of being foreign invaders." She brought a hand to her mouth and turned toward Cuss. "How did he know the kidnap victim was a woman? At the end he referenced missing women and prestigious awards."

Cuss was stunned by the idea that Royale could somehow be involved, revealing himself with a careless slipup. But an instant later he remembered. "Right up front I said it was Moby's granddaughter."

She slumped back. "That's right. It would have been so sweet to learn he'd implicated himself in some nutball scheme."

Ygo interjected from the front display. "I've gained access to surveillance feeds from Nick's workshop."

The front display shifted to a view inside a building: a barn with a wide-open floor plan and big sliding doors at each end. Nick had organized the equipment in the barn so there was a central walkway down the middle. On each side, workbenches projecting from the wall defined informal U-shaped workspaces. Some had wall racks holding hand tools. Some had sophisticated-looking shop machines. All had shelves stocked with parts.

He couldn't see any people in the building. Two bots stood motionless at one end.

"Are these the stations of an assembly line?" Cuss asked aloud. He knew Nick built small rocket engines, but the details of the construction process appeared to be more complex than he'd imagined. "Or does he build different models at the different stations?"

"I'd say some of both," said Ygo. "There's only one nav control station, so all engines would stop there. But some of the other stations seem more specific to things like the kind of thruster being used. What's curious is I don't see any engines nearing completion."

Cuss agreed that construction activity seemed light for someone complaining of overwork. The benches were littered with scraps and rags and small tools, but none held a near-completed rocket engine. At best, a couple held what looked like the beginnings of an engine assembly.

"I don't see any signs of a fight," said Cuss. "There's a stack of boxes tipped over and a few tools on the floor. But that could be normal for this operation."

The display switched to an outside view.

"Here's what I have for exterior angles," said Ygo. A quick tour of the outside revealed an attractive building clad in faux pine boards. All the images were closeups, none offering a view beyond the building.

"You can't show us the house?" asked Cuss.

"The barn is a workplace," replied Ygo. "Turns out when Nick first moved here, he enrolled in a crime watch program that gave the police access to his business-monitoring feeds in the event of an emergency. I don't even know if he remembers doing it, but the credentials he'd established back then still work. The family home next to the barn was never included in the program."

"Any way we can get a look over there?"

"Soon. I spoofed the voice of a neighbor and reported a disturbance. Shouting. Possible gunfire. Patrol officers should be arriving in about four minutes. They'll activate their live feeds when they reach the home. We can watch those."

It was closer to six minutes. Cuss used the time to solve a different problem. "Peanut, bring two waters and six bars. Include a savory beef, a spicy chicken, and an almond crunch." He looked at Julie. "One of the waters and three of the bars are for you. Any requests?"

"Would you have an apple?"

"An apple nutrition bar or an apple apple?"

She looked at him but didn't respond.

"Peanut, add an apple."

Just as Peanut arrived with the food and drinks, the display came alive with a view of Nick and Patsy's family home, a two-story box set near the north canyon wall in Armstrong, Nova Terra. Simple design. Modest construction materials. Few adornments.

The feed they were watching came from a camera in the cop's field goggles. The view centered on the front door, but the view was wide enough to show the cop's partner, a youngish man in a dark blue uniform, moving into position. The partner put his back against the wall of the home, his shoulder near the door, his hand on his holstered gun, nodding that he was ready to provide support should things go south.

The cop with the camera reached out and knocked on the front door. It was a small hand. Smooth skin. Finished nails. A wedding ring with precious stones. A woman. When she knocked, the door, a smooth white panel with hand-painted filigree, moved inward far enough to reveal a splintered jamb near the door latch.

Using the tip of one knuckle, the cop pushed the door all the way open. On the floor, not three steps inside, a man lay prone. Hands spread wide. Face pointed toward them.

A thick trail of blood running down his temple and across his cheek.

Nick. He wasn't moving.

The blood had dried to a sticky sheen, suggesting the wound was maybe twenty or thirty minutes old, but not hours.

"We got a body," the cop warned her partner. Then she called to Nick, "Hey Mister! You hear me?"

The cop stepped inside and pointed a small device at Nick. A display appeared in front of her showing a thermal image of a body with wounds highlighted. The device gave a formal identification: Nicholas Navarro; Age 57; Deceased 42 min.

While the time of death was an estimate, it was likely accurate to a few minutes. Which meant Nick had been murdered about twenty minutes after they'd spoken to him. And the doers were now forty-two minutes away.

"I'll finish this," the cop told her partner, who was looking over her shoulder at the display. "Coordinate with Central."

While the partner stepped back outside and began talking in a low voice, the cop with the device pointed it around the room. When she swung it in the direction of the kitchen, it found a second body, this one on the floor behind the counter.

"Second body in the kitchen," she called to her partner. The display identified the victim: Patricia Navarro; Age 55; Deceased 44 min.

"He watched her die," said Julie, who'd been sitting quietly up to this point.

Cuss had been thinking the same thing.

The cop swung the device upward and panned it across the ceiling. "We have three bedrooms and a bath upstairs," she said. "All clear."

"Crime Scene is on the way," said the partner. "Central's working POTS to see if they can track 'em."

Then came the wait. The cops had to stay outside for fear of contaminating the scene. They couldn't leave until the ME finished the medical exam and the detectives finished the scene eval.

"Are they having any luck with POTS?" Cuss asked Ygo. Then to Julie, "The system only tracks public spaces and the career assholes know that."

"The doers rode a lorry to the exchange and disappeared inside," said Ygo.

"I don't follow," said Julie.

"Not sure I do either," admitted Cuss.

"This section of Armstrong is zoned mixed light industry. So it's a bit of everything. Homes. Shops. Mom-and-pop manufacturing. The businesses out here use lorry carts to move goods. And they do most of their commercial business through a central exchange, a cooperative that gives the group leverage in buying and selling."

The display switched to show a holo of a lorry—a cart with an enclosed cab—as it pulled up to the loading zone at the side of the exchange building. Two men stepped out, both wearing pressure gear that masked their identities. They entered the building through a side door.

"By the time the cops can get a warrant," said Ygo, "the doers will be long gone."

Chapter 17

Aurora opened her eyes, saw a blur of light, and closed them again. Not because the light was bright. Quite the opposite, it was a gentle glow. She closed them because she was tired. She drifted off to sleep.

After a bit, she surfaced again, this time keeping her eyes closed as she floated in a murky fog, struggling to awaken, waiting for her senses to sharpen. When she finally looked, she focused on the light. It didn't seem that far away. Maybe three steps.

But nothing made sense. The place she was in, a room of some sort, appeared to be cylindrical. Not much wider than she was tall. And the smell of new materials, some sort of chemical off-gassing, made her think of the time she'd ridden in Moby's brand-new car all those years ago.

Running a dry tongue around a parched mouth, she thought about water. But before the thought gelled, she fell asleep.

Her eyes popped opened. This time she remembered being awake before. She remembered the light. Being thirsty. But everything before *that* was a muddle. She looked at the light and the faint shadows it cast. She listened to a quiet hum, and thought how the chemical smell bothered her sinuses.

She sat up, or tried to, but the action tangled her in bedding. She stopped moving and analyzed her situation.

The sense of floating hadn't been a dream. She was weightless. Which meant her tiny room, whatever it was, was in one of Lagrange's spaceports. Either that or she was floating in space. Her bed was a sleeping bag, one side attached along its length to the wall, the other side floating freely.

She closed her eyes and tried to reconstruct events. She was at the spaceport, walking with the crowd, and then everything went blank. She had shadowy memories of men talking near her. Of loud noises. Of being bundled up. More talking. Being moved.

Of being dressed.

Goosebumps tingled down her body as she ran her hands down her front. The clothing didn't feel familiar. She opened the top of the sleeping bag and looked. She was dressed in a white jumpsuit. Lightweight. Nothing she'd seen before.

She opened the front of the jumpsuit and took a peek. She wore her own bra and panties. She wasn't sore down there but touched herself anyway. No tenderness.

Part of her wanted to think more about the clothing incident. But for now, she dismissed it. She had larger issues to deal with. Concerning issues.

She had no idea how much time had passed from when she'd entered the spaceport until now. Had no idea where she was. And she was thirsty as hell.

"Hello?" Her voice came out cracked and scratchy. She cleared her throat so she could call louder.

"How may I help you?" said a male voice. Deep. Soothing.

She sat up, the reflex causing her to tangle in the bedding yet again. Holding onto a strut on the wall, she wiggled her body out of the sleeping bag. When she was floating next to it, she surveyed her surroundings.

She was in a cylinder. There were struts and ribbing on the walls that reminded her of the inside of a storage tank. A single light source glowed at one end. If she put her toes on one side of the cylinder and stretched her hands up over her head, she could just about touch the other side.

"Hello?" she said again.

"How may I help you?" the voice repeated.

"Where am I?"

"You are in a Bish 1200 Fluid Storage Module."

"Why?"

"I don't know."

"Who are you?"

"I am a message button, here to answer your questions."

She knew about message buttons. They were coin-size communication devices used in a million temporary applications, throwaway things like instructions, greetings, warnings, and apparently, information for kidnap victims.

"Where is the storage module right now? Where am I?"

"You are in a Bish 1200 Fluid Storage Module, and you and it are on a ten-day orbit around the Moon."

"Why?"

"I don't know."

"Who put me here?"

"I don't know."

"What happens in ten days?"

"A ship will meet you and transport you home."

Nothing made sense and her disorientation grew. "How long have I been here?"

"Six hours forty-four minutes."

Her eyes welled with tears and she fought to stay in control. "Why is this happening to me?"

"I don't know."

She tried to clear her throat, but her mouth was too dry. "Is there water?"

"Yes. Find the large blue bladder on the wall. A tap is at one end."

She was looking at the bladder as the message button spoke. It was a blue bag mounted between two struts on the wall opposite her bed. The thing was big, maybe as long as she was tall. It had the words *Potable Water* stamped on the front in several places.

She floated to the end nearest the glowing light and found a length of tube with an on-off valve. Putting the end of the tube between her lips, she cracked the valve. Liquid flowed into her mouth.

The water was cool. A little stale. Wonderful going down her parched throat. After three big gulps, she closed the valve, choosing to wait a bit to see how the liquid settled in her stomach before drinking more.

While she waited, she took a quick inventory of her cell, a disconcerting way to think of her predicament. First off, she didn't see any other blue bags, meaning this one would have to last ten days. She studied it, trying to estimate her daily ration. She traced a three-by-three grid on the front of the bag with her finger, but it didn't tell her much. She pushed softly in the middle and watched the whole bag undulate. In the end, she used gut feel. It seemed certain that she'd have plenty to drink. And she *probably* had enough to bathe with a cloth every day or so.

Toward the front, she saw a row of four bucket-like things attached to one wall. Across on the other wall was a row of four loose bundles. Overhead, a row of small machines, boxes of polished silver metal, were lined up between two struts, humming quietly. They had small operating lights on the front, and two had tiny pipes running between them. A tube ran from the last box in line down along a beam to a device stowed at the back of the cylinder.

Her stomach felt fine, no cramping from the water, so she drank some more.

As her body hydrated, she acknowledged that she was still tired. Weak. Like she'd run a marathon. She figured it was from the drugs they'd used on her, whoever "they" were.

"Can you call the people who put me here?"

"I cannot."

"Because they told you not to, or because you don't have the equipment to do so?"

"I don't know."

She looked up and down the cylinder. There were no window ports that would let her see outside, something she needed to do if she were to confirm her situation. Was she really in free flight? It seemed so unlikely. "Is there any way to see outside?"

"There's a viewer at the rear of the cylinder."

She moved back to find a round door hatch at the back end of the cylinder, answering one of her million questions. This was the way in and out.

Above the hatch was an eyepiece. Looking through it, she saw a field of stars. The eyepiece had simple controls to direct the view. Left. Right. Up. Down. There were stars in every direction for as far as she could see. Dense. Bright white. Never-ending.

She began to whimper. Then she began to sob. She felt her way back to her sleeping bag, climbed inside, closed it up tight, and hugged herself, rocking gently until she cried herself to sleep.

. . .

"How long before we land?" asked Cuss, sounding a bit like a kid at the start of a family vacation. Then he remembered that Ygo was appearing as a fellow marshal helping from a remote location, which meant Cuss was supposed to be piloting the ship.

To save the situation, he scanned the pilot's display. As he did, Ygo spoke to him privately. "Fifty minutes before we start landing maneuvers."

"Fifty minutes before we start landing maneuvers," he said aloud as if talking to himself, but speaking with enough volume for Julie to hear.

He turned to Ygo on the front display. "You said you had a background briefing. Can you give us the ten-minute version? Then I want to call Brace. We can't wait until we get there to hear what he has to say. The clock's ticking."

"Can do." Ygo filled the display with holos to help Cuss and Julie follow along. "So, we saw the Bendolin Sprint heading outbound from Earth. Since it never landed in Lagrange or Port Collins, next best guess is the lunar surface."

"Could they loop around and return to Earth?" asked Julie.

"A possibility. Girish has Arron Gutierrez and Sara Beagley scouting Earth. So far, they've come up empty. They'll continue that effort while we look out this way."

He paused for a moment, and when there were no follow-up questions, the display switched to show an aerial view of the Nova Terra canyon. Through the clear dome, it looked like an irregular oval, with meandering walls created from multiple impact craters, and several smooth arcs that were excavated by explosives and machines.

"This is the Nova Terra canyon," said Ygo. "Those flashes you see due south of it are from the Port Collins space complex."

Cuss looked at the circular installation below the dome. As he watched, an arc of light rose from it. Two other light trails were descending toward it.

"Think of the canyon as a clock," said Ygo, "with Port Collins at six o'clock."

"That's one Salvador Dalí lookin' clock," snarked Julie.

Cuss smiled. She wasn't wrong.

"No doubt," agreed Ygo. "But if we go with it, can you see the surface activity at eight o'clock, one o'clock, and four o'clock?"

Cuss could see three distinct concentrations of activity. Buildings, lights, landing pads, and roadways concentrated in spots roughly corresponding to the clock positions.

"These are the three surface airlocks out from Nova Terra: the West, North, and East Gates. Most of the infrastructure you see near the gates are food factories and manufacturing plants. Highly automated. Minimal storage onsite except what's being used for production."

The display zoomed in on one of the three clusters. The larger buildings were either big domes or fat cylinders with domed roofs, shapes that allowed for a modular construction while having the strength to hold pressurized air inside.

"What you're seeing here is the activity at the North Gate. These are food and manufacturing installations, and this over here is a waste recovery plant." The view broadened until several enormous tracts of glistening squares were visible. "And these, obviously, are solar installations."

The display blinked and now centered on a different cluster of buildings. "This is the East Gate. No surprise that it's laid out like the North Gate, since the Nova Terra government built the infrastructure."

The camera view widened to show two solar installations. Next to them sat an oversize igloo-shaped building, a sturdy structure with thick walls. "These solar fields are under construction. This odd building over here is the nuclear power station. Been around almost as long as Nova Terra itself."

The view switched to a broad panorama showing the Nova Terra canyon and a huge tract of lunar landscape next to it. Rough terrain with craggy hills and impact craters. Sharp features. Long shadows.

"The West Gate is similar to the others. What makes it different is the activity out on the plains." The camera zoomed in on a cluster about a third of the way out on the desolate terrain. "These are water mines. Telltale for them is this pipeline running all the way back to Nova Terra." He highlighted the thin pipeline trail, a faint scratch on the stark landscape. "They harvest ice, melt it, and pump the water to market."

The view shifted out to the far edge of the display. "And see these clusters way out here?" He zoomed in on one of them. "These are ore mines."

Ygo zoomed in on one of the clusters to reveal a hive of activity. Big sheds and small huts and launchpads and remote power stations and buildings of unknown use, everything linked in a crisscross of dirt roads, with huge excavators and transporters crawling through the massive hole.

"What are they mining?" asked Cuss.

"Platinum, palladium, rhodium, iridium. Stuff the worlds can't seem to get enough of."

"What's that long thing to the north?" asked Julie.

"This?" The image shifted to a high-tech straightaway, a kilometer-long length of rail, perfectly flat except at the very end, where it had a gentle curve upward. "It's a kinetic launch system. It tosses payloads of ore up into orbit, something possible when you have low gravity and no atmosphere. Ships catch the loads and ferry them to Earth."

Ygo interrupted himself with a yelp of surprise. "Whoa. Check this out!"

The image shifted back to the mine site, stopping on a silo-shaped object tucked up against one of the larger buildings. The view was from above, but as the camera panned down, Cuss saw the blunt nose. The octagonal carriage. The external fuel packs. The grasshopper legs. All gray. "The Bendolin Sprint!" He sat forward. "Who owns the mine?"

"Let's see." A pause. "It looks like Kolour Limited. They're midlevel players in lunar mining. And before you get too excited about this being *the* ship, I saw three of them in orbit when I was preparing for this briefing."

"Is this one of those?" asked Julie. "Or is this a fourth ship?"

"At this point, I can't tell." Then, "Heads-up. I'd sent a call request to Brace Harde, and he says he can talk now or you'll have to wait an hour."

"Go for it," said Cuss.

A holo of Brace appeared in the display. The man was standing in an aisle of his hardware store, shelves of goods on either side of him. He appeared to be restocking a bin of pipe fittings from an impossibly large crate he was holding in one hand. "I heard about Nick and Patsy. Give me a sec."

Setting the crate on a high shelf where it would be out of the way, he moved down the aisle in long strides. They followed him through a twist and turn, and when he reached his office, he hopped over a cluttered desk in a practiced move, settling into a broad chair, a big pillowy seat that caught him like a glove.

"How can I help?" He spoke in a somber tone, jaw set, brow level.

Cuss started. "Nick's and Patsy's deaths are a senseless tragedy. Now we're searching for their daughter, Aurora."

Brace sat forward. "I know Aurora. Saw her here in the store every so often a few years back. She's missing?"

"She's been taken by the killers."

Brace inhaled sharply.

"Kidnappers usually make their demands in the first days. I think that's what happened a few hours ago with Nick and Patsy, and the doers didn't like their answer. Now that her folks are dead, Aurora loses value as a bargaining chip. We are time critical at this point."

"Nick wasn't rich. What was their motive?"

"Not sure yet. Nick's dad is dead and his daughter's been taken. What do you think it's about?"

"Absolutely no idea."

Ygo displayed a holo of the Bendolin Sprint taking off from the Albacete Spaceport.

"Our best lead is this ship," said Cuss. "It's an old craft. Heavily repaired. Painted all gray. Have you seen it before?" He studied Brace as he spoke, gauging his reaction, looking for signs of recognition. Perhaps deception.

But Brace shook his head, this time broadly. "Sorry to be the one to tell you. There are a bunch of those flying around here. Joey Sprints is a rocket shop located just off the Port Collins complex. Run by Joey Spigliano. They rescue and refurbish old ships as a business, and Bendolin Sprints are a specialty of the shop. Thus the name. Show him your holos and he'll know something. If he didn't build it, he can probably tell you who did."

Brace's words—that the ship was one of many—hit Cuss like a kick to the gut. He'd convinced himself that the ship was unique enough to provide a direct path to the doers, and from there, to Aurora.

He was back to probing. "We think a company on the surface might be a home base for the pirates. An outfit that has launch and landing capabilities. Uses lasers in their business like the one we showed you earlier. Lots of storage space. Away from scrutiny. Has a need for heavy industrial components like valves, pumps, compressors, piping, staging. A ruthless approach to business…"

Brace barked a laugh and then held up his hands in a plea for forgiveness. "Sorry. As I listened to your list, I was thinking of the mining companies. But when you said that ruthless thing, it was like a home run. Those assholes think they're their own nation."

"Which ones?"

"All of them. Believe me. *All* of them. I make sure they clear payment at pickup because the law runs thin out there."

"So none of the food or manufacturing or power companies would fit the profile?"

"Not in my first or even second pass. I suppose it's possible in a hypothetical world. Keep them in the picture if your instincts tell you to. I'm just saying that if it's a surface company, I'd look at the miners first." He calmed a bit and continued. "Maybe part of my suspicion is because whenever they visit the city, they behave like obnoxious tourists. People who don't care about the place. Don't respect it. Locals hate that shit, including me."

He gave an unapologetic shrug. "But beyond that, distance puts them away from scrutiny. Ships land and launch out there, but who knows what they're doing?

Mining is equipment heavy and they're always importing more of it. They have onsite storage for their equipment and the material they mine. Hangars for some of their ships. They use lasers on a daily basis. And they don't seem to care about anything but meeting quota."

Chapter 18

The *Nelly Marie* landed in Port Collins, and as a tug pulled the ship into the massive underground hangar, Cuss brooded from the pilot's seat. It bothered him that he was back to tilling soil. He'd expected to be harvesting by now.

He glanced up the stairway to confirm Julie was still in the bathroom and then said to Ygo, "I'm bringing my gun to Joey's. And if I think it's that dangerous, then she can't come."

Ygo had called ahead to Joey Sprints to arrange a meeting at the rocket-ship rehab shop. Joey's response had been noncommittal. Evasive. Once that behavior started, Ygo knew to suggest that the proposed meeting take place in a couple of days. So when Cuss showed up an hour or so later, Joey wouldn't be ready for it.

Ygo had also reached out to the mine bosses. It turned out that there were seven active ore mines near Nova Terra, each with its own head of operations.

When Ygo called, all the bosses took the time to understand that Cuss was an Interworld Marshal who would be arriving soon in Port Collins. That he was interested in meeting with them to ask for their help in an investigation. And that he would like to meet them at their mine site, where he would provide further details and answer questions.

None of the bosses asked what the investigation was about. Or why Cuss wanted to meet them onsite. Or if he'd be coming alone. Or whether he had a warrant. Instead, they all made up an excuse to close the call and then set their contact status to unavailable.

"Joey has three employees with him today at the shop," said Ygo, speaking to Cuss privately. "He acted the tough guy during the call. But he and his crew have no priors. No warrants. Still, though. I think you're making the right call with Julie."

While Ygo was talking, a quiet thump told Cuss that the tug had disengaged from the *Nelly Marie*. As it trundled off to its next task, a mobile stairway was moved into position against the side of the ship.

"Perhaps we could have Julie interview Brace Harde in person while you're at Joey's," continued Ygo. "I bet she can tease something useful out of him. And with the time crunch, you two should split up anyway."

While Cuss thought it through, he heard a knock on the ship's main hatch. A polite tap.

At the ports in Lagrange, the hangar crew always gave a courtesy tap soon after he docked. It was their way of saying "welcome home" and to let him know that the *Nelly Marie* had cleared the port safety check, which meant he was free to take on water, air, and fuel, and to dump waste.

If he was near the hatch when the knock came, he'd crack it open and thank the crew. Let them know their efforts were appreciated. Maybe shoot the shit for a bit if he was in the mood.

But the culture was different at Port Collins. While the people there dressed in colorful garb, they tended to be more reserved in their behavior. More private.

So knocking was out of character. He knew that. But he was so absorbed with the challenge of finding Aurora, his mind racing as he struggled to narrow the investigation, that he opened the hatch anyway.

A woman stood in the opening. Cute. Short skirt. Low-cut top. Big smile. Red hair piled in a complicated swirl of braids. Eyebrows leveled in concentration.

Her right hand came forward like she wanted to shake. A pretty hand. Polished red nails.

A hand that held a stunner, a compact cousin of the stun gun.

When Cuss saw it, his brain signaled for his right arm to swing forward, for his hand to open, for his wrist to flex, the series of motions required to swat the weapon away.

But before that action could be completed, his head exploded in an electrical storm, searing his brain, the energetic torment causing overwhelming agony and confusion. Every muscle flexed at the same time, locking his body in a painful grip. He couldn't breathe, though in his agony and confusion, he didn't realize it.

His body vibrated as his brain crazed. After an eternity, it stopped, leaving his voluntary muscles limp. He sagged to the deck.

He could vaguely sense the hard deck coming toward him. He could hear the sound of his body hitting it. His face slapping against it. But he couldn't feel any of it.

And then he blacked out.

. . .

Beyond idle curiosity, Ygo didn't have any concerns when Cuss opened the hatch. He normally screened visitors in advance, but he'd been so immersed in prioritizing a suspect pool that he'd been deflecting the low-level warnings sent by the AI linked into his brain.

He started paying attention, though, when he saw the woman standing there. She was out of character. Not an invited guest. Not dressed like a Port Collins tech.

And then Cuss began to writhe in a horrific dance, grimacing in pain before collapsing. As he fell, two men stepped from behind the woman and entered the ship. Big men. Tough-looking bad guys wearing thin film masks that hid their identity. Unlike the woman, these two were dressed in ill-fitting port employee outfits.

Ygo fought a rising panic. His den was just a dozen steps from where Cuss lay, but he was unable to intervene himself. He cast about for something he could use as a weapon. Some way to slow them down, or better yet, harm them. But his choices were meager.

The killing weapons, the disabling weapons, the shocks and beams and projectiles were all mounted outside the ship to repel aggressors. He was mortified that the sophisticated defensive installation he'd helped create had become his very own Maginot Line. Once the invaders got past the elaborate fixed armaments, the weapons lost value in the fight.

Ticking through an evolving list, his first act was to protect Julie, doing so by locking her in the bathroom. Posing as the ship's AI, he told her that an emergency was in progress and she must shelter in place. "The door is a fortified barrier," he explained. "It will protect you if you remain inside."

At the same time, he broadcast emergency calls for help. Armstrong police. Port Collins security. Disaster response crews. Off-duty officers. Anyone and everyone with a crisis channel received the message to come on the run.

One of the men picked Cuss up and tossed him across the command deck like he was pitching hay into a loft. Cuss hit the far wall with a solid thud and then fell to the deck in the slow motion of low gravity. The two thugs laughed and bumped forearms in a show of camaraderie.

In desperation, Ygo activated Peanut, knowing the bot needed to exit its closet and load its tool carousel with "weapons"—a nail gun, a hatchet, and an extra-long screwdriver—before it could enter the fray. It was a delay of almost a minute, a delay long enough for the toughs to do some serious damage.

Groaning, Cuss bent a leg at the knee and used that as leverage to turn on his side. Moving slowly, he placed a hand on the deck and lifted his head, squinting to see his attackers.

Tough Guy One, the guy who'd thrown Cuss against the wall, took it as an invitation. He moved toward Cuss, first with a short stutter step, then a long stride, and then a kick, a full swing with a follow through, a brutal assault to the face. Like he was kicking a ball downfield.

Cuss's head snapped back. He stayed up on one hand by sheer will. Then he exhaled, deflating as he collapsed onto his back, arms sprawled at his sides, head facing away from his attacker. His nose, almost certainly broken, was a fountain of blood, gushing a stream of thick red liquid that drooled across his cheek and onto the deck.

"Halt!" bellowed Ygo. "Or I'll shoot."

The *Nelly Marie* had equipment that let Ygo project lifelike holos inside the ship, something he used when fighting Cuss in a sim. Using the projector tech, he created the image of a man standing up on the middeck, a brute looking down at the intruders from the top of the ladder. Thick shoulders. Weathered face with sharp features. Buzz cut. Dressed in an Interworld Marshals Service shirt and pants, an impressive and intimidating uniform.

Ygo's brute was pointing a Tosic 325 Hybrid at Tough Guy One's center of mass. He twitched the gun toward the exit. "Now move toward the hatch."

"You alone?" asked Tough Guy Two.

"Why? You faster than a bullet?" Ygo was unnerved that the two were immediately suspicious of the situation. But at least they weren't hurting Cuss.

"Maddy!" shouted Tough Guy Two, staring up at Ygo's holo while he talked. "Is there anyone out there?"

The redhead, who'd been standing outside, poked her head through the hatch. "What?" She saw Ygo's muscleman for the first time and her eyes widened.

"Is there anyone out there?" The exasperation in his voice was clear.

She pulled her head back out and looked. "Just random traffic."

The tough guys looked at each other, agreeing on a plan.

"Hold on!" Maddy called over her shoulder. "There's a cart with flashing lights headed this way."

Ygo checked the exterior cameras. A Port Collins emergency team was racing in their direction. He'd reported an uncontrolled fuel leak. Of all his calls for help, that one proved to be the winner.

"I'd say ten seconds," she said, now sounding nervous.

The two men looked at each other again. Tough Guy Two tilted a head toward the hatch. "Let's go."

Tough Guy One gave Cuss a quick kick in the stomach, and then followed his buddy out of the *Nelly Marie*. They jumped from the stairway down to the roadway, and then jackrabbited away, bobbing and weaving through the maze of spacecraft and cargo and service vehicles. Maddy couldn't keep up, so she stopped running and hid between two trucks.

Ygo was able to track the men for a while, co-opting cameras where he could to follow them as they hopped and ducked their way through the obstacles of a busy spaceport hangar. But they were experienced at evading modern surveillance, likely using assets pre-positioned to help, blending with and then disappearing into the muddle in just over two minutes.

Ygo guided the cops to Maddy. They took her into custody without incident.

Then he unlocked the bathroom door, freeing Julie, suggesting she grab the med kit and attend to Cuss.

. . .

Cuss's face throbbed, a wash of pain with every heartbeat. His ears were ringing like shrill sirens. Something was affecting his breathing. And his eyes were watering so much that he couldn't see.

He could hear people talking above him. A back-and-forth. He felt pressure on his nose. And then his face exploded in pain so intense, he blacked out again.

He awoke. This time the pain was gone, though he still couldn't breathe through his nose. A woman was leaning over him. Warm smile. Kind eyes.

"How do you feel?" she asked. "Headache? Nausea?"

"I feel good," he said reflexively. He tried to sit up.

She pressed a hand on his chest to keep him down. "I'm Dr. Wallach. Tiffini Wallach." She looked into his eyes and nodded, reassuring him. "I'm a responder from the Pahala Med Center. Your nose was broken and I just reset it."

He lifted a hand to his face. She intercepted it and squeezed his hand in hers, preventing him from completing the act.

"I put a med pac on it. It's why you don't feel pain right now." She released his hand and then held hers straight out, karate-chop style. Wrapping her other hand over the top of the first, she said, "The brace straddles the bridge of your nose like this, providing support so it heals properly, protecting it from further injury. It's also dosing you with meds."

She sat back on her knees, giving him space. "You may touch it. Be gentle."

Cuss used his lens to see a view of himself as if he were looking in a mirror. He touched his face with his fingertips, pressing gently, probing. He could see his eyes swelling, already turning black. The patch bridging his nose looked just like she'd said. She hadn't told him about the white rolls of gauze stuck up his nostrils to control the bleeding.

"Do you know who this is?" Dr. Wallach motioned to Julie, who leaned over him from his other side, her face scrunched in worry.

"Julie!" He was happy to see her. "Are you okay?" He tried to sit up again, and they both held him down. He relaxed and put a hand on her knee, making a physical connection he found comforting. Then he lifted his head at the neck to look around, hoping Ygo would fill him in.

He could tell he was lying on the command deck. A number of strangers were milling about, something that made him very uncomfortable. And his head ached, perhaps worse than he could ever remember.

"Welcome back, pal." Ygo spoke inside his head. "You had me worried."

"You took a beating," said Julie. "The ship locked me in the bathroom or I would've been here to help."

"Exactly," said Ygo. "The woman at the hatch used a stunner on you. Two toughs kicked the crap out of you after that." A pause. "I did the best I could."

Cuss was beginning to remember. Yet there were blank spots.

Dr. Wallach said, "We're going to bring you to the hospital now for an evaluation."

"I'll stay with you," said Julie.

Cuss normally would resist going to the hospital, his macho coming to the fore. But this time he thought it was a good idea. Someone had scrambled his brain, and he needed to be well so he could find Aurora. Or learn what happened to her so he could take his revenge.

He also needed to square accounts with whoever kicked him in the face.

"Everyone needs to clear out," he said. "I can't have people in here while I'm gone."

. . .

Aurora opened her eyes just enough to see the light at the end of her prison cylinder, a monster's eye staring back at her. Unwavering. Challenging. She lifted her head and squinted, searching for an on-off switch. She couldn't see one from her current vantage point and figured she'd check again when she got up.

Lowering her head, she mulled her situation. Nothing made sense. What could anyone possibly gain from launching her into space? She believed that Georgio and her dad would be looking for her, and felt a surge of energy when she thought to signal them. But as she studied the equipment in the capsule for a way to do that, she acknowledged that she didn't have a clue where to start. She was a cook, not a tech.

Her stomach grumbled and her attention shifted to the bags attached to the wall. She hoped they held food. Clothing. And maybe a clock.

How long had she been asleep? Five hours? Ten? Without a timepiece, how would she know when ten days had passed, the time of her promised rescue? Looking overhead, she considered the electronic boxes attached between the struts, thinking that one of them might have a display that showed the date and time.

She decided to check.

As she wiggled out of her sleeping bag, she got tangled in the floating folds yet again. She kicked her feet in frustration, waited a moment for her anger to diffuse, took a deep breath and exhaled, then patiently worked herself free.

She hovered in the spot between her sleeping bag and the blue water bladder, her eyes on the silver boxes overhead. Grabbing a wall strut, she pulled herself up, turning her body so she hovered right in front of them.

Viewing the setup, she shivered. It was definitely colder than she remembered. She rubbed her hands together and hugged herself as she studied the devices.

There were four boxes in a row, each a different size and shape, each with different attachments and wire connections on the outside. Two had tubing connected to them. They had brand names she'd never heard of: Hezelt, Baxaton, two of them were ChalSource.

The Hezelt and Baxaton units had tiny control pads. She touched a button gingerly on the Hezelt but nothing happened. "Don't screw it up," she scolded herself, worried she'd change something and not know how to put it back.

Then she stopped what she was doing and looked around the vessel. "I need to pee." She considered the notion for the first time. "Where's the toilet?"

"The four buckets on the wall are portable toilets," said the message button. "Use each one for three days, if possible."

She was startled by the button's voice. For some reason she thought she'd used up whatever wisdom it had to offer. Starved for company, she engaged it. Her companion. Her oracle.

"How will I know when ten days have passed?" She pulled herself over to the bucket-like things attached to the wall.

"I can tell you."

"How many days until my rescue?"

"Ten."

"That's what it was when I went to sleep."

"It has been two hours and six minutes since we last interacted."

The news hit her hard. Two hours, not ten. Time was going to pass slower than she'd imagined.

The pressure on her bladder short-circuited her frustration. The toilets were hooked to the wall in green plastic bags. She unhooked one, and as she removed the bowl from the packaging, she read the ad copy printed on the outside. "These are portable toilets for boating and camping."

The button didn't comment. It took her a moment to realize she hadn't asked it anything. "Are these portable toilets intended for boating and camping?"

"Yes," said the button.

"These don't work when there's no gravity. Weightless toilets have suction to collect the waste. With these, it will end up drifting around the cabin."

The button remained silent.

"How do I use a camping toilet in weightlessness?"

"I don't know."

"Perfect."

She looked inside the one she was holding. The bowl was filled with some sort of absorbent material. Still, though, she needed a way to trap the waste because anything not absorbed would float freely.

Holding the green plastic bag in front of her, she turned it this way and that, thinking about the best way to wrap it around her and the bowl while she did her business. She studied the seams to see if they'd pull apart, figuring she'd need to unfold the bag to maximize coverage.

Then it came to her, a memory from a documentary she saw years ago. Space travelers improvised during a power outage by making diapers out of plastic bags filled with tissue paper.

She was about to ask the button if there were bags included anywhere in the stuff still hanging on the wall. Then she giggled—a release of pent-up angst more than anything else—when she realized she was holding one.

Using her teeth, she clipped the bottom corners out of the green bag to make leg holes. She pulled a portion of the absorbent material from inside the potty bowl and transferred it into the bag. Then came the next realization. Since her jumpsuit was one piece, she'd need to remove it completely.

She opened the garment down the front, pulled out her arms, and then slipped it off her legs. During the process, she learned that she still wore her own socks, a small comfort for reasons she couldn't explain.

Casting about for a place to put the jumpsuit, she decided to tuck it inside her sleeping bag, securing it from drifting about while she was busy. She pulled off her panties and tucked them away as well.

And then, floating in slow circles in the middle of the vessel, she climbed into her diaper bag. As she folded the top of the plastic tight around her waist, she decided she'd moderate her drinking and stay on the dehydrated side until her rescue.

Chapter 19

C uss lay on his back, a warm tingle on his face, a somewhat annoying hum in the background. He was in a rejuv pod, a machine located in the trauma unit at the Pahala Med Center. Julie sat next to him, something that made him uncomfortable because the commitment was significant.

Rejuv was a four-hour treatment, a time when he wasn't supposed to move, which included him talking. They'd put something over his eyes, so while he could hear her, he couldn't see her. He spent most of the time drifting in and out of sleep.

Afterward, they were shuffled down to a small meeting room so the doctor could report on the med tests. "Your brain trauma eval ticks a couple of boxes at the low end of our assessment." He crossed his arms over his white-coated chest and assumed a stern expression. "That doesn't mean you're home free. There's no such thing as a mild concussion. You need to take it easy. Be careful."

"Am I restricted from duty?"

The Interworld Marshals Service had a policy of asking the doc treating an injured agent to weigh in on their fitness for work. Girish Mannan knew that Cuss was in the hospital because Ygo, very worried at the time, had told him.

"I'm clearing you." The doctor was nodding as he spoke, but the motion soon transitioned into a headshake. "But take it slow. If you start feeling tired or weak, if you have a headache, queasy stomach, weakness, anything out of the ordinary, sit down and drink fluids. If you don't recover straightaway, give us a call."

He moved on to Cuss's external injuries. "The nose is set well and the lacerations will heal clean, so no worry of lasting damage to your face."

"Thank God," said Julie, who grinned and winked at the doc when she said it.

"If you do three more rejuv sessions, you should be mostly healed in about ten days. If you don't, you'll have raccoon eyes for at least that long and your nose will be tender for a month."

"I understand," said Cuss. He understood that he wouldn't be delaying his search for Aurora, or for Moby and Mia's killers, just so his black eyes could heal a little faster.

He was discharged, and he and Julie were riding a cart through Port Collins' massive hangar on their way back to the *Nelly Marie*, when Ygo reported some news.

"They interviewed the redhead, Madaline Hyacinth. She scored truthful for all but a few questions. Claims she was hired by the two men yesterday. Calls herself an entrepreneur, but the only thing she peddles is her body. Her criminal record includes using a stunner on a couple of clients. Says they stiffed her. I guess the doers liked her skill set and hired her."

"She doesn't know them?" Cuss was incredulous.

"Bullshit," said Julie.

"She claims they approached her. Practiced her on the initial assault. What she should do. What she should say. Then afterward, she was to stand on the top of the stairway and watch for trouble. She was paid a grand in advance, is owed another."

"This made sense to her?" asked Julie.

"They told her Cuss was a rich asshole who rapes because that's what rich assholes do. She swears she didn't know he was law. They never talked with her about the escape and she didn't know to ask. She's realizing she'll never see the rest of her money. That's why she's talking."

"How did they work her through it all?" asked Cuss. "She had to have seen them during practice time."

"They did it with avatars. They told her that anonymity was a security feature. That impressed her. Made it feel professional, as weird as it sounds."

"I still call bullshit," said Julie. "Stand outside and look at the *Nelly Marie*'s decals and tell me you don't know she's law."

"That was one of the questions that raised flags. Her answer was rated 'somewhat deceptive.' The interviewer believes that she didn't know until she was outside the ship. Then she decided to go for it anyway."

They sat for a moment lost in their thoughts, the cart bouncing along in the weak gravity. "So who are they?" asked Julie. "What's the motive?"

"Maybe one of the mine bosses?" said Cuss. "Or the mine owners. Maybe Joey the ship builder. We're perceived as a threat to someone and they're responding."

"What about Brace Harde?" asked Ygo.

"Maybe," said Cuss. "But my instincts say he's one of the good guys."

"Seriously?" Julie's exasperation was on full display. "You were attacked in Hermes right after the conference, and then again on the Drome. Now here. Do you really think this is someone different?" She shook her head. "If it's one of the miners, we should be able to link them back to the conference someway, somehow."

Cuss turned in his seat to face her. Even though he was floating from pain meds, he still felt a surge of desire. Smart women were a weakness. "You're right. But we're also certain that one of those Sprint ships is involved, and that brings us here."

"And we're stumped from that end," admitted Ygo. "We've been back and forth on the meeting attendees and can't find the missing link. Georgio and Aurora connected with Cuss as conference support workers, so we expanded the investigation to include custodial, management, security, the whole list. Nothing pops. That leaves us working it from this end."

The *Nelly Marie* came into view. Next to it, a truck was unloading something the size of a small couch.

"What's this?" asked Cuss. He zoomed in with his lens for a better look.

"I found a used rejuv bed in a consignment shop," said Ygo. "A portable unit. It's tired. A little beat-up. But should work well enough to help."

"Wow," said Cuss. Ygo was generous to him on a daily basis, but he was still moved by the thoughtfulness. "Thanks, pal."

"What an amazing colleague," said Julie.

"Amazing friend," said Cuss.

. . .

Exhausted and hurting, Cuss climbed into bed and slept through to the morning. When he awoke, he sat on the side of his bed, sore but determined. He popped one of the pills the doctor had given him and sat for a minute, waiting for it to kick in. Then he started his day.

After a quick breakfast, he crawled into a cart and set out to visit Joey Spigliano, owner of Joey Sprints Rocket Shop.

"Julie's made the tram okay?" he asked Ygo. While he rode the cart through a connecting tunnel to see Joey, she was traveling across Armstrong to meet with Brace Harde at his home near the North Gate. Cuss didn't want to check in with her himself, fearing she'd think he doubted her abilities. Or that he was smitten.

"She's underway and on schedule," reported Ygo.

The tunnel Cuss rode through skirted the huge Port Collins Field, the launch and landing portion of the spaceport. The tunnel opened into a tall cavern, the so-called Service Center, and his eyes widened. The display of gleaming technology inside a primitive stone cavern created a striking image.

"Pretty impressive," he said.

Indeed, caverns had rock ceilings overhead instead of a clear polymer dome. And here, the ceiling was sloped in a dramatic fashion, the highest point to the right at five or six stories tall. From there, it sloped down across a ballfield-size floor space to the wall on the left, where it hit at about two stories.

On the right, the tall wall had an imposing airlock built into it, an enormous black composite door crisscrossed with ribs and bracing, sized to permit the passage of ships as tall as the *Nelly Marie*. Just inside the door was a service area. Three spaceships stood side by side, filling the available work bays.

On the left, a row of service shops was built into the low wall. Some of them had adverts: propulsion, life support, waste management, electronic systems.

As Cuss scanned down the row looking for Joey Sprints, the smell of ozone irritated his already inflamed nose. An impact wrench screeched, the sound echoing from wall to wall. Bright sparks flashed from a welding bot overhead. A worker shouted something in an unfamiliar language.

"I don't see Joey's," he called over the din.

"Across the floor and to the left," said Ygo. "Around that far corner. See the opening?"

Cuss saw it when Ygo used his lens to enhance the view. He started the vehicle across the open floor but then stopped. Two bots were carrying a long bundle of pipes in front of the cart, blocking his way. While he waited the few seconds it took for the path to clear, something thumped to the ground behind him.

"They should require hard hats in here," said Ygo.

Cuss agreed, but instead of saying so, he started the cart moving, swerving behind the trailing bot in his impatience. He zipped across the open floor. At the far corner, he made the turn and stopped.

He was at the entrance to a narrow street, an alley with a rock ceiling overhead. There were four shops in a row along the wall to the right, each marked by a pair of tall roll-up-style garage doors. None of the shops had any sort of signage. All had shabby exteriors. Broken lights. Dirty walls.

Ygo used Cuss's lens to highlight each business as he spoke. "This first one is a custom fabrication shop, then a speed and racing shop. Joey Sprints is this third set of doors. And then a rehabbed-parts outlet at the far end."

The alleyway had the same grungy feel as the shops. Or perhaps it was the street mess that set the tone for everything else. Parts were everywhere, with most pieces mounded into loose piles, suggesting the collection had been curated at some level. Broken machine tools, tangles of electronics, metal scraps, even a pile of broken furniture.

And to complement the junk, a half-dozen young toughs were leaning against the wall across from the row of shops, hanging out, watching Cuss. Each had their own dramatic hair style, yet all had the same shiny chains around their necks. Sleeveless shirts that showed off their skin decorations. Two were smoking enhancers, an artificial cloud forming when they exhaled.

Cuss left the cart at the mouth of the alley and started toward Joey's on foot. When he passed the first tough, he nodded, looking down the row as he did, telling the rest of them that this was a communal acknowledgement.

Then he turned his attention to Joey's rocket shop. One of the garage doors was open to shoulder height. Cuss ducked under it, stepped inside, and paused to look around.

The place was bigger than he'd expected, running deep and with a high ceiling, giving them plenty of room for big projects. And like the alley out front, the space wasn't wasted. There were pieces of spaceship everywhere. Old motors. Landing gear. Pilot seats. Electronic racks. Air systems. Cowlings.

"Do you see any Bendolin Sprints?" asked Cuss.

"A bunch of these pieces are from Sprints. And those that aren't could be fit onto one."

Cuss saw five people in the shop. All men. Two of them were working deeper in the store, teaming with a bot on a project of some sort. The three other were standing not too far away, talking in a group.

"Joey is the gnome in that near group," said Ygo.

Cuss zoomed in on the man, easy to find with his wild red hair, full beard, and bushy eyebrows. In a mirror of his workplace, Joey had a disheveled appearance: smudges on his face, hands that were stained with grease, and clothes that were frayed and grubby.

Cuss approached him.

Joey was doing the talking, something about a special coating that added life to pulse rods. When Cuss crowded the group, Joey ignored the incursion, continuing his pitch, moving on to the value of extended wear resistance.

Knowing it wouldn't be received well, Cuss dove in anyway. "Excuse me, Mr. Spigliano? I'm Cuss Abbott. I wonder if I could have a moment."

"Happy to help, pal, *after* I finish here." Turning to look at Cuss when he said the last part, he pulled his head back in surprise, the black eyes and brace over Cuss's nose catching him off guard. "Holy shit, I hope the other guy looks worse."

Joey's friends laughed, and he turned back to accept the glory. Then he resumed his conversation.

Cuss felt that Joey was being reasonable. That, like he said, he was currently engaged and would help when his business was complete. Perhaps this was a big sale. Maybe he was excited to see old friends.

But Aurora was missing and Cuss didn't have the luxury of time. He fished his badge wallet out of his inside coat pocket and held it up.

"I'm Interworld Marshal Abbott here on official business. Sorry, but I'll need to interrupt."

This time Joey turned around, his face reddening. "Well, shit. *I'm* sorry because my lawyer says never to talk to cops without her being here. I told your assistant I needed a few days to arrange it."

"Yeah, right," said Ygo.

Cuss exhaled a huge sigh. "It's just a few questions. No need to make it complicated. A woman's been kidnapped in a Bendolin Sprint. I'm hoping you might be able to help us identify the ship."

Joey stepped back and frowned. "And you're looking at me?" He crossed his arms. "This is bullshit."

Cuss heard a quiet exchange and turned to see the other two men in Joey's group making for the exit. He was happy to let them leave. Now Joey could focus.

"No, sir. I'm not accusing you. But if you choose not to help, which is your right, then I'll wonder why you wouldn't answer a couple of questions to save a life. Your lawyer will tell you that you don't have to answer, that I can wonder about it all I want."

He paused his lecture while he put his badge wallet back in his pocket, letting Joey stew before he piled it on. "But I'll bet I can convince a judge to sign a warrant that lets me bring a crew in here to have a look. Wouldn't surprise me if one of the pictures on the wall in your office matches our ship. Or a picture in your archive. If we dig deep enough, we'll get our answer."

Cuss made a show of looking around, his sweeping gaze intended to convey that everything was on the line. "And while the cops are crawling through your stuff, you won't be open for business."

Joey took a quick glance toward the back of the space, making Cuss suspect he was worried about the two working there.

Ygo solved the problem for him, broadcasting over the shop speakers, "The police will be arriving momentarily to question everyone. If you were *not* involved in the crime, please wait outside."

The two men in back looked at each other, exchanged words, one nodded, and they both scurried for the exit, avoiding Joey and Cuss's gaze as they passed.

Cuss waited until they were gone. "The sooner we clear this up, the sooner I'm out of your life. I just need help with a ship."

"Jesus, you're brutal." Joey's fierce expression communicated his displeasure. He turned and started walking. "Let's go to my office so I can enjoy disappointing you."

His office turned out to be a small conference room set next to the supply closet. It held a heavily marred table surrounded by six chairs, none of which matched. Cuss guessed it was his place to take breaks, eat lunch, maybe meet with clients to discuss their projects.

The pictures on the wall were of a younger Joey. In one, he was sitting in the pilot's seat of a racer. A sleek ship, high tech, nothing like a Bendolin Sprint. In another, he was holding a trophy so big it took both hands to lift it, a huge grin on his face.

Joey went to the far side of the table and slumped into a chair.

"How will you disappoint me?" asked Cuss, choosing the seat across from him.

Joey moved his fingers and a hoverview display opened at the far end of the table. "Show me your ship."

Cuss cast up a holo of the Sprint hovering in space next to Mia's transport.

Joey fiddled and Cuss's image moved to one side. In the open space, another Bendolin Sprint appeared. This one looked more like a brochure image. Artful lighting. Pale background. Clean.

"Do they look the same?"

Both ships had the same distinctive blunt nose. The octagonal carriage. The external fuel packs. The grasshopper legs. All gray. But Joey's ship didn't have any rectangular patches on the exterior surfaces. No random weld lines. No rivets along the seams.

"Help me understand," said Cuss.

"We make a modest profit by following a recipe. Make each build the same. That way you know ahead of time about the challenges and the fixes. You don't waste time figuring out workarounds when you've done it before."

He highlighted the seams and weld patches on Cuss's craft. "Everything here was done after they bought the ship. The plates on the outside are bracing to support something they've added on the inside. Maybe a shelf. An extra toilet.

Instrumentation. A partition. Some want to travel in comfort to Earth. Others want to carry as much cargo as possible."

Joey sat back, his agitation thawing. "Each one becomes unique, but *after* they've left my shop. Anyone with modest skills can do the retrofits you see. Nothing hard about 'em, especially when they look as shitty as those." He smiled at his wit. "And at least half my builds have been out there long enough to have two owners. Some three. So, no. I can't identify your ship." He shrugged. "I told you I'd disappoint you."

"C'mon," said Cuss, anxious to rescue something from the exchange. "Since they're built from old ships, each one is unique at the parts level. Can't you look at an external fuel pack or a nose cap and identify something unique?"

"Perhaps if I kept records."

"What does that mean?"

"Part of the Sprint mystique is the outlaw image. Modern-day cowboys bucking the system." He scratched his cheek through his beard. "Something I agree with, by the way. I'm sorry about the kidnapped girl, I hope you find her. But cops are involved in a lot of bullshit." He broke eye contact. "For all I know you're making up the kidnapping to trick me into helping you fuck somebody over."

"I promise I'm not making it up. She's young and innocent and in deadly danger." Frustrated, he pointed at the Sprint in the display. "Someone local is using that ship. How can I find it? Or them?"

Joey sat back and toyed with his beard. "Maybe do spot visits and hope to catch it on the ground." He continued stroking his facial hair, acting as if he were done with his contribution. And then he popped forward like he'd received an electric shock. "Or maybe I've just become your best friend."

He wiggled and waved his fingers, working an interface Cuss couldn't see. He kept at it for several seconds. Then he looked up at the hoverview.

Cuss saw a lunar horizon on the display, a camera image looking across the surface of the Moon from an elevated position.

While they watched, a rocket ship descended in the distance. Joey moved his fingers and the camera zoomed in on the ship. It wasn't a Bendolin Sprint. But they could see full details of the hull and were able to follow the vessel all the way down to landing.

"I'm an umpire for the Tycho Sport Racing Series. We have cameras placed around the circuit to track the ships during a race. But we keep them running all the time so we can watch the teams practice." He pointed to the scene on the hoverview. "A few of the cameras offer great views across the plains."

Cuss was confused. "Why aren't they looking up?"

Joey gave a knowing smirk before explaining. "Sport racers run low to the ground. Max height is a thousand meters. One kilometer. Go above that and you're disqualified." Joey looked off in the distance, like he was remembering earlier days. "It's hard to go fast and stay low. Danger lurks near the ground. It really tests a pilot's skill."

Returning to the present, Joey tapped and swiped, and the lunar landscape on the hoverview was replaced by a map. "The race track is twelve hundred kilometers, with these six mountains serving as race pylons." Six spots on the map glowed to show the mountain locations. "The start and finish line is the central peak of the Tycho lunar crater." A lone spot in the middle of a vast crater glowed as he spoke.

"The track is set way out on the plains where you don't have to worry about collisions with the locals. So none of the cameras see action near the cities. But it just so happens that a couple of cameras catch the ore mines." Two spots on the map glowed to highlight the camera locations.

Ygo asked Cuss, "Why would we be interested in the ore mines?"

Cuss asked the question.

This time Joey's smirk was driven by chagrin. "Because six of them have one of my Sprints. Three of them have two. You should be able to catch them launching or landing by searching our race archive. We save everything."

Cuss felt a surge of energy. Finally, some good news.

"They're not positioned to see the water mines, though," continued Joey. "You'll need a different solution for those."

"How do we access the archive?"

"I'll connect you with Irma Liu, CEO of the Tycho Sport Racing Corporation. I don't have the authority to give you permission. But she can give you access, no problem."

"Found it and copied it," said Ygo. "They have really weak security. Anyway, I've started searching."

"I appreciate the offer," Cuss said to Joey. He stood to end the meeting. "I promised I'd be out of your hair after a few questions. Please send me the introduction to your CEO."

He shook Joey's hand and made for the exit.

Chapter 20

Ygo shadowed Julie as she made her way across Nova Terra, changing trams twice before arriving at the Alberton Station near the North Gate. Alberton was one of the older stations in Armstrong, its age reflected in its severe aesthetic: stone construction, hardpack floors, drab vines covering the walls, small displays providing traveler information and commercial adverts.

She made her way outside, climbed into the first cart in line, and gave Brace Harde's home address on Lansing Street. When the cart was underway, she asked, "Are you there?"

Julie had tech she used to stay linked with her company. Ygo tapped into her audio feed and replied, "I'm here."

"I'm trying to think through our priority questions." Her body swayed as the cart zigzagged its way through the neighborhood, a blend of homes and small businesses. Like the tram station, this section of Armstrong was older, with most of the structures built from dark basalt brick, rock mined during canyon excavation. "Any suggestions?"

"Let the conversation evolve. Your instincts are superb."

Though Julie had personal tech, it was nothing like Cuss's lens, a device that allowed Ygo to follow him everywhere. So while Julie rode, Ygo explored how to access the cameras inside Brace's house so he could be there with her.

His initial frustration gave way to a smile. Brace Harde's hardware store was a partner in the same crime watch program as Nick Navarro's rocket shop, allowing the police access to his business feeds in the event of an emergency. But unlike Nick, Brace had included his home in the agreement, which meant that Ygo could follow Julie inside with minimal effort.

"He knows why you're coming," Ygo continued, happy to be relieved of a burden. "That means he's thought about what you'll ask. He's even practiced answers to some of the questions."

"How do I get him off his script?"

"Patience. He'll give his rehearsed answers at the beginning. I'd guess that after ten or fifteen minutes, he'll be through them and back to natural responses."

The cart turned onto a block with row houses on either side, dark brick buildings pushed one against the next. The homes were tall and narrow, four floors each, with windows in front that marked the levels, low gravity making the stair climb easy. The cart stopped midway down the street.

As she got out, a door opened on a house to her right. Brace Harde stepped onto the porch, his broad grin revealing his excitement, the expression having the unfortunate side effect of amplifying the crow's feet around his eyes. He was wearing a sharp outfit. Somewhat formal. His hair was washed and brushed, hanging loose down to his shoulders.

"Welcome!" he called, looking both ways down the street before turning his attention to Julie.

His behavior made Ygo wonder if he was looking for Cuss.

Brace came off the porch and met Julie halfway, greeting her with a hug that seemed a bit too cozy. She took it in stride, exchanging pleasantries with him as he ushered her inside, keeping the patter going as they toured the first floor: a living area, then a dining room, followed by a kitchen, all in a line toward the back. The place felt cluttered to Ygo, with lots of stuff on the walls, and gizmos and appliances in abundance. At the same time, it seemed fitting for a single male hardware store owner.

"Please, make yourself comfortable," he said when they'd returned to the front of the house. He motioned to a three-cushion couch and she sat.

Ygo was growing increasingly uncomfortable with where this was heading. The fancy clothes. The deferential manners. The room as neat as a pin. A plate of goodies on the coffee table.

"What can I get you to drink?" Brace asked her.

"Tea, please. Green if you have it. Black is nice as well."

"I have a bottle of Screaming Octopus. It's from the Frothier Distillery over in Aldrin. Won all types of awards. Makes a wonderful cocktail."

"It's a bit early for me."

He seemed disappointed but went into the kitchen, pressed a few buttons, and while he waited for the brew process to complete, called, "Cream or sugar? It's green, by the way."

"Cream would be delightful."

Moments later, he carried two cups of tea back to the living area, placed them on the coffee table, and sat next to her on the couch.

Brace's actions from there only compounded Ygo's concern. He complimented Julie repeatedly. He steered the conversation back to her on a personal level. He pointed out instances where they shared a mutual interest or belief. He never stopped studying her face and body.

But Julie proved to be a master of deflection. She never encouraged him. Never rebuffed him. She just guided the conversation to ways to find the pirates.

"We think the killers have Aurora. She's in grave danger and we need your help."

"The Bendolin Sprint, right? What did Joey Spigliano say? He couldn't help?"

"He seems to be pointing us out to the mining companies, just like you did. What is it you and he know that we don't?"

Brace sat back on the couch and crossed his arms. "First off, you were the one who said that it was a surface company. The marshal did, anyway. All I'm saying is that if that part is true, I would start with them. But it's not that I know something. It's my guess based on yours."

"Suppose I said it was a group operating from within the city. Who would it be then?"

"Using lasers and Sprints and all that equipment?" Brace fidgeted for a moment. "Okay. I'd still look out there."

Julie turned on the couch so her knees pointed toward his. "Why, Brace? Tell me."

"Beyond the fact that they suck as people, it's that they burn through equipment at an incredible rate. The kind of stuff the marshal mentioned as being stolen. And they're doing it way out on the plains where no one can see."

Julie pressed. "I saw a vid of the ore mines. It's bone dry out there. Nothing but dust. What do they need with so many pumps?"

Brace sat forward again, like he knew an answer for a change. "Washing rock."

He let the statement hang there for a moment before continuing. "They mine the ore, crush it, and then wash it to remove the fine particles, stuff they don't want to pay to ship back to Earth. Wash water is expensive, so they filter and reuse it. Big volumes for the tonnage they mine. Anyway, it's hard stuff to filter, and fine particles get through and eat at the seals and bearings. A pump that should last ten years with clean water lasts them a couple of months. They replace parts until the pump dies, then toss it on a pile and swap in a new one."

"That knowledge is so specific," Ygo said to Julie. "How does he know it?"

Julie asked.

"Believe it or not, a fair chunk of my store profit comes from replacement parts for that kind of stuff, and the mines are my main customers. They ship in most of what they need from Earth. But they're screwups, so they still come running to me for emergency parts." He smiled. "I get them up and running fast for a very steep markup."

"Do they fly to your shop in Bendolin Sprints?"

His smile turned into a grin and he shook his head. "No idea. They land outside the gate and I don't see them until they're inside the store."

He started to take a sip of his tea and stopped. "I assume you've checked the gate logs? If it's them, there's likely a record of the ship landing there. With all the activity at the gates, though, it may be quite the chore to find."

. . .

Aurora was shivering when she woke. To warm herself, she pulled her knees up to her chest and scrunched into a ball. Then she pulled the sleeping bag over her head and blew into her cupped hands, hoping to warm her fingers.

Her teeth started to chatter.

Looking out through the opening at the top of the sleeping bag, she eyed the bundles of stuff hanging on the wall. The third one held extra clothing, something she desperately needed.

Steeling herself, she decided to make a dash for it.

Wiggling out of the sleeping bag as fast as she could, she pulled herself to the front of the small cylinder, screaming, "Fuck, it's cold!"

Reaching the bundle, she struggled to open it, her frozen fingers refusing to cooperate. Teeth still chattering, she dug out a sweatshirt, extra socks, and sweatpants, and put them on over her jumpsuit. Then she dug out a T-shirt and wrapped it around the top of her head as a makeshift cap.

"Can I turn up the heat?" she asked the button, still shivering.

"Yes," the voice replied. "The silver box labeled Hezelt has a green up-down arrow. Press the up direction to raise the temperature."

Studying the box, she saw the arrows and pressed the up arrow once. A red number lit up, moving from seven to eight. She pressed the arrow a second time and moved it to nine.

Still shivering, she waited for something to happen. The extra clothes weren't helping much, and she eyed the sleeping bag, thinking maybe she should climb back inside. Then she heard a clicking noise behind her. She recognized the sound. In her kitchen, it was the noise appliances make when heating up.

Pulling herself to the rear of the cylinder, she located a box on the wall and put her hands near it. Warmth radiated from the surface. She positioned herself so her head and torso were in front of the heater, her hands on either side.

As her body warmed, her teeth stopped chattering. She sighed.

Looking at her sleeping bag, she decided to unhook it from the wall and position it so it was next to the heater. She didn't believe there was a fire risk. And the heat source would feel wonderful.

Moving the bed was more of a chore than she'd guessed. The bag was held to the wall with a dozen metal rings along its length. She couldn't break or open the rings, so she used a jackknife her kidnappers had included in one of the bundles to cut each ring free from the bag.

Floating the bed to its new position near the heater, she fastened it to the wall by tying the bits of torn cloth to a pipe. It wasn't as secure as before. But it would work.

That chore complete, she eyed the bundles of stuff hanging on the wall and thought about eating. But then she had an inspiration. She floated to the front, unhooked the four bags, and moved them to the center of the cylinder, attaching them around the wall in a circle like the points of a compass.

She shifted her growing pile of waste to the front of the chamber. Then she moved herself into the back half and draped the corners of a clear plastic sheet over each bag, creating a crude see-through wall. It made her prison smaller. But now the heater had less space to keep warm, and that could only be a good thing.

Hunger turned her thoughts back to food. They'd given her prepared meals, most of it dehydrated. No fresh fruits. No fresh vegetables. There were ample quantities, but everything had a mushy texture, or chalky if she didn't allow enough time for the water to penetrate and moisten the food.

Squirting a cold goo of red beans and rice into her mouth, she thought about who would do this to her and to what end. It had something to do with Moby and her dad, that part seemed certain. But after hours and hours of thought, she couldn't imagine who or why.

Chapter 21

Cuss flew above the barren lunar landscape in a Viperion, the zippy skimmer creating a cloud of dust behind him as he cruised out to visit the ore mines. Small and fast, it was the perfect vehicle for surface travel, designed to carry two passengers with limited baggage over a craggy moonscape.

He was riding alone. Telling Julie "You can't come" had not gone well.

The mine bosses had been evasive when Ygo first called, so Cuss had asked him to contact the corporate CEOs and work his way down. The CEOs all proclaimed support for the Interworld Marshals Service and promised that Cuss would be welcome at their mine.

Still, Cuss had worried that he would stumble across the doers, criminals who had shown a casual willingness to kidnap and kill. If things turned ugly, he'd have to split his attention between confronting them and protecting Julie. It was a recipe for disaster, and he'd put his foot down. But he hadn't broached the subject as tactfully as he might have, and the conversation built to a prickly edge.

While she acknowledged that he would feel driven to protect her, she insisted that it wouldn't be necessary, at one point hinting that his attitude felt condescending: male macho out of control.

They were at an impasse until Ygo stepped in to save the day.

He offered her the job of screener. An observer. Someone who viewed the feed from afar, but not with the goal of watching Cuss and whoever he was engaged with. Her job was to study everywhere else. Look for hidden danger. Or something that didn't belong. Maybe a place where criminals could hide evidence. Or activity that had little to do with mining.

She hemmed and hawed, behaving like they'd offered her a booby prize. But when Ygo reminded her that his role was similar, had been for years, and that through his vigilance he'd saved Cuss's life on more than one occasion, she began to teeter. Cuss closed the deal by offering the *Nelly Marie*'s pilot's seat as her station, never telling her that Ygo was doing the same job from his private room in the hold beneath her feet.

Cuss's first appointment was with the Castile operation, the northernmost mine. From there, he would work his way south.

Ygo had sent a flock of microdrones ahead to map the place and establish a basis for their assessment. As the mine site came into view, Cuss communicated his observations aloud, confirming what the drones had found. It was his way of internalizing the scene.

"They're working twin craters. I see the two warehouses set between them. Plenty big enough to hold stolen goods and a Sprint. Let's see, eight small buildings in a cluster to the right. Four trucks in motion in the mine pits."

Ygo and Julie spoke at the same time, both with urgency in their voices, warning him of an approaching skimmer.

"Is it what's-his-name?" asked Cuss.

"Yup," said Ygo after a pause. "Miko Korhonen, the Castile mine boss. He's alone. You're meeting in the near warehouse. The one with the green roof."

Cuss was still a few minutes out when Miko's skimmer touched down on a small landing pad next to the green-roofed warehouse. An airlock door opened on the side of the building, and a mechanism pulled the landing pad and Miko's skimmer inside.

"How many people work out here?" asked Cuss

"Eight, according to their business profile," said Ygo. "But during the scouting run, the drones located only four humans."

"Any priors?"

"The four are clean. No record in any of the worlds. Well, one was arrested in her youth during a political protest in Boston and was given probation."

"Why did she get probation for protesting?" asked Julie.

"She handcuffed herself to the door of a federal building."

"Good for her." Julie's voice sounded wistful.

The airlock on the side of the warehouse opened again and the now empty landing pad moved out to its original position. Approaching from the front, Cuss plopped his tiny craft onto it. Mechanisms engaged, and he felt a small jolt as he and his skimmer were pulled inside.

While Cuss waited for the airlock door to close behind him, he activated the compact detector he'd placed in his coat pocket. Built to Space Watch specifications, the miniature device would read equipment ID tags from everything within a hundred meters and send the data to Ygo, who would be monitoring the feed for stolen goods.

Stepping from the skimmer, Cuss was greeted by Miko, a tall, fair-haired happy sort. Miko was polite in that he didn't gawk at or comment on Cuss's obvious facial injuries. And he was cooperative when it came to providing information about the Castile mine site.

He gave Cuss a tour of the buildings. Showed him their Bendolin Sprint. Gave him access to the in-house camera archives. Took him out to the boneyard, the place where broken equipment was piled high. Introduced him to the other three humans. They even sat together for a nice lunch.

The visit was a bust. The external patchwork on Castile's Sprint didn't match with the ship used to attack Mia. The pocket detector didn't locate any stolen goods. None of them saw anything to contradict the obvious conclusion: Castile wasn't involved.

The only curious interaction occurred when Miko was walking Cuss to his skimmer. Cuss had asked, "Of your neighbors, who comes to mind when I say 'piracy and murder'?"

Miko gave an assortment of answers, none of them completely believable, things like, "I don't know them," and "We all keep to ourselves," and "Beats the hell out of me."

Cuss tried to balance that against one of Miko's earlier comments, something he'd said when they were touring the boneyard. He'd allowed that when they were in a pinch trying to fix a broken machine, they'd sometimes reach out to their neighbors in search of parts.

Yet even with that minor discordance, the complete lack of physical evidence told Cuss to move on. He thanked Miko, climbed into his skimmer, and flew south to the next mine site, Kolour Limited.

The outcome there was similar to the Castile visit. Friendly people. Open. Cooperative. Not involved.

Cuss was flying the Viperion to the third mine site when Ygo yelped, "I found it!"

He projected a holo of a Bendolin Sprint flying in space. "They're about to leave lunar orbit, outbound for either Lagrange or Earth."

"You sure it's ours?" asked Cuss.

The display switched from live action to a fixed image of the ship Ygo was tracking. Next to it, he projected the Bendolin Sprint used in the attack on Mia. The external patchwork matched to the finest detail.

"Thank fucking God," said Cuss, his excitement rising. "It's about time we got a break." After a pause, he added, "Please don't lose it."

Turning the skimmer back toward Port Collins, he fretted because at top speed, he was still ninety minutes out. "Can you launch a tracker?" he asked Ygo.

Since the *Nelly Marie* would be leaving orbit a few hours behind the Bendolin Sprint, the two ships would be traveling on different paths through space. Piloting the *Nelly Marie* so it was within camera range of the Sprint would require extreme gee forces and enormous amounts of fuel. A tracker was a nimble missile that could accelerate and turn in ways the *Nelly Marie* couldn't. Once in place behind its target, its suite of sensors would provide Cuss and Ygo with front-row seats no matter where their quarry traveled.

"Not until we launch, but Space Watch has assets we can use until then." Ygo paused. "The Sprint's a tub, Cuss. We can leave four hours from now and track her easy."

As Cuss thought through the details, he realized he had another sticky situation on his hands. "If they're after a cargo ship, they'll want to take it when they're heading back home. It'd be too much exposure otherwise. That means they'll loop behind Earth and approach it on the return trip."

"If this is a piracy run, I agree," said Ygo. "But they could be on a supply run, out for a visit, or a hundred other things. We'll have to wait and see."

"Which means it could be a multiday chase." That comment was for Julie. Ygo already knew this.

"You got lucky this time," said Julie. "Glen's back from his dad's soon, so I need to head home anyway. I'm happy though. I have *a lot* to discuss with Gastrow. Should lead to more business."

"I can get her home in style if you want to offer," Ygo told him privately.

"Losing you means I'm unlucky," said Cuss. "Hang around until I'm back so I can say goodbye. In fact, Ygo, would you please arrange first-class travel home for our provisional assistant deputy marshal?"

"It would be my honor."

"I'll wait," said Julie. "But I need to get my staff started on our reports. Do you mind if I sit on the middeck and make some calls?"

He couldn't help but smile. "Make yourself at home."

Riding across the plains after that, Cuss listened to the hum of the skimmer, watched the holo of the Bendolin Sprint leaving lunar orbit, and thought about Julie.

She'd turned his head like few women had. It wasn't just that she was gorgeous. Had enchanting lips. Eyes he could get lost in. Hair that smelled intoxicating. He liked how she challenged him. Offered mind-blowing insights and creative solutions. Was open and honest. Upbeat and positive at every turn.

And because he cared for her, he was hesitant to include her in his life. His was an itinerant existence.

Chasing evil, confronting it, battling it into submission. Too often in ways that involved frightening violence.

He'd lost his new bride years ago to a madman he was chasing. And since then, colleagues, friends, and lovers had been threatened, wounded, a few even killed. Associating with him put the other person in danger. It was his curse. And the more he respected someone, the less he wanted to inflict his chaos on them.

A flash from the Bendolin Sprint pulled his thoughts to the present. He turned to the display, trying to determine the source of the light.

It wasn't hard to figure out. The ship's hatch was swinging open. A six-armed industrial bot stood just inside the doorway.

The bot crawled out onto the exterior surface of the ship, a giant insect making its way to a flat section. There, it took a square weld patch from a stack it was carrying and pressed it onto the hull. When the bot moved on, the square looked like the other exterior patch panels.

"Are you seeing this?" Cuss asked in amazement.

"It explains why we couldn't find them," Ygo replied.

As he spoke, the bot pressed a fake weld seam onto another open expanse.

"How did they know we were IDing off the external patchwork?" said Cuss. "Someone we shared details with has passed that tidbit on to them."

"You think this is a new behavior?"

"They weren't using camouflage when they attacked Mia."

"Good point."

Cuss scratched his chin. "Where did they launch from?"

"Don't know. They were already in orbit when I spotted them."

The miss was out of character for Ygo, making Cuss wonder if something was bothering him. But before he could ask, a call chime pulled him in a new direction.

It was Darlena Washington, assigned by Chief of Detectives Toni Carrabelle to be his liaison partner for police matters within Armstrong proper.

"Goddammit, Cuss," said Darlena, a full-figured black woman who spoke her mind. "Every time you show up, dead bodies follow." Shaking her head, her tall hair moving with it, she demanded, "Who are they?"

"Nick and Patsy Navarro."

Darlena snorted. "Don't fuck with me. I know their names. Why are they dead in my town?" She met his gaze and stopped talking, her eyebrows raised. "What the hell happened to that beautiful face? Oh my God, Cuss. Tell me there's no permanent damage."

Cuss had worked with Darlena on a number of investigations over the years, and at no point had she ever commented on his looks, good or bad. So he was pleasantly surprised by her concern. It softened an otherwise brash persona. "The doc says it's nothing permanent."

She nodded. "Good." And then she got back to business. "So why are the Navarros dead?"

"Truthfully? I don't know. Nick is the son of Moby Navarro, a pilot killed during a pirate raid a few days back. I was on my way to talk with Nick and Patsy about Moby, see what they knew, when I found them dead. What's worrying me now is their daughter is missing. Aurora. Either dead or kidnapped."

"She a kid?"

"No. She's thirty."

"Thirty-one," Ygo told him privately.

He didn't correct himself.

"Was she taken from Armstrong?" continued Darlena.

Cuss shook his head. "Earth."

She tugged on an ear, and Cuss could almost see her brain working toward the obvious conclusion. Since the crime took place outside Armstrong, it wasn't her problem.

She steered the conversation back to the part that was. "Did you learn anything about the killers?"

"I tracked a lorry from the Navarro house to the co-op exchange down the street. Two men masked in pressure gear went from the cart into the building and disappeared inside. I lost them there." Hoping to mollify her, he added, "I sent the feed to the cops who'd discovered the bodies and suggested they look into it."

"Did they?"

He shrugged. Before she could follow up, he asked a question of his own, "What did Crime Scene find?"

"The two were killed by blows to the head. There was a pipe on the kitchen floor with both their blood on it.

Crime Scene says it's from their front yard, staking a plant or something."

"Any ideas on motive?"

She shook her head. "Best guess is an argument turned deadly. But about what, who knows. He had defensive wounds on his arms and shoulders, which means he fought back. The missus got clocked once and that put her down." She studied him for a moment. "If you've been working this for days, you must know something."

Cuss shrugged. "His business is small rocket engines, something he did with his dad. Most of me says that's an important piece of the puzzle. But it beats the hell out of me how it gets them both killed."

"Their business records are secured. Know who might have the credentials to open them?"

"There's Nick's dad, Moby, the pilot who was killed. Nick's mom died a few years ago. There's Nick's daughter, who's missing. His nephew, Georgio, is still alive. He might be your best shot. He lives near Valencia, Spain."

Cuss hesitated, trying to decide. Softened by her concern for his well-being, he made a rare offer. "I've been working with Georgio on Moby's case. If you want, I can reach out and see if he knows how to access Nick's books."

Darlena looked offscreen for a moment. Cuss figured she was consulting with Hobby, her partner. She turned back to him and nodded. "Let us know what you learn." A pause. "Speaking of access, Chik Gambier has been pestering me for a story. I'd like to pass her off to you."

Chik Gambier was a crime news muckraker with a huge following, in part because she splashed buckets of blood across her stories. And she liked to attack, accusing the cops of incompetence or corruption or brutality, whatever she thought made the story more appealing to her fans. Shock was her coin. It didn't matter to her or her followers that in the modern world, everything was recorded and false accusations could be debunked.

Cuss knew her better than he cared to admit. They'd had a few drinks a year ago when Cuss was working a case she thought might have enough gore for her fans. In a moment of weakness, or perhaps it was the half-bottle of wine, she'd allowed that her vampire style of reporting had begun by accident.

Her first job was for a man who believed in the classics, his favorite being, "If it bleeds, it leads." In an effort to impress him, she'd reported bloody details about a recent murder, her gruesome imagery painting scenes of carnage and butchery.

Her boss loved it, and their audience *loved* it. The rest was history.

As Chik worked deeper into the bottle that evening, her filters began to fade.

Cuss liked her in an odd sort of way. She was an openly sexual creature, lewd, horny. As they finished their drinks, she'd invited him to spend the night with her, an invitation that stoked wild fantasies.

He'd walked her home but declined the invitation, admitting that he felt a strong desire but couldn't accept because of the alcohol. He'd made it clear that if she reissued the invitation when she was not impaired, he'd be delighted to accept.

Since that night, she'd reported on two more of his cases. She portrayed him as a ruthless detective motivated more by revenge than the law, something he didn't like. But she let him guide the timing of her installments to ensure she didn't interfere with his investigation, a behavior he valued.

She'd never reissued her bedroom invitation.

"Have her call me," he said to Darlena. "There's a bigger story if she'll work with me."

Darlena crossed her arms and flashed a frown so fierce, Cuss gulped.

"You gonna tell *me* about it? Or do I need to hear it from your girlfriend?"

Chapter 22

When Cuss stepped through the *Nelly Marie*'s main hatch and onto the command deck, Julie was waiting for him in the pilot's seat, the chair swiveled to face him. Her hair was wet. She wore only a towel, one big enough to preserve her modesty. Barely.

As he closed the hatch, she stood and approached him. He tried to look into her eyes but spent most of the time focused on the towel, staring at the tucked bit that kept the cloth snugged around her, willing it to release.

Taking his hand, she led him to the ladder and began to climb.

He followed, the view a spiritual experience for him.

She continued up to the third deck. By the time they reached his bedroom, he was burning with desire.

They faced each other, her back to the bed.

He enveloped her in his massive arms and kissed her on the lips, his tongue probing her mouth. She moaned, and then her tongue danced with his.

In the hotel tub, their lovemaking had been tentative. Exploring. Caressing. Gentle kisses. Checking to make sure she was comfortable.

This wasn't like that. When he came up for air, her towel was on the floor.

He looked her up and down. "You are a beauty, Julie."

Pushing her back onto the bed, he stared at her naked body as he undressed. She propped herself up on her elbows and mirrored his stare.

He climbed onto the bed beside her.

They kissed and caressed for maybe thirty seconds, and then he took her. She said his name with a sigh.

They began moving together, matching rhythm, building intensity, Cuss whispering words of endearment into her ear.

They finished together. He had the presence of mind to roll his huge body off her before collapsing on the bed.

She moved up against him, swung a leg over his, and laid her head on his chest. After spending a moment basking in the afterglow, she said, "You need to get moving."

"Give me ten minutes, love. He has to rest between performances."

She giggled and gave him a playful slap on his chest. "You know what I mean."

He kissed the top of her head. "You're right, of course."

"We both travel a lot. I'll bet our paths cross more than we realize."

"Absolutely." When he traveled, it was to hunt criminals. Not the best situation for romantic diversions.

She climbed out of bed and he watched her dress. When she was covered, he threw on his space travel uniform: shorts and a T-shirt.

At the main hatch, they hugged and kissed. Expressed the desire for continued intimacy. Made vague promises, things neither of their schedules would allow.

He waved when she rode away in a cart.

As he shut the hatch, he asked Ygo, "How far off did I set us?"

"We're fine. Launch in six minutes."

. . .

Low gravity and no atmosphere made for a smooth and easy liftoff from the Moon. As soon as the *Nelly Marie* cleared the Port Collins restricted zone, Ygo launched a tracker. The spritely missile would need sixty minutes to get within sensor range of the Bendolin Sprint.

Cuss released his restraints, checked his messages, and found a note from Darlena. They were friends again because he'd briefed her on what he thought he knew.

To wit, pirates were using a refurbished Bendolin Sprint to steal industrial equipment, most of it the kind used in mining operations. The thieves were targeting ships owned by the Gastrow Group because they were able to corrupt the security feeds during their raids, and that allowed them to hide their identities.

After a couple of dozen robberies with no casualties, the pirates killed Moby Navarro, a retired Gastrow employee. Mia Moreau of the Lunar Organized Crime Unit confronted the pirates in a sting operation and was killed. Moby worked with his son, Nick Navarro, to make small rocket engines for specialized use. Nick and Patsy were killed for reasons unknown, and Aurora, their daughter, was missing.

Common threads were the Gastrow Group, the Navarros, and stolen mining equipment. No solid suspects. Yet.

The video message from Darlena included an update and a plea. "Hobby and I got a warrant for that exchange cooperative down the street from the Navarros," she reported. "The perps somehow avoid getting their faces on any feed before they disappear. Hobby thinks by hiding in an outbound shipment, a crate or something. I don't have anything better. But it makes us both think they have someone powerful helping them." She shook her head. "Most criminals are too dumb to figure out something like this. Give me your ideas, I want to hear them."

Closing the message, Cuss sat back in the seat and gently rubbed his tender eyes. Her report was in line with everything else he knew about the doers. He didn't have any clever ideas to suggest.

"Do we know yet if we're going to Earth?" he asked Ygo as he climbed to the middeck.

"That's their current trajectory. It will take half a day to transit at this speed. If they loop around Earth and head home like we expect, multiply that by two."

Cuss grabbed a nutrition bar from an overhead cabinet, opened it, and as he munched, his eyes fell on the big parcel sitting at the back of the middeck, Ygo's gift of a previously owned rejuv. He wandered over to it.

He was growing tired of the commentary about his face. And unless the Sprint changed course, he had a lot of time to kill. Stuffing the rest of the bar into his mouth, he dusted his hands of crumbs and worked to unwrap the unit. As the pieces were revealed, the machine seemed to be in good shape. No dents or loose wires. Easy to assemble.

That is, until he got to the patient platform, the flat bed he would lie on while an electronic box above him did its thing. The platform was dirty. Not like dust-settling-from-the-air dirty. More like the sweat and grime of the previous owner. Cuss wasn't a germophobe or clean freak by any stretch of the imagination. But the thing looked disgusting.

"Peanut!" he called to the air.

He ate another nutrition bar while he waited for the bot. When Peanut was out of its closet and ready for work, Cuss motioned to the device. "Clean and sanitize the machine. Pay special attention to the patient platform." He pointed to the streaks of filth to help the bot understand the assignment. "Make it pristine."

To Ygo he said, "I'm going to take a shower. After Peanut is done, would you mind checking that it runs like it should? I'd prefer not to bake my head like a potato."

"You sure? I stocked up on sour cream and chives."

Cuss smiled and then climbed up to his bedroom on the third level.

Studying his face in the bathroom mirror, he saw that some of the bruising around his eyes had gone from purple to a sickly green, the first steps in the healing process. He lifted the medical cover off the bridge of his nose and had a look. His nose was slightly swollen, bruised along one side, scabbed where the boot had connected, but seemingly on the mend as well. He tossed the nose cover into the trash and then shaved, showered, and dressed.

Climbing back down to the middeck, he felt mentally ready to fulfill his promise to Darlena. "Would you call Georgio?" he asked Ygo. "I'd like to filter my face when we talk. The attention isn't helping."

Some people altered their holo as a matter of routine. Most did so occasionally, perhaps when caught in a state they didn't want to immortalize. Cuss couldn't remember the last time he'd filtered his image. It wasn't how his mind worked. But he did care if his appearance was so disturbing that it interfered with the dynamic of his interview.

"Got him!" called Ygo.

A hoverview display opened in front of Cuss. On it, Georgio was red-faced and bleary-eyed.

"Make it make sense," he wailed.

In three separate acts over the span of a few days, his grandpa had been murdered, then his cousin was taken, and then his aunt and uncle were murdered.

Uncomfortable with the raw emotions, Cuss sat quietly while Georgio spewed venom and sadness and outrage and frustration. Eventually he wound down, and Cuss was able to ask about accessing Nick's business records. Georgio didn't know anything about it.

After closing the call, Cuss felt discouraged and said so to Ygo.

"I hate to make it worse," replied Ygo. "But we have an issue."

"I knew something was bothering you. What's up?"

"As soon as the Sprint committed to Earth, I started working to identify their target vessel. I can compute when they reach Earth. They loop around behind and start their return. At that point they need to be matching the trajectory of their mark. So I look at what's moving out on Dependable Delivery with the right flight path. Turns out the most likely target is carrying large-diameter pipe. Lots of it."

"I didn't see any pipework like that at the mines. What are they doing with it?"

"More to the point—how are they carrying it back to the Moon? The load won't fit in a Bendolin Sprint. Not even close. And as I thought it through, I realized most of the stolen loads wouldn't. I hadn't even considered that aspect of the thefts until I was searching out likely targets. And now it's so obvious that I'm furious at myself. It means we're still missing a huge piece of the puzzle."

Cuss hadn't thought of it either, something so apparent in retrospect that he felt his own level of shame. "They cut the feed before they move the cargo and that trick kept sidetracking us." He'd said it hoping to make them both feel better. In his case, it didn't work, so he said something that did. "Let's follow these assholes to the end, pal. We'll get our answers and put them away for good."

Ygo's revelation left Cuss feeling discouraged in brain, body, and spirit. As he looked at the rejuv, now shiny clean, the thought of lying still for a few hours suddenly sounded appealing.

Climbing onto the patient platform, he stretched out on his back. His feet hung over the end, a casualty of his height, and he scooted up as best he could. Ygo powered the machine, and as it warmed up, Cuss covered his eyes with a special protective pad.

"Ready?" asked Ygo.

"Full speed ahead."

For the next twenty minutes, Cuss's brain twisted and turned as it tried to force the facts of the case into something that made sense. And then he fell asleep.

. . .

"Rise and shine," called Ygo.

Cuss opened his eyes, felt his eyelids rub against the protective pad, and lifted it off. Taking care not to bump his head on the silver box suspended above him, he slid out of the rejuv and stood. He felt refreshed and checked the time. Seven hours had passed since he'd climbed into the machine.

"I shut off the power after five hours and let you sleep. How do you feel?"

"Royale Anderson," Cuss replied.

One of the things he liked about his brain was that it would toil away at problems while he slept. It meant he didn't have to force himself to concentrate, something that always felt like work. And often he'd awaken with a solution, or at least a plan. This time it was neither a plan nor a solution, but a curious anomaly.

"Royale made a big stink about us crowding his investigation. That we'd trip over each other when we visited the mine sites. But no one mentioned seeing him out there."

"You didn't ask," said Ygo.

"I didn't. But if he'd been there, it would have been in the last two days. *Everyone* who's being questioned by multiple interviewers will say at least once, 'I told all this to the cop before you.' It makes me wonder if he has a different lead and was blowing smoke up our ass so we'd chase our tails."

"Let me contact a few of the mines and confirm whether they've seen him."

Cuss nodded. "Any guesses on his real line of attack?"

"Only that whatever he's doing, it can't be better than following the pirates as they make a strike."

Cuss agreed, though Royale's childish behavior deepened an already intense dislike for the man. "How's that going?"

"The Sprint has moved into a standard approach trajectory as it nears Earth. If this is a pirate's run, it means they're perfectly aligned to take that shipment of pipes.

When they strike is still an open question, but they've always hit when the target is far from help."

Cuss's brain was wrestling with the seed of an idea, one he hadn't fleshed out enough to express in words. He decided to go with it anyway. "Can you see if Chik Gambier is free?"

"She called while you were asleep. Hold a sec." A moment later, he said, "She's on a call but wants to talk. She's available in twenty minutes. Asked if you'd wait. Begged actually."

"That'll work."

Cuss used the time to start his workout. He normally would launch a fighting sim and battle Ygo. But those were violent sessions and he wanted to give his nose more time to heal. So instead, he worked through a short kata, practiced movements designed to strengthen his muscle memory and physical conditioning.

He was breathing hard when Ygo said, "Here she is."

"Filter me again. I want to keep her focused."

A hoverview opened and Chik appeared. She was a pretty woman in her midthirties, but Cuss was old school and thought she undermined her traditional good looks with spiked silver hair, plump green lips, and sparkly makeup around the eyes that carried back onto her ears.

"Hey, Marshal Abbott."

"Hi, Chik. How've you been?"

"You got something for me?"

"I do. It's about the new director of the Lunar Organized Crime Unit. His name is Royale Anderson."

"Is this related to the Navarro killings?"

"In a roundabout way. It's a good story."

She ignored him and plowed ahead. "What was the motive behind the Navarro murders? And how could the perps escape so easily?"

"Chik, stop." He said it forcefully and waited a moment before he continued. "I've got a huge case and I'll give you an exclusive. But you need to work with me for the next three or four days."

"Fuck you. That's an eternity in the news cycle. Three eternities. I'll be scooped by a dozen losers."

"None of them will have anything close to what I'll give you. I promise. But I need your help."

"When you get all serious like that, it puts my panties in a quiver."

Cuss pretended he didn't hear. "Royale Anderson became the new director of LOCU when his competition was killed in a pirate raid."

Chik became all business. "When did this happen? And where?"

He took her through it. The competition between Royale and Mia Moreau for the director's job. Both of them believing the recent wave of piracy was *the* burning issue for the selection committee. Solving it, or at least making a dent, was their chosen contest. Mia took an unnecessary risk in a sting operation and the pirates killed her. Royale got the promotion.

Cuss finished with, "Royale asked me to step aside so he could be the one to capture Mia's killers."

"And…"

"And so I did. But he hasn't. And now I'm curious to know where he's at. Who are his suspects? Who has he cleared? When does he expect to make an arrest? Like that."

"You can't ask him?"

"I'd get a much different response than you will."

"He's not going to tell me details. Not for an ongoing investigation."

"Of course not. But how does he behave when you push? Defensive? Angry? Evasive? Smug?"

She studied him, seemingly suspicious of his motives. "Suppose I do it and report back to you that he was angered by my questions. Where does that get you? What's your takeaway?"

"It will mean that you stirred the pot. When an investigation is at a crossroads, stir things up and see what happens."

"That's really your plan? It sounds…desperate."

"It could lead to nothing, but my sense is that he'll react in some fashion."

"Will I be in danger?"

Cuss gave an apologetic shrug. "You'll be in danger of being insulted. Shouted at. Demeaned. The guy's a supreme asshole. But drama is a reaction you're used to; one you know how to handle. That's why I'm asking you."

She seemed on the verge of accepting the role, so he kept selling. "LOCU is an elite investigative unit and he's just been elevated into a high-profile position. I don't see any physical risk. Help me stir the pot today and I'll give you a treasure trove of insider stories later this week."

"I want to hear those stories in person."

"Of course." He said it without thinking what might come next.

"Sitting by a fire. Or maybe during a walk in the park at sunset." Her nose scrunched as she grinned. "Hell, I'd settle for a simple romantic dinner."

"We can have dinner."

"Done."

. . .

An hour later, the *Nelly Marie* began the loop behind Earth. The ride was bumpy, and Cuss stayed strapped in the pilot's seat.

Halfway along, Ygo reported that of the five mines that responded to his query, none had been contacted by Royale. Then he said, "Girish will want to know why we're going it alone on this raid."

Cuss gave his reasons, most of them unconvincing. "How do we coordinate a group when we don't know when or where the pirates will strike? And once word gets out that we're organizing a sting, I'll have to referee who gets to do what, which could even include LOCU and Royale." He saved his best reason for last. "And the pirates seem to have inside information on the investigation. If we share our plans and they hear of it, Aurora will surely die, if she isn't dead already."

He had a another good reason, but he wasn't going to say it aloud, even to Ygo. And that was the likelihood that at some point, he'd have to hurt people to get answers. He didn't want to make Ygo a party to such behavior. And he especially didn't want outsiders witnessing it.

"Girish will remind us that we're members of the Marshals Service," said Ygo. "Not vigilantes."

"Then let's call him when we're leaving orbit. That's too late for anyone else to be at the scene if the pirates strike, and soon enough to help us on the Moon when the doers return home."

"Why didn't we call him sooner?"

"Because we didn't recognize it was our Sprint at first. Because we were uncertain of the pirate's intentions until now. We weren't sure of their target vessel. The cargo didn't seem appropriate for our suspects. I was in the rejuv. We forgot. Whatever you tell him doesn't need to make him happy. Just not angry enough to call us in."

And then they were outbound, two hours behind the Bendolin Sprint, which was twelve minutes behind the Dependable Delivery van carrying the load of pipe.

Chapter 23

Just minutes after leaving Earth orbit, the Bendolin Sprint disabled its transponder, causing the craft to drop from the VICO flight monitoring system. That action ensured that the Dependable Delivery pilot wouldn't see the pirates, allowing them to approach at will. But since Ygo's space tracker was following the pirates, he and Cuss would see everything.

Feeling the tug of professionalism, Ygo called Girish Mannan to update him on their situation. He didn't lie. But he picked his facts carefully.

"We've spotted the pirate's Bendolin Sprint, the one involved with Mia Moreau's murder, the same one seen lifting off from the Albacete Spaceport about the time Aurora Navarro was kidnapped. They've been disguising it, making it look like different craft each time. We're a couple of hours behind it now."

"What's the plan?"

"We believe they're about to make a hit on a Dependable Delivery van carrying industrial pipe. We're going to witness the theft and then follow them home."

"What about the pilot?"

Ygo hesitated for the briefest moment, at first thinking that Girish was talking about the pilot of the pirate ship before realizing the obvious. He winged it. "Except for Moby Navarro, the pirates have always given instructions to the van pilot. How to behave to ensure their safety. If they do that this time, we wait and watch. If they don't, we'll do our best to intervene."

He didn't mention that getting the *Nelly Marie* to the scene in time to make a difference would require impossibly high gee forces and more fuel than they had aboard.

"Who are you working with?"

"It's been unfolding quickly and we haven't connected with anyone yet. If we could have a marshal waiting for us in lunar orbit, someone to partner with when we follow the ship down, that would give us backup during the arrest."

"Two of our ships landing in an unknown situation where the people there have attacked twenty-plus delivery vans with industrial lasers? That's the plan?"

"Sorry, sir. I was spitballing and you caught me. In truth, Cuss and I are still brainstorming how it will play out. The situation is dynamic and we've been reacting more than planning. It's clear we'll need help when they reach their home base. And Cuss will expect them to produce Aurora. Backup would let our favorite agent do that with minimal drama."

"I don't have favorites," said Girish, his voice stern. "We don't beat information out of suspects. And you should have called much sooner, something we'll discuss when this is over." He paused, letting the silence develop while he scowled. "For now, I'm going to pass you off to

MFOD. Work with them to refine your plan and get your backup in place. By the book, Ygo. I count on you for that."

"Yes, sir."

Girish closed the call, sending Ygo's stomach flip-flopping with anxiety.

Committed to the service's mission, Ygo worked hard to be a faithful marshal. Reliable. Logical. Effective. He loved the job. Believed he made a difference.

He'd applied to the service seven years earlier on a lark, a man with congenital limitations that kept him from experiencing life the ways others could. He'd thought the action and adventure might provide him an exciting life.

They'd offered him an interview, and it started worse than awful. The pitch was for him to sit in a back room, where he would use his quantum AI link to tackle the agency's most difficult challenges. The isolation wasn't the problem. It was that they were treating him like a piece of equipment rather than a person.

Midway through the interview, he'd decided the Marshals Service wasn't the answer he'd been seeking. A polite man, he kept his doubts to himself and stuck it out to the end.

His last interview was with the director of the Interworld Marshals Service, Girish Mannan.

Girish spoke with passion, focusing in the beginning not on Ygo's role in the agency, but about that of a new hire, Cuss Abbott. He explained that Cuss was an accomplished agent. Gifted. Seemingly charmed. One willing to put himself at risk without hesitation to protect the sheep from the wolves. One whose streak of successes put him in rarified territory. But one who sometimes took shortcuts to achieve his goal. Who too often left death and destruction in his wake.

Girish had pitched it as the perfect match. Ygo could use his talents to help Cuss be even more successful as a marshal while at the same time providing guardrails to keep him out of trouble.

Soon after Ygo met Cuss, he developed a full-on bromance. Not the "let's cuddle" kind. More like a deep respect. A joy in sharing his company. He admired the guy's selfless attitude. Was amazed at the way women threw themselves at him. And instead of being a jerk about it, he treated them with respect. Outside of Ygo's tight circle of family and doctors, Cuss was one of the few people he cared about, living in anticipation of their next interaction.

And as such, instead of riding herd on him, Ygo began protecting him from burdensome oversight that interfered with his success. He knew it was wrong, and compensated by using his own moral compass to limit Cuss if he strayed too far. And the "being bad to do good" behavior felt wicked and naughty, which made him feel wonderful.

It had been a narrow path ever since. Helping Cuss without provoking Girish.

"Girish is unhappy, no surprise. He's going to help, but warns us to follow procedure."

"He didn't wave us off?"

"No. He's going to hold court after it's over, though. He wants us to coordinate with the field operations desk, which lets him keep an eye on us."

"That's okay. He'll forgive us after we've captured the pirates and saved Aurora."

Ygo couldn't help but grin at the over-the-top confidence. He knew from experience that it wasn't empty bravado. "He's concerned about the van pilot. I am, too."

Cuss nodded. "I've been thinking about that. We need to send a couple more drones, anyway. Let's make one an Arrow."

Ygo had already concluded that they'd need three drones to monitor the action after the robbery: one to follow the Dependable Delivery van, one to follow the Bendolin Sprint, and one to follow the cargo, however it was being transported. An Arrow could do everything a tracker could, plus it had visualization tech that let it see through walls. And it had a stabilized precision laser, a weapon either of them could point and shoot from the safety of the *Nelly Marie.*

"Agreed." Ygo sent the drones on their way, distinct *thups* marking each launch.

The next hours were spent waiting for something to happen, an activity that was both stressful and boring.

Cuss spent the time finishing his workout, drinking coffee while he cleaned his gun, and finding chores for Peanut to do so he could watch and critique the bot's performance.

When the Arrow reached the delivery van, he took time to practice with the Arrow's laser. He first synced the weapon with his lens. Then he used the "look inside" viewfinder to target random items around the ship, verifying that he had options should the pirates threaten the pilot.

Ygo spent the time replaying every conversation and interview he'd collected from the case, starting from when Cuss first met Mia on the *Dependable Delivery 8*, the ship where Moby was killed. He knew he was missing something. Hearing it but not registering it. But whatever it was, it remained elusive.

And then the Bendolin Sprint began moving up on the van.

"We have action!" Ygo called to Cuss. He projected the view from the drone's camera onto the big front display, airing the pirate's comms so Cuss could see and hear everything.

The raiders were approaching silently, and Ygo feared the worst. "They should have sent a warning to the pilot by now."

"They will," said Cuss.

Ygo appreciated his partner's confidence, but he still squirmed as the ships closed.

The Bendolin Sprint was just a few hundred meters behind the van when the pirates finally broadcast, "Attention *Dependable Delivery 44*. You are about to be boarded. We are taking your cargo." A pause. "Pilot of *Dependable 44*. We are coming aboard. Lock yourself in your stateroom. Stay inside with the door sealed. Do not call for help. Do not maneuver your ship. Do not resist. If you do, you will be killed. You have one minute to comply."

"Thank God," said Ygo when the van pilot moved into the stateroom and sealed the door. He sent a message to MFOD telling them that the robbery had started, relieved that he could include the pirate's warning to the pilot in his report.

The first part of the action was similar to what they'd seen happen to Mia. Two people dressed in pressure suits—a big man with a laser on his hip and a smaller pirate—attached a seeker explosive ring around the van's hatch. They blew it open and entered.

Then came the part they hadn't yet seen. The broad cargo bay door lifted along the side of the van, exposing a hold packed with large-diameter pipe. The pipe was strapped together in five big bundles, something they realized when two industrial bots floated the bundles out of the van and into space between the two craft. Working methodically, the bots lashed the bundles together into a single unit and wrapped a large gossamer cloth around the whole assembly.

"Any ideas?" asked Cuss, wondering about the mesh.

"I'd say it blocks Space Watch from reading the equipment tags."

"Are they towing it in?"

"Maybe." Though Ygo doubted that was the plan. Spaceships used tiny maneuvering rockets to guide their flight. If the Bendolin Sprint used its maneuvering rockets to slow down or change direction while pulling a load, inertia would carry the pipes forward into the ship.

One of the bots returned to the Sprint and emerged with a rectangular item the size of a hay bale. It had a tubular framework that surrounded a collection of components: canisters, valves, pumps, manifolds, nozzles.

While the bots worked together to attach it to the rear of the pipe load, Ygo zoomed in for a closer look, confirming what he'd suspected when he first saw the device. "That's one of Nick Navarro's custom specials."

"Pal, we've just answered so many questions," said Cuss, his voice animated. "I'd say our boy Nick was supplying rockets to the pirates. Either Moby got in the middle and had to be removed, or Nick was acting up and Moby was a message for him to behave. Same with Aurora." A pause. "With Nick dead, Aurora is worthless as motivation."

Ygo agreed that if she was still alive, she wouldn't be for much longer. He kept the thought to himself, though, instead asking about a different issue. "That engine is way too small for the load. No way could it control a landing. That means there's a ship somewhere waiting to carry it down."

"A cloth-wrapped rig is so distinctive. Why hasn't anyone reported seeing one before?"

They were still mulling possibilities when the pirates returned to the Bendolin Sprint and sealed the hatch. Moments later, Nick's rocket engine sputtered to life.

The flicker behind the huge load of pipes was almost comical, more like Fourth of July sparklers than a mighty rocket engine. But even a small force can make a difference in weightlessness.

After spewing flame for most of a minute, the bundle began lumbering forward. The rocket labored, moving the pipes ahead, struggling to gain speed. After about twenty minutes, with the rig traveling at a modest clip, the rocket engine flared and went dark.

With the engine dead, the bundle was coasting, following a fixed path that Ygo could forecast. When he saw the results, he whistled in admiration.

"Check this out," he told Cuss, projecting a map on the big display. "The pipes pass wide of the Moon by a good thousand kilometers and continue out into space."

"Wide enough to be ignored by Space Watch," said Cuss.

"That's right. What's clever is that the Moon's gravity pulls the pipes around. See how they return in a flyby that's only two hundred and sixty kilometers out? This will happen sixty-one days from now."

"Space Watch monitors out to two hundred klicks?"

"Yup. And at Julie's conference, they said they drop stolen items from their ID tag database after six weeks."

"Well goddamn. I'm beyond impressed."

"It's beautiful in its own way. But with Nick dead, the game's over until they find another source for their engines."

Cuss crossed his arms. "All this requires insider knowledge, and my gut keeps screaming Royale. The guy's a huge prick, and I was thinking his assholery was swaying my instincts. But it's him. I know it. Find our motive, Ygo. It's out there."

Ygo had looked at Royale along with everyone else. Twice. "I'll run him again."

All he could think to do differently was start with the man's childhood and work forward from there. He proceeded methodically, pursuing every detail. Tracking daily routines. Examining anomalies.

And he found his answer, not in the man's childhood, but at a regulatory meeting five years ago.

Gurby-Dent, a private company, sought to open a third water mine on land they owned near the two water mines operated by the Nova Terra government. The proposal included transporting their water through the existing pipeline that snaked across the plains.

Pushback on the proposal had come from a number of sources, with the two strongest arguments coming from Nova Terra's regulatory agency. The notion of having a vital life source owned and operated by a private firm was wildly unpopular. And the two mines controlled by Nova Terra were on track to grow their production to fill the pipeline, which meant there was no spare capacity.

At the meeting, Royale had spoken passionately in favor of the independent mine, talking of the need for redundancy, capacity to fuel growth, options during an emergency, as well as the efficiency of private enterprise.

As Ygo listened to his testimony, he realized the thing he'd been hearing but not registering.

"It's a water mine, not an ore mine," he said to Cuss. "The private one under construction. And you called it. Royale is the inside source."

Chapter 24

Aurora pushed as much of her body as she possibly could against the surface of the heater. She wore multiple layers of clothes, was snugged deep in her sleeping bag, and still her teeth chattered from the cold.

She'd already raised the heater to its maximum setting, but either it wasn't working properly, or it didn't have enough power to keep her prison canister warm.

The water in the blue bladder was icing up, so she'd soon be out of water to drink. Her fingers were turning numb. She couldn't feel her toes.

She had something like a week to go, but she was unsure because the message button had stopped talking.

No way can I make it, she thought, afraid that if she fell asleep, she wouldn't wake up.

. . .

When Cuss heard it was a water mine, he was confused. "Then why did Brace Harde point us at the ore mines?"

"I thought so, too, but he didn't."

Ygo played a clip of Brace answering a question from Cuss earlier in the investigation:

Cuss: *We think a company on the surface might be a home base for the pirates. An outfit that has launch and landing capabilities. Uses lasers in their business like the one we showed you earlier. Lots of storage space. Away from scrutiny. Has a need for heavy industrial components like valves, pumps, compressors, piping, staging. A ruthless approach to business…*

Brace, laughing: *Sorry. As I listened to your list, I was thinking of the mining companies. But when you said that ruthless thing, it was like a home run. Those assholes think they're their own nation.*

Cuss: *Which ones?*

Brace: *All of them. Believe me. All of them.*

"He switched focus to the ore mines after that," said Ygo. "But that was about where he makes his money. Them wearing out pumps and all. It wasn't about piracy."

Cuss was flummoxed. "What about Joey Spigliano?"

"Have a listen."

Joey: *The track is set way out on the plains where you don't have to worry about collisions with the locals. So none of the cameras see action near the cities. But it just so happens that a couple of cameras catch the ore mines.*

Cuss: *Why would we be interested in the ore mines?*

Joey: *Because six of them have at least one of my Sprints. Three of them have two. You should be able to catch them launching or landing by searching our race archive. We save everything. They're not positioned to see the water mines, though. You'll need a different solution for those.*

"Goddamn, Ygo. I make fun of people for their tunnel vision."

"We'd dismissed two of the water mines because they're essentially government facilities. The third one isn't operating yet."

"That doesn't make me feel any better. So how is Royale involved?"

Ygo played the clip of Royale testifying at the Nova Terra regulatory meeting.

"This is what pointed me to water. It's the only time he spoke publicly about the issue. After his testimony, the agency gave Gurby-Dent a provisional license. And for the next three years, the company invested heavily, working to develop the site."

Ygo's face appeared in the display as he continued the story. "Two years ago, an election shuffled the regulatory board members. The new board modified the license, removing permission to use the existing pipeline."

"That must of hurt. Piracy was their solution?"

"It seems so. They needed money for high-capacity pumps and compressors, big valves, and lots of pipe. It more than tripled their investment costs. They filed lawsuits, appealed to the citizenry, and donated campaign funds to sympathetic politicians. It didn't work. After six months of noise, they went quiet and began construction of a new pipeline."

"Where was Royale in all this?"

"He never testified again, but he was involved behind the scenes through his investments. I'd previously reviewed the financial disclosure he'd submitted as part of his application for the LOCU director's position. I was aware that he had his money in a trust with his wife and kid. His wife inherited a nice bundle from her folks, and trusts are a common way to protect money. Theirs was spread across three different financial houses, something I also knew about. What I hadn't checked before was where the three houses had put the funds. Turns out about eighty-five percent of it is with Gurby-Dent. He'd made the investments after the regulatory commission issued the provisional license. He stood to lose it all if the company went bankrupt."

"Imagine telling wifey that you lost all her money."

"Eighty-five percent of it, anyway."

"I don't think I've said it even once this week. You're a goddamn genius."

"Actually, it's been nineteen days."

"You're a genius. You're a genius. You're a genius. Put those in my bank to catch me up."

Cuss heard the whine of the *Nelly Marie*'s Paulson drives cycling up. The pressure from acceleration pushed him into his seat.

"Girish has assigned Arron Gutierrez and Sara Beagley as our support." Ygo spoke in the all-business tone he used when he had a long agenda to get through. "They were at Julie's conference and have been working the case from the piracy viewpoint. We'll be catching up to them in lunar orbit about three hours ahead of the Bendolin Sprint. As for the pilot of the Dependable Delivery van, she reports that she's safe and secure. Space Watch is in contact with her and expects to be there in about four hours. And I reached out to Toni Carrabelle about local police support. He asks that we coordinate through Darlena and Hobby. I think you'll need to make that call."

"Agreed."

"Before you do, remember Danika and Paval, the sweet couple who broke into our ship at the Drome? Pina has questioned them and believes they don't know who was paying the tab."

Cuss thought back to that incident, as well as to the attack by the Rodneys in Julie's hotel. "Since we didn't have a suspect back then, I remember saying that the person behind the attacks was responding to our reputation. Fear based on perception. That insecure little weasel Royale fits the mold perfectly. He's always dick-measuring his progress against ours."

"Cops have access to bad guys, so he definitely had the means. And think about him cheering on Mia and her perfect load. Doesn't it seem like he set her up?"

Cuss felt a tingle of excitement as pieces fell into place. "Remember when I was on Aurora's balcony and I saw Royale in the street? We thought he was watching me, but I'll bet he was scoping out the kidnapping."

Then he felt a different tingle. "Oh shit, I need to call Chik."

He did. She was unavailable so he left a message, marking it urgent. "Hi Chik. I have concerns about Royale Anderson and your safety. Do *not* call him. And definitely *don't* meet with him. Call me and I'll explain."

Next, he called Darlena using her Armstrong detective's link. She answered immediately.

"Hi Darlena. Things are heating up and I could use support."

"Whatchya got?"

"Guess who the inside source is?"

"It's not me."

"Duh. Wanna guess or should I get to it?"

"Royale Anderson."

Cuss sat back in his seat, his face flushing. "Yup. When did you know?"

"I didn't. I just picked the biggest asshole in the business."

Ygo said privately, "I wonder where Hobby is on that list?"

Cuss resisted the impulse to grin. "I sent Chik to meet with Royale before I knew he was dirty. I just called her but she isn't answering. Could you track her down? Make sure she's safe?"

"If she's in the cities, I'll find her." She nodded. "So, who're the pirates?"

"We have Gurby-Dent in our sights, the ones building the water pipeline. It seems Royale bet his wife's fortune on the project. They're stealing the equipment they need to finish it."

"Sort of makes sense, except for the part where they thought no one would notice."

Ygo said privately, "Yet they went a year and a half without detection by sending the stolen cargo on a two-month loop."

Cuss said aloud, "I'm still looking for the woman they took. Best guess is they have her out at their mine site. If Royale is in the cities, I'm hoping you could gear up your network to find him and sit on him."

"Why not arrest him?"

Cuss tilted his head to the side. "We haven't run our case past a municipal attorney. Until then, we need to be cautious, though I don't anticipate any issues."

Darlena looked off camera, nodded, and turned back to Cuss with a scowl. "We find him and watch him, but you get the arrest?"

Cuss raised his voice so Hobby was sure to hear. "You and Hobby will get full credit for the arrest." He knew that Girish was results-oriented, happy to share the spotlight if it greased the wheels of cooperation.

Darlena's face softened. "Done."

After a few moments of friendly chitchat while Ygo sent Darlena what they had on Royale, Cuss closed the call. From there, his thoughts turned to rescuing Aurora, starting with the Gurby-Dent location.

"Can you show me the mine site?" he asked Ygo. "I have no sense of size or layout or anything."

An aerial view appeared on the front display. The largest building was a white dimpled half-sphere, like a gigantic golf ball had been sunk halfway into the ground. The golf ball building had an airlock on one end with two landing pads just outside it. Both were empty. The other end connected to a cylindrical building, a modest-size structure of unknown purpose.

And outside, halfway between the airlock and the cylindrical building, sat a concrete blockhouse. The gray cube was small compared to everything else. A pipeline snaked from it out over the plains, following alongside the existing pipeline, offset from it like a shadow.

"I take it the mine is under the ball?" said Cuss.

"The entrance is. The mine itself is a hundred meters below ground."

"It looks like they could hide a lot of cargo in there."

"With room to spare for a Bendolin Sprint."

Cuss began framing a rescue operation. If there were several people inside, he'd have to go with a broad assault, which meant coordinating with the locals. If it was Aurora and a couple of guards, he'd go in alone, a quiet infiltration.

"What does the company list for staff?" he asked.

"Locally there are five humans in management and legal roles. They spend most of their time in the cities. There are a couple of supervisors who take turns visiting the site. The underground work is done by industrial bots, the kind we saw in the raids. And then there are these two, who I'm guessing are our actual pirates."

Two holos appeared on the front display. One was a tall, lanky Caucasian male. The other, a short, pudgy Hispanic male.

"They're contractors, not employees," said Ygo. "They both have priors. The big one is wanted for capital crimes in Southeast Asia. Laos and Cambodia specifically. The small one is something of a tech wizard, the kind capable of figuring out how to erase selected bits of the record from Gastrow's archive. He's been charged a couple of times on Earth but never convicted."

"Can we tell who's onsite right now?"

"Not from here. Arron and Sara might be in position to look."

"They're there already?"

"They've been in lunar orbit for a couple of hours."

Cuss called his fellow Interworld Marshals, both pleased and confused that they were in a position to help. After an exchange of greetings, he got to it, "I thought you were working Earth?"

Arron, sitting in the pilot's seat of their ship, the *Ruby Belle*, answered. "We were. Girish assigned two other crews to team with us, and we became a fricking machine, running ID scans on every big water project we could find. We spotted a mountain of stolen property, but none of it was from the pirate raids. We'd even put a swarm on the Drome to watch stuff passing through there and it found zippo. So we figured either the doers had learned how to mask ID tags, or the stuff is somewhere else."

Arron glanced at Sara in the seat beside him. "The Lagrange environment is too controlled for pirates to home-base there, so we moved to the Moon and Sara identified Gurby-Dent as a player. No lie, we just got here but it's looking interesting."

Cuss felt his face flush for the second time. He hated being late to the party. "We've zeroed in on Gurby-Dent ourselves. I'm thinking that's where they're holding the kidnap victim."

"She's still missing?" asked Sara.

An innocent question that hit Cuss hard. "She is. And it's way late in the game. Honestly, if she's not there, I don't know where else to look."

"How can we help?" asked Arron.

"Maybe send a VuBuoy for a scan of the site? See what it finds?"

Pronounced "view boy" by the marshals, the VuBuoy drone offered an attractive mix of maneuverability, stealth, and scanning technology.

Arron studied something offscreen for a moment. "We could be in position to drop one in twentyish minutes."

"Thanks. I'll take it."

After closing the call, Cuss couldn't contain his frustration. "It's killing me that we're behind everyone else."

"We aren't behind anyone," said Ygo. "We're working a kidnapping and murder. Our goals and methods will be different from someone working a robbery."

"I guess."

Ygo was pushing the ship hard, so Cuss stayed seated, eyes closed, letting his mind float as he worked through the steps Arron and Sara would follow. They'd need to get their ship into position before they could launch the drone. The tiny craft would need time to fly down to the surface and travel to the mine site. And then it would need to visit the different buildings, using its various instruments to peer through the walls, mapping the rooms and locating the people.

He cast a plea to the universe that the drone would show Aurora with just one or two guards. He could move so much faster if he were alone. And the odds of reaching her alive were higher with a quiet infiltration.

But how to approach the big ball undetected? Landing the *Nelly Marie* on one of their pads would surely trigger a response before he was even out of the ship.

He was puzzling through options when Ygo called out, "We have signal."

Cuss opened his eyes and looked at the display. It showed the white ball on the horizon, growing larger as the VuBuoy skimmed over the bleak gray regolith—the rocks, soil, and dust coating the Moon's surface. The sun was low in the sky, its oblique rays hitting spires of rock, creating long black shadows across the plains that added a surreal texture to the scene.

"We need a way to get me inside," he said as the ball loomed larger.

"We'll know if it even matters in another minute."

The drone slowed as it approached the curved white wall. The display flipped from the visible color spectrum to an ethereal image of gray tones. The drone circled the building to gather readings and construct a holo of the happenings inside.

The first images showed that the big ball served largely as a cover, a pavilion sheltering a broad open area. Equipment, crates, and lengths of pipe were gathered in piles underneath the cover. Big piles. Lots of them.

It also showed that the cylindrical building sitting at the end of the ball was glowing—a giant oven bathing the things inside in electromagnetic radiation.

"Any ideas?" asked Cuss, stumped by the glow.

"Just wild guesses," said Ygo. His voice changed to one of excitement. "Here we go!"

The display zoomed on a row of five rooms tucked along an inside wall of the pavilion. The first two rooms and last two rooms held furniture and equipment. The middle room held furniture, equipment, and two people.

"These two are all the drone found," said Ygo. "No one else onsite."

"Above ground, anyway," muttered Cuss, thrilled he could act without the delay of organizing a larger assault, wary of the danger he faced by going in alone.

The holo showed a gray-tone image of a larger person seated in a chair. A smaller person was stretched out on a couch. Neither was moving. He waited for the image to sharpen, but it never resolved enough to discern gender, let alone see faces.

"I can't tell shit about them. Why the poor resolution?"

"I don't know. Maybe it's the material covering the ball. Maybe it's interference from the glow."

Cuss studied the ghostly images. "That isn't the contractors."

"No. The Sprint is still a few hours out."

"So it could be Aurora and a guard."

"Could be. The person on the couch is similar in size. It could also be two employees taking a break."

"Oh, for fuck's sake." Cuss shook his head in frustration. "We're the ones who need a break."

"It's been challenging."

Cuss fought the impulse to say, "The understatement of the year," instead asking, "How far out are we?"

"Fifty minutes to orbit. About the same for a hot landing."

The VICO flight monitoring system normally guided ships through a staged approach: enter orbit, take a loop or two around the Moon while the system orchestrated traffic, and then land. But if circumstances warranted, VICO could guide a ship on a hot approach where it didn't loop, instead threading the needle as it screamed between the ships in orbit before landing directly.

"Given the lack of options," said Cuss, "my instinct is to go for it. Even if she's not there, one of those two should know something. Or at least know who knows."

"Did you figure out a way to get inside?"

"I have an outline of an idea but it needs details. We land hot at a neighboring water mine. I borrow a skimmer from them and ride to the ball, maybe approaching near the glow so they can't see me any better than we can see them."

"How do you get inside?"

"Backing up, I don't know anything about the other water mines. We need permission to land, and permission to borrow a skimmer. Can you work your magic on that one?"

"Already started. My only worry is if they even have a skimmer for you to use."

Cuss gave a dismissive shrug. "For getting inside, I need Peanut to build me a plastic airlock, a simple flexible booth I can stand in. It should roll up small. One side has adhesive that I stick to the dome. My idea is to approach the ball, unfold the airlock, press the sticky side to the wall, inflate it enough to crawl in, get inside, seal it up behind me, and inflate it all the way into a booth. Now I have the room to cut my way in using a laser cutter. The airlock lets me pierce the wall without getting blown away by the air rushing out. And if that's Aurora on the couch, it keeps the air inside for her."

"Not bad. I'll work with Peanut to get that assembled. Oh, and we caught a break. The mine nearest Gurby-Dent confirms they have a skimmer, so we're a go from that standpoint."

"You see?" Cuss smiled. "We're winning already."

Chapter 25

Ecstatic to be moving into action phase, Cuss climbed up to his bedroom, a bit of a workout given the high gravity inside the *Nelly Marie* from Ygo's aggressive acceleration.

He stripped to his boxers and, before dressing, removed his gun from its hold in the wall. He performed the ritual of pulling the magazine and verifying it was full, returning it into the handle of the gun, cycling the slide to load a bullet into the chamber, then putting a last bullet into the magazine to give him eleven rounds in all.

The weapon, a Tosic 325 Hybrid, was a modern combination of an old-style Taser and a pistol. The ammunition would pierce most things like a regular bullet. But as soon as it touched flesh, it collapsed to deliver one of three jolts depending on the position of the gun's selector: stop, drop, or dead.

He worked the selector as part of his ritual. Using his thumb, he pushed it forward from safety to stop, then dead, and then drop. With the selector on stop, the zap from a bullet felt like a hard punch with a fist. Pushing the selector all the way forward set the gun to the drop option, a position easy to find in a panic and the most useful choice for a cop. Drop brought the target to the ground rather

DOUG J. COOPER

decisively, unharmed but out for a good twenty minutes. The dead option was in the middle, a harder position to find in an emergency, requiring a deliberate choice on the part of the shooter. The result was exactly as it sounded.

He set two extra magazines next to the gun, moved his Damascus-steel combat knife into its strap-on leg sheath, and added it to the pile.

Then came the toil of putting on his safe suit, a second skin covering his arms, legs, and torso. The thin material acted as light armor, offering limited protection against bullets, knives, and similar nasties.

Some people lathered themselves in lotion so it slid on smoothly. He hated the squishy feeling afterward, so he took the time to struggle his way in. When he finally had it adjusted to his satisfaction—binding in the crotch area was always a problem—he dressed in shirt and pants, finishing with special shoes that paired with his flexible spacesuit.

With gun, cartridges, and knife in hand, he moved down to the middeck, pulled his flex suit from a closet, and climbed in, leaving the hood hanging down in back. He stowed the gun in the suit's built-in holster on the right hip, put the spare cartridges in special loops at his waist, and strapped his knife to the lower portion of that same leg.

While he loaded the other pockets with typical cop tools—flashlight, shrink cuffs, multitool—he flip-flopped on whether to bring a med kit, a pouch with meds and dressings that could help get him back into action, or even save his life. It felt like bad luck to bring it, like he was preparing for failure. But then he thought that Aurora may need medical attention, so he snugged the kit into its special suit pocket.

"How we doing for time?" he asked as he pulled the laser cutter from Peanut's tool closet.

"Fourteen minutes." Then, "I had to add to your cutting-booth idea. Come down to the command deck and I'll show you."

Cuss hustled down the ladder to find Peanut holding a tool he didn't recognize, a pipe with a bulb-shaped grip at one end. A rolled-up bundle of plastic sat on the deck next to the bot.

"I did some research on the big ball," said Ygo as Peanut handed Cuss the tool. "It's a self-healing shell. When you cut into it, bloop will leak into the opening and harden like a clot, closing it back up."

"Bloop?"

"The company says it's a portmanteau of blood and goop."

Cuss held the tool by the bulb and swung it back and forth as if wielding a sword. The pipe part, about as long as his arm, had rows of holes along its length. He saw a release pin between the bulb and the pipe that reminded him of an old-style hand grenade.

"The idea is to cut your way into the shell just like you planned. When you're through, poke the wand all the way in. Bloop will ooze around it. While the bloop is still liquid, pull the pin to release the foam. It will expand into the cut and harden, and the bloop will harden around that. When it's solid, laser the foam away and climb through your hole."

"Neat."

"The plastic booth is like you designed. The one difference is you'll have to peel off a backing from the sticky side. I wanted to protect it from dust until the last moment."

"Makes sense." He squatted next to the roll of plastic and had a look. "Anything more on the two people?

"The big one in the chair went to the bathroom and returned. He's a male."

"Peed standing up?"

"It's a solid tell. The small one on the couch is either asleep or tied up."

"Alive?"

"Yup. There's been some shifting on the couch. Just not enough to learn more."

Hot landings could get rough, so Cuss strapped into the pilot's seat and then called Arron and Sara to finalize details. After outlining his plan for them, he made his ask. "If I call for help, you're my cavalry. Come runnin' with guns a-blazin'. Short of that, wait for the Bendolin Sprint. After they land, disable their ship and knock out anything that comes to their rescue. Strand them good until we can arrest them safely."

They refined details in a quick back-and-forth, Arron wondering if it would be best to disable the ship with a laser pulse from orbit, or if they should send a drone for a close-up attack.

"I trust your judgment," said Cuss, adding, "Happy hunting," before closing the call.

"Godspeed," replied Sara as the signal faded.

Minutes later, the *Nelly Marie* hurtled through orbital traffic like a meteor about to make yet another crater on the Moon's pockmarked surface. Drives roared and the ship slowed, vibrations causing something on the middeck to rattle. A thump, and they were on the pad at the water mine.

From there, events went pretty much according to plan. Cuss rode in another Viperion skimmer, giving him plenty of room to carry the foam wand and the booth. The craft zipped right along, but the trip to the ball still took twenty minutes, a frustratingly long time when racing to save a life. Setting up the booth also proved to be straightforward, though fastening it closed after he got inside was a challenge in suit gloves.

Things began to deviate from Cuss's mental image of how it should play out when he cut his way through the ball wall. The laser cutter sliced a clean opening. Bloop began to flow. Cuss inserted the wand and pulled the pin. Foam filled the opening. He waited for everything to harden. Then he waited some more. And some more.

"Christ, Ygo. How long does it take to set up?"

"Two more minutes."

"Two *more* minutes. I'm a target here."

"They're both in the room. You have time."

While Ygo's words made sense, Cuss couldn't help feeling vulnerable standing in a plastic booth outside a building he was breaking into. He used calming techniques he'd learned in the past, and they helped, only because it gave him something to do besides waiting to die.

"Go," said Ygo after an eternity.

Cuss fired the cutter and worked the beam in a circle. The foam vaporized, leaving a round hole.

"Good," confirmed Ygo.

It was all Cuss needed to hear. Dropping the laser cutter, he dove through the opening headfirst, rolled forward on the packed dirt floor, and pulled his gun as he rose to his feet, thumbing the selector all the way forward to the drop option. He looked over the top of the weapon as he swept his surroundings, scanning from left to right and back again, Ygo processing for threats along with him.

"Clear?" Cuss posed it as a question, asking for confirmation of his own assessment.

"Clear."

Keeping his weapon raised, Cuss oriented himself. The inside of the ball was as big as a medium-size warehouse, the floor area filled with rows of crates and pipe and equipment on pallets. To his left was the tall airlock door, his view of it partially blocked by what looked like a small construction project.

"That'll become the main pumping station once they're up and running," Ygo told him.

To his right was the doorway that led to the cylindrical structure outside the big ball, the one that glowed on the drone's sensors. The door was a sturdy black thing. An overhead pulley system that rode on a track passed through it. Crates were stacked in small piles outside the door, like they were waiting their turn for whatever was happening inside.

"Should have brought the pocket detector to check ID tags," said Cuss as he lowered his flex helmet.

He turned his attention across the floor to the far side of the ball. To the left was what looked like a massive rock poking up from the ground. A composite door had been fitted into the forward face, one that rode on tracks as it opened and closed. A cart and a small forklift were parked outside.

"Is that the entrance to the mine?" he asked.

"It is."

To the right of the mine entrance was the row of five offices they'd seen with the drone. His target was the middle door.

After a last look for danger, he started toward it, accelerating into long strides. A row of crates blocked his way, and he leapt over them like a high hurdler, landing for two steps and then leaping over a row of pipe.

"Show me," he said as he closed on the center door.

Ygo showed Cuss the room in his lens. The big male sat in a chair just past the door. The smaller person was on the couch in the far-right corner.

Three steps out, Cuss leapt, the heel of his right boot leading the way. While he weighed just thirty-five pounds on the moon, he counted on the physics of momentum to carry him through the door.

Momentum is determined by mass, not weight. His mass was the amount of matter in his body, the total of his blood, bones, organs, and everything else. His weight was the pull of gravity on that mass. So while he weighed two hundred ten pounds on Earth and thirty-five pounds on the Moon, in both worlds, his mass was the same. Perfect for busting through doors.

When his heel hit just above the door handle, the jamb splintered with a sharp *crack*. The door flew open and he was carried inside, hurtling across the room.

Cuss turned in midair as he sailed past the man in the chair and shot him in the back, putting him down for a good twenty minutes. In the split second before he hit the wall, he twisted again to catch the impact evenly with his back shoulders.

Righting himself, he made for the couch. The person lying on it faced the rear cushion, a blanket pulled up to the neck.

Cuss had intended to shake the shoulder through the blanket and say, "Wake up." But as he approached the couch, he realized it wasn't Aurora. He raised his gun.

His hand was still in motion when the person turned, arm swinging through the air in a blur, flexed hand chopping at the base of Cuss's wrist.

Few assailants had the ability to disarm Cuss, but this was the strike of a skilled fighter. The gun flew from his hand.

And then the person sprang from the couch, a flurry of arms and legs, punching and kicking at him like a buzzsaw. That's when Cuss got his first glimpse.

Though he was working hard to protect himself, deflecting blows as he was driven back across the room, inside he was smiling, a feeling of primal satisfaction.

It was a man. Wiry frame. Ugly sunglasses.

Royale.

The man was clearly skilled in hand-to-hand combat. Skilled at defending himself. Skilled at using every part of his body to inflict fatal injury.

But so was Cuss. He began his offensive with a jab to Royale's chin.

Royale responded by pushing off a wall and somersaulting in the air. The acrobatics showed he was practiced in low-grav fighting, perhaps more so than Cuss. And as a small guy, his hands and feet seemed to move faster.

But Cuss was no slouch. And he held a tremendous advantage in height, weight, and reach.

As much as he wanted to damage Royale—to punish him, to hurt him—he needed the man conscious so he could point the way to Aurora. Royale had no such limitations in his attack, making the battle lopsided.

Even so, the fight didn't last long. They began a back-and-forth, and Cuss used a boxing trick he'd learned years earlier from an old-timer at Chaparral, the Marshals Service training school.

Find a seemingly unimportant part of the body your opponent is leaving exposed. Doesn't matter what it is. Start hitting it. For the first couple of blows, your opponent will think they've deflected an attack on a more vulnerable part of their body. But by the third or fourth blow, the spot will start to get sore. They'll move to protect it, something they haven't practiced. Now you've taken them out of their game.

Cuss picked Royale's rib cage below the left armpit, hitting it from the side once with his fist and moments later with an elbow. He deflected a flurry before hitting it again with his fist.

Royale grunted and lowered his left elbow to protect the area, in the process moving resources away from the left side of his head.

Cuss feinted at the rib cage with his knee before launching a left hook to Royale's cheek. He connected, snapping Royale's head back, sending his sunglasses spinning off his face and into the wall.

The man paused, stunned. Cuss used that moment to slap him, a hard, open-handed smack across the face, connecting with his palm more than his fingers, dazing him further.

Then, in a practiced motion, Cuss pulled a shrink cuff from his waist pocket, looped it over Royale's head and down to his neck, and gave it a tug, activating it. The cuff shrank until it reached the design tension for securing wrists and ankles.

During training, marshals were specifically warned not to put a self-tightening cuff around a suspect's neck. As it shrank, the cuff would restrict the flow of air to the lungs and blood to the brain. If not removed, the victim would pass out inside of a minute and be dead within two minutes.

Royale began to gasp and buck, clawing frantically at the noose, struggling to loosen it or at least get his fingers under it to create space.

Cuss shouted several times, "Put your hands behind your back and I'll take it off!"

Royale either didn't hear or couldn't get his body to comply, because while his face turned purple and his eyes bugged out and saliva flew from his mouth, he continued to struggle.

Cuss held a second cuff at the ready. When Royale collapsed to the floor, Cuss secured his arms behind his back and then used his multitool to clip the cuff from around Royale's neck.

Royale was slow to respond but then rolled onto his back, his arms underneath him, and gulped air, taking deep, dramatic breaths.

As color returned to Royale's face, Cuss put another cuff around his ankles, asking in a firm tone, "Where is she?"

Instead of answering, Royale continued his recovery histrionics. Cuss used the time to retrieve his gun.

Scooping it from the floor, he shot the big man in the chair a second time, then used shrink cuffs to secure his arms and legs. Tipping the seat back, Cuss dragged the big guy out the door and into the office next door. After looping him to the heat register on the wall, Cuss grabbed an empty chair from that room and returned to Royale.

He lifted Royale off the floor, threw him into the seat, and secured him to it.

"Where is she, asshole?" he said again. "Your choices are to tell me or die. The dying one comes with impressively horrible pain."

Standing behind his prisoner, Cuss probed the man's shoulders, much like a masseuse checking for knots. He was searching for the suprascapular nerve, which ran through a small notch in the upper part of the shoulder blade.

When he'd located the nerve on each shoulder, he asked again, "Where is she, asshole?"

"Who?" Royale whined. "I don't understand."

Cuss pushed down with his thumbs, compressing the nerves against the bone, causing an electric pain in Royale's shoulders similar to the pain of hitting your funny bone. Except hitting your funny bone was a one and done. By maintaining pressure, Cuss put Royale in a continuous, overwhelming state of agony.

Royale wailed and bucked, getting increasingly violent, struggling until he succeeded in tipping the chair over to gain relief.

Cuss righted him. "You're pissing me off. Keep it up and I'll do something you'll regret."

"I want to help. Who is it you're looking for?"

"I warned you." Cuss, still behind him, cupped his right hand and smacked it hard against Royale's right ear. The slap sent a sharp pulse of compressed air down the ear canal, rupturing the eardrum.

Maybe it was the disorientation from the trauma to his inner ear, or the horror of losing a vital sensory organ. The pain certainly contributed. Royale screamed.

"Stop!" he cried. "Let me talk."

"I'm taking an eye next." Cuss put a hand on Royale's face and pushed on an eyelid with his thumb, pressing it hard enough to make the message clear.

"Oh my God!" he shrieked. "You're a fucking animal."

"Much worse. Five, four, three…"

"She's here! Right here. I swear it."

Cuss let go of his face. "Where here?"

"In the mine. She's down in the mine." Royale was nodding as he spoke, reinforcing his message. "In the operations office. There's a bedroom in the back the super uses for all-night shifts. She's there."

Cuss felt a surge of excitement because Royale had just admitted to playing a role in a woman's imprisonment. He fed him the next part.

"Show me." He opened a hoverview. "Access the mine feed and show me Aurora. I want to see her alive and healthy."

"I've never accessed that feed before," he stammered. "I'm not sure how."

Royale hadn't questioned the name or denied that Aurora was the prisoner. While Cuss believed the man was saying whatever it took to stop the pain, he felt certain that if Royale hadn't been directly involved in a scheme involving Aurora, his behavior at this point would be different.

"Royale. There are so many ways to hurt you. Why are you being stupid?"

"I'm serious. I don't know how."

The desk behind Cuss had a shelf at the back made from a board sitting across two bricks. He lifted the board, upending the items resting on it.

"Show me," he said again.

"What are you going to do?" Royale squealed in panic, his eyes glued to the board.

"Last chance."

Royale tried to shrink into the chair. "Are you going to hit me?"

Holding the shelf like a bat, Cuss swung for the fences, driving the edge of the board into Royale's right kneecap. The sound of impact wasn't much different from when Cuss had kicked his way through the door.

Royale shrieked and began to cry.

"Where. Is. She."

"Oh my God. Fuck, that hurts. I need a doctor! Goddamn it, I'm in crisis."

"Keep it up and you won't need a doctor at all."

Cuss started a back swing with the shelf board, lining up Royale's other knee.

"Jesus fucking Christ! Okay, stop!"

Cuss motioned to the hoverview.

Facing the display, Royale wept. Cuss believed that his pain and fear were overwhelming, and thought to give him a minute.

He gave him twenty seconds. "Enough. Show me."

Between snuffles and whimpers, Royale began to chant, accessing his personal AI assistant and using it to open the feed. He spoke longer than seemed necessary, adding cryptic commands, words Cuss had never heard.

Ygo said in an urgent tone, "He's doing more than opening a feed. Do *not* let him close the display."

Cuss understood. Inside Royale's private area were secrets, and the door was now open. Ygo wanted it to stay that way so he could look around.

Cuss decided to interrupt Royale's scheme. "You've got two seconds."

No sooner had he spoken when the hoverview resolved with a holo of Aurora. She was sitting on the edge of a bed. The room was dark. The spartan setup looked about like what Cuss imagined a super's overnighter might look like.

"I knew you'd come." Her voice was quiet. Sad. "Get me out of here, Cuss. Please."

"Are you okay?"

"I'm fine. Just scared."

The lighting in the room was poor, making it hard for Cuss to see her.

Ygo told him, "The holo's being filtered. That's a sim."

"Aurora, I can't see you very well. Could you stand up and turn right a bit so the light hits your face?"

She stood and moved as he asked. "Like this?"

"That's perfect."

In a sudden move, Cuss turned and put his massive mitts over Royale's face, covering the man's mouth so he couldn't speak, covering his eyes just in case.

The Aurora that Cuss saw on the hoverview was wearing a sleeveless white blouse and jeans. When she stood and turned, it wasn't her face he wanted to see. It was her left shoulder, and a fine-line tattoo of a Christian cross inside a triangle inside a circle.

It wasn't there, so he'd acted to stop Royale from closing the display.

Chapter 26

While Cuss dealt with Royale, Ygo focused on gaining access to the man's secrets. But he'd just begun sorting through his options when Cuss dragged Royale out of the room, moving him to an office down the hall.

Royale's AI assistant would soon conclude that he was no longer part of the conversation and act to protect his privacy, leaving Ygo with seconds to find a way in.

"What's going on?" the Aurora avatar asked Cuss when he'd returned from securing Royale. "Are you coming for me?"

"Keep her talking," urged Ygo.

"The mine is a maze of tunnels," Cuss replied. "Royale is getting a map to show me where you are. He'll be back in a moment."

Ygo's objective was to enter Royale's private area, the place where he kept things he didn't want others to see. Like the source for the Aurora apparition they now watched on the hoverview. And the details of where he was actually keeping the woman.

While his private area was highly secure, by necessity it was connected to external feeds that carried the comms and data he used in his daily activities. One of those external feeds was from the Nova Terra financial system, a tool that

Royale, as director of the Lunar Organized Crime Unit, used to monitor budgets, approve expenditures, and forecast balances.

Ygo had long ago established a presence inside the Nova Terra financial system. And it was easy enough for him to find the LOCU accounts. His challenge was to connect an action Royale took from his private area to its counterpart in the financial system. The connection between the two would give him a pathway inside.

But he needed the hoverview open so he could send himself a confirmation signal, a visual cue that told him he had it right.

With little time to act, Ygo pinged the whole lot, sending a complex injection command back through every LOCU transaction made in the past month. All eight hundred ninety-two of them. He started with the most recent transaction and worked through the list, watching the hoverview, looking for his confirmation.

The move was undoubtedly creating havoc. Administrators and their support teams would soon be wondering what the hell was going on. He'd deal with it later, perhaps by placing evidence to make it look like an equipment glitch.

Royale's personal assistant realized something was afoot. "I'm going to close this link until Director Anderson returns."

"Wait," said Cuss. "I hear him coming. If you close down, what should I tell him? I need to locate Aurora. Can you show me on a map?"

While Cuss worked his delay tactics, Ygo kept going, the quantum AI wired into his brain allowing him to proceed at the speed of thought.

"C'mon," he said again and again, the anticipation weighing on him.

Aurora's avatar in the hoverview sprouted a black-and-white tattoo of a rose on her shoulder, the confirmation signal he'd sent to himself. Ygo smiled.

"Goodbye," said Royale's personal assistant, having decided Cuss was wasting its time.

That's when Ygo realized he'd been moving so quickly, he wasn't sure which of the last dozen commands had been the winner.

He backed up and repeated them.

As the hoverview image faded, Aurora's black-and-white tattoo became a full-color red rose.

Ygo's smile became a grin. He was in.

But the moment he entered Royale's private area, his face tingled in alarm.

"Uh-oh," he said, showing Cuss a feed he'd found.

An industrial bot—the six-armed kind—was scrambling up the mineshaft. Its objective seemed certain.

Cuss had been threatened by bots in the past, and Ygo had solved it by sending a "stop" command from the manufacturer's home feed. He accessed the link and issued the command.

It had no effect.

The bot reached the door that led from the mine out into the big ball. It toggled the mechanism that opened the door.

Ygo issued the "stop" command again. And again.

The bot kept coming.

"Holy shit, pal. Run!"

. . .

Ygo rarely swore, so when Cuss heard the expletive, he knew it meant big trouble. And from what he was seeing on the feed, it wasn't hard to discern the threat.

He dashed out the office door and started across the open floor, high-hurdling his way toward the bloop hole.

"Is this right?" he shouted, lifting the flex helmet over his head as he jumped a row of pipes, hoping he wasn't supposed to be heading in a different direction.

"Through the hole!" Ygo shouted. "Fast as you can!"

Even though Cuss could see the bot in his lens, he glanced back as he ran. The mineshaft door was open and the bot had started toward him, its six arms twirling to propel it much faster than Cuss could run.

"Fuck me," he muttered, willing his legs to stretch farther.

The bot's body was too big for the bloop hole, so if Cuss could get through it before the bot got to him, he'd escape.

It would be close.

Three steps out, he leapt, arms outstretched, hands together as if he were Superman, hoping his aim was good.

It was, though his heels scraped the edge of the hole when he passed through. He ended up tumbling to the ground inside the plastic airlock.

Lying on his back, Cuss reached for his knife, planning to cut a slit in the bottom of the booth and crawl out. But as he moved a hand toward his sheath, his elbow hit the laser cutter, the one he'd dropped on the way into the big ball.

Changing plans, he snatched up the tool, scrambled to his feet, and pressed himself against the wall of the structure so he was looking at the bloop hole from the side. Extending the blade, he raised it overhead, ready to strike.

One hand of the bot slithered out through the hole, a sinister metal-composite snake coming for him. Cuss swung the laser cutter downward, slicing hard at the wrist.

He got lucky. A small spark and exposed circuit told him that he'd hit the embedded camera lens, blinding that arm.

Instead of pulling the damaged limb out and using another, the bot pushed the arm all the way in, an appendage as long as Cuss was tall. It waved the arm around, perhaps believing it could connect with his body and end his resistance. In its zeal, the bot caught the side of the booth and tore open the airlock.

Air poured out through the bloop hole, through the damaged booth, and into the stark vacuum of the lunar landscape. The humidity in the air froze when it hit the cold, creating a growing cloud of ice crystals.

Cuss's rational brain told him to escape while he could. But instead of listening to reason, he stayed, slicing the cutter down at the base of the arm near the bot's shoulder. The blade dug in, exposing internal mechanisms. After a second hard slice, the arm drooped, the severely damaged limb hanging from the shoulder by a hinge of material.

The bot made a series of sharp jerks in an attempt to pull the arm free, but the appendage just flopped about, caught up on Cuss's side of the bloop hole. For the moment, the bot was trapped.

Instead of celebrating his success, Cuss focused on his new worry. If he didn't plug the bloop hole, enough air would eventually escape that Royale and his partner would suffocate. He wasn't done with the guy by a long shot, so he couldn't let that happen.

"How do I plug it?" he asked Ygo.

"Try cutting into the wall next to the hole, then angle in and cut a wedge out of the hardened shell. Once the bloop starts flowing, it'll seal itself."

His cut into the wall went quickly. But with a fearsome machine jerking so hard that it shook the structure, each tug causing the dangling limb to thump about right next to him, every second seemed too long.

When he reached the hard shell holding open his original hole, instead of cutting a wedge out of it as Ygo had suggested, he pierced it with a couple of quick stabs. Bloop began to flow in around the bot's arm. He didn't wait to watch it harden, instead slipping out through the tear in the plastic booth and running for the skimmer.

"Good work!" crowed Ygo. "I'll be there in twenty seconds."

Cuss looked over his shoulder to see the *Nelly Marie* descending onto a landing pad at the front of the big ball.

Pausing at the skimmer, he reached into the cab and activated the "home" feature, sending the vehicle back to the water mine without its passenger.

Then he ran for the ship.

. . .

The *Nelly Marie*'s sharp acceleration pushed Cuss deep into the pilot's seat. Still shaken from his harrowing escape, he rubbed his face with his hands and took some deep breaths, the calming routine centering him.

Then he asked, "I take it we found her?"

"We're close," said Ygo. "Royale's private area was a gold mine, but we're not there yet."

Cuss was waiting to hear what hurdles remained when he received an urgent call.

It was Arron. He was frowning. "Where are you going?"

As Interworld Marshals who had worked with Cuss and Ygo in the past, Sara and Arron were aware that Ygo was an enhanced human who helped Cuss from a special room in the *Nelly Marie*. They'd even seen a portion of his true capabilities.

This allowed Ygo to appear as himself when he gave the group a quick summary of Cuss's escapades in the big ball. He edited out his partner's brutality, instead highlighting his success in gaining evidence against Royale and the Gurby-Dent leadership.

"While I'm no lawyer," he concluded, "I'm pretty sure we have enough to convict the group of murder, kidnapping, and space piracy."

Next, Ygo showed them a design schematic of a storage cylinder. Arrows pointed to various details: equipment for life support, supplies of water and oxygen, stores of food.

"We've learned that they've launched her in this space capsule."

"Oh my God," said Sara.

"The plans we found call for it to be sent on a ten-day loop out into space. It's been about three days so far."

"A lazy loop like the stolen cargo?" asked Cuss.

"That's right."

"Wait, what's this about stolen cargo?" asked Arron. "What's a lazy loop?"

While Cuss and Ygo were focused on murder and kidnapping, Arron and Sara were tasked with catching thieves. So Cuss understood Arron's interest, but chose not to respond.

Ygo continued his presentation, replacing the holo of the cylinder with a diagram that showed its pathway through space. A line on the image rose up from one side of the Moon, peaked high above it, and returned on the other side in a steep arc.

"This is the ten-day pathway," said Ygo. "That blinking dot is an estimate of Aurora's progress."

"Can we communicate with her?" asked Cuss.

"Not that I can find."

"Do you think she's still alive?" asked Sara.

"I think we need to get to her as soon as possible."

"How long to reach her?" asked Cuss.

"With lots of luck, inside four hours. But it could be never."

Cuss felt his stomach twinge. "What's the luck?"

"We've got two problems. One is that there's a lot of debris out that way. Even if we knew her location, picking out the capsule from the scatter of space junk will be a challenge."

"We can help," said Sara.

"That brings us to the bigger problem. What we got from Royale are plans. Construction schematics. A proposed flight trajectory. But we haven't found a record of the actual launch of the cylinder."

Ygo cast a holo of the Bendolin Sprint on the display, along with images of the two pirates.

"When these two launched the capsule, they were supposed to measure its trajectory so they'd know where to pick her up."

Sara nodded, her face grim. "We'll follow 'em down and get the data you need."

"Exactly right," said Cuss, happy to hear her aggressive proposal. He'd worried that they wouldn't have his resolve when confronting the assholes.

"The Bendolin Sprint lands in about twenty minutes," said Ygo. "If you bring a boost, I can help with the search."

Like Cuss, Arron and Sara wore eye lenses that enhanced their capabilities in the field. Ygo could share their lenses and use the features in the same way he did with Cuss. But sharing was an intimate experience. Ygo would not only see what the others saw but how they saw it. What drew their attention. Where their eyes lingered. Their reactions to different scenes.

It was like baring your soul to a work colleague, something few wanted to do. That's why Ygo didn't ask. Instead, he would use a boost, a device that when in close proximity to the Sprint's command deck would provide him the ability to interact with the ship's electronics.

"I'll carry one," said Sara.

"Thanks, Sara," said Ygo.

This was the third time she'd volunteered to support him in the past two years. Arron had never offered.

Ygo cut the drives after that, leaving the *Nelly Marie* in a weightless environment as they coasted through space. The lack of background thrum made the ship quiet, an eerie silence broken by occasional clicks and hums as devices cycled to maintain environmental conditions and ship readiness.

On the front display, Cuss watched as Ygo scanned the space detritus along their path, combing it for items that were the approximate size of the capsule and that were moving in the general direction of Royale's proposed trajectory. When he found something, he'd image it to see if it was the capsule. It was tedious and frustrating work.

"My challenge," said Ygo, "is that while pushing ahead might put us closer to Aurora, it could just as easily be carrying us farther away."

"Makes sense."

"Until we get the flight path numbers, I'm guessing."

"We should have them soon." Cuss could tell Ygo wanted to say something, so he made it easy for him. "What are you thinking?"

"That we should call Girish and ask for help."

Cuss nodded. "I agree. But in a few minutes, the assholes land. I want my full attention there. We'll call after."

Releasing his seat restraints, Cuss changed subjects. "I have just enough time to change. Yell if something good happens."

Floating up to his bedroom, Cuss struggled out of the body suit. The suit stank of fear-laced sweat, and so did he. With no time to shower, he wiped himself down with a handcloth and threw on shorts and a T-shirt. He was back on the command deck thirty seconds before the Bendolin Sprint landed in front of the big ball.

The tracker Ygo had sent to follow the pirates was still in position. Ygo was also able to see inside the *Ruby Belle*, though Arron and Sara were unaware of his presence. He sent both feeds to Cuss, giving him a front-row seat for what came next.

The Bendolin Sprint took a standard approach, orbiting the Moon once before beginning its descent to the pad in front of the big ball. The *Ruby Belle* jockeyed into position during the orbit and followed the pirates down.

The *Ruby Belle*, like the *Nelly Marie*, was outfitted with a selection of modern tactical systems. When the Bendolin Sprint landed, Arron issued a general command to his ship: "Disable the propulsion, comms, and weaponry of the Bendolin Sprint while sparing all life and life support systems."

The *Ruby Belle* responded by proposing six precision laser pulses that would achieve the objective. Arron approved. With the *Ruby Belle* still a kilometer above the Bendolin Sprint, Cuss caught the blink of multiple laser pulses in his lens.

The *Ruby Belle* landed on the pad next to the Sprint moments later. A half-dozen perimeter drones flew from its belly and into a patrol formation that encircled both ships.

Chapter 27

Ygo's heart thumped as Arron and Sara exited the *Ruby Belle*. The next minutes would tell if this went easy, or if it would become an unfortunate mess. It was up to the pirates.

The two marshals walked halfway to the pirate ship and stood together on the gray lunar soil. Arron called to them. "You have one minute to enable the utility airlock and stand back. If you choose not to cooperate, use the minute to put on your pressure suits, because we'll be coming in through the hull."

Ygo fretted at that point, concerned that the pirates would look out at Arron and Sara, and scoff at the threat. The two marshals carried pistols, Stymer 311s that delivered a stop, drop, or dead outcome like Cuss's weapon. The guns were hardly capable of cutting open the spacecraft hull. He hoped the doers understood that it was the *Ruby Belle* that would deliver on the promise.

He also worried about Arron and Sara entering through the airlock. It made them easy targets for the pirates inside the ship.

Like the *Nelly Marie*, the Bendolin Sprint had a main hatch that opened directly to the outside, used when there was air beyond the door. That would include anywhere on

Earth, or if the ship were docked in a pressurized hangar, or if a second pressure door were provided by a port facility. And like the *Nelly Marie*, the Bendolin Sprint had a separate onboard airlock: the maintenance compartment used to service the ship's drive.

In fact, Arron and Sara would be entering the Bendolin Sprint the same way that Paval and Danika entered the *Nelly Marie*: pass through the utility hatch at the bottom of the ship to get into the maintenance compartment. Once there, pressurize the compartment, and then open the cabin hatch into the ship.

All eyes were on the tiny pilot light next to the utility hatch. After half a minute, it cycled from red to green.

"This is crazy," Cuss said to Ygo. "It's too easy for this to be a trap."

"When Sara gets closer, I should be able to see."

Sara stepped up to the ship, in the process moving the boost she carried within reach of the pirate ship's electronics. Through it, Ygo linked to the Sprint's command console.

He'd expected to find outdated electronics, but the equipment was truly archaic. It took him several seconds to parse through the different quirks and peculiarities. When he had it figured out, he accessed the Sprint's internal camera and sent the feed to the group through their lenses.

The big pirate, a gawky, unkempt, middle-aged man, was standing on the deck, the stock of his big laser rifle up against his shoulder, the barrel centered on the cabin hatch that Arron and Sara would be coming through. The small pirate stood off to the side. Neither was wearing a pressure suit, reflecting either their supreme confidence, or in Ygo's opinion, an astounding lack of foresight.

"I can use the *Ruby Belle* to neutralize the threat," Ygo told the group.

Sara exchanged glances with Arron. "We need them alive to get Aurora's flight numbers."

"I'll be putting a small hole in the back of the shooter's hand. He'll be in pain, but he'll be wide awake. Get in position and I'll let you know when I have a shot."

Sara commanded the *Ruby Belle* to give Ygo access to its weapons systems, and then she and Arron climbed through the utility hatch, closed the door, and started the airlock cycle. As the maintenance compartment filled with air, they watched the big pirate respond to the hissing sound by pressing his cheek against the stock of the weapon, the barrel still aimed at the cabin hatch, his finger gently stroking the trigger.

Ygo accessed the *Ruby Belle*'s tactical laser, charged it, and aimed a precision shot at the firing circuit of the pirate's rifle. The circuit was buried in the stock of the gun, a part now covered by the pirate's right hand.

He had a clean shot.

"I'm go on three," he announced. "One, two, three…"

He sent the signal to fire.

The *Ruby Belle*'s tactical laser flashed. A narrow beam blinked across the desolate moonscape, traveling through the hull of the Sprint and into the back of the big man's hand. The beam continued through the flesh and bone, drilled into the body of the rifle, and hit the firing circuit as intended.

The pirate reacted by jerking his hand and turning away. But in a freak outcome, a one-in-a-million chance, Ygo's shot didn't disable the weapon. Quite the opposite, it somehow shorted the circuit in a way that caused the laser to fire a continuous beam.

So as the injured man turned, the beam swept across his partner's chest. From there, it moved onto the side wall of the Bendolin Sprint, cutting a long slice through the hull before the energetic beam drained the gun's power reserves and shut down.

Air began venting from the cabin with a roar. Ygo heard the ship's alarm, but as the air carrying the soundwaves spilled into the vacuum, the noise faded.

Either dead or dying, the small pirate dropped to the deck, the weak lunar gravity making it appear as if he were falling in slow motion.

The big pirate didn't notice. Instead, he was staring at the gash in the hull, realizing that his tiny ship was breached in a way he couldn't possibly repair in time for it to matter.

Dropping the gun, he lunged for a closet and succeeded in fumbling open the door. He got his hand on his pressure suit, a solid grip. And then he collapsed to the deck, dying from the same horrific trauma he'd inflicted on Moby Navarro a week earlier.

"I did not mean to do that," said Ygo.

No one seemed to hear him.

Arron struggled to open the cabin hatch, but it wouldn't respond because the pressure inside the maintenance compartment no longer matched that of the cabin. He cursed and banged the door with his fist.

Sara found the manual override beneath a red flap on the wall, smacked it, and the cabin hatch opened with a *whoosh*.

They rushed to the pirates and knelt beside them. Both were dead.

"Well shit," said Arron. "This is a disaster."

Ygo tried to apologize again, but the group wanted to focus on finding the launch numbers for Aurora's prison capsule.

Arron and Sara searched physical things: drawers, shelves, shirt and pants pockets. Ygo searched the ship's electronic record.

They couldn't find the data.

"Let's go back and help," said Cuss.

Ygo heard the anger and frustration in his voice. It stung.

Sulking, he prepared to turn the ship around, but paused when he noticed an old-style ranger mounted above the pirate ship's command console. It looked like an oversize pair of binoculars fitted with a smatter of buttons and dials.

The ranger was an outdated tool used to measure the location, speed, and direction of objects moving in space. Absent modern equipment, the tool provided nav guidance when approaching another ship, when docking at an orbiting pier, when chasing down a lost item adrift in space, and perhaps when tracking the orbits of prison capsules.

Taking a measurement with a ranger was much like taking a picture with a camera: aim the viewfinder at the object of interest, center it in the display, and press a button. Most models retained the last few readings in memory. So if the pirates had used the ranger to track Aurora's capsule, and if they hadn't taken too many readings since, then her flight trajectory data should still be available.

"Sara," said Ygo. "Would you please activate the ranger? Don't touch anything but the power button."

Sara glanced around the cabin and then motioned to the device. "You mean this?"

"Yup. Press the red power button in the upper right."

Sara did. The display came alive. Flight data from its last reading showed in black numbers on a white background.

"Hold on." Ygo processed the information as fast as he could. The launch point was ballpark of what he'd expected. So was the speed and angle of flight.

"I think we have it."

Sara cheered. "Go get her."

While Ygo plotted an intercept course, he told Cuss, "Strap in. We'll be there in two hours."

. . .

The Paulson drives fired, again pushing Cuss into his pilot's seat. He got as comfortable as he could, and then he reached out to Sara and Arron.

"All's well that ends well?" He smiled, hoping to calm their nerves while he worked to protect Ygo.

"Find her first," said Sara. "Then we'll decide how to categorize this mess."

He paused a moment before asking, "I need a favor."

Arron frowned. Cuss didn't wait for him to respond. "Royale and his buddy are tied up in one of the side rooms inside the white dome. I promised Detective Darlena Washington that I'd give her the bust. Would you mind babysitting them until she gets there?"

"How long will she be?" asked Arron, his manner making it clear he did mind.

"I imagine a few hours. It's outside her jurisdiction, so she needs to work that out. She also needs a way to travel from Armstrong out to you."

"Why are we doing this?" Arron was still scowling.

Cuss firmed his tone. "Because I promised it when I needed her help."

Sara nodded. "We'll handle it. Tell her we'll deputize her as a provisional marshal, and that we'll hop over to meet her and bring her here. You focus on your rescue."

"Thanks, Sara. And thanks, Arron."

Arron grunted, but he didn't question Sara's offer.

Cuss closed the call, spent a minute messaging Darlena about the arrangements for Royale, and then called Girish, who was available for a brief update.

Cuss began by praising Ygo for finding the flight numbers they needed while defending the deaths as unfortunate. He kept the account factual because Arron and Sara would be reporting on the incident as well. But he made it clear that it was the pirates' fault, that Ygo's actions had been appropriate, that they had been supported by the group beforehand.

He finished with, "We have her location, but you know how space searches can go. We'll need help."

"I'll reach out to Space Watch, but interagency coordination takes time." Girish rubbed his cheek as he thought. "Ygo told me about a rocket jockey who organizes Moon races. You know who I'm talking about?"

"Joey Spigliano of Joey Sprints Rocket Shop."

"That's the one. Maybe he can get his members to organize a search party?"

Cuss thought it was a brilliant idea.

"I found her!" yelled Ygo. "Ninety minutes out."

"You sure?" asked Cuss.

"I'm sure." It was the old Ygo talking. Confident. In control.

"Gotta go," Cuss told Girish. "We'll let you know."

After closing the call, he said to Ygo, "Show me."

A holo of the capsule appeared on the front display. It seemed to shimmer, an artifact of long-range imaging. But Cuss could see that it was a white canister with the words *Bish 1200* written on the side in stylized blue letters.

"It's a liquid storage tank like we saw before." Ygo displayed the schematic of the canister he'd found in

Royale's private area, the one with arrows pointing to food, water, air, and heat. "See in the notes that the design is for a Bish 1200? We have the right tank in the right location flying on the right trajectory."

"Nice job, pal." Then, "Do you think she's still alive?"

"It depends on their engineering skills and how seriously they took the build. Space habitats can be tricky."

Cuss imagined the horror of finding yourself alone in that tiny prison and shuddered. "Hang on," he called, willing her to survive.

"Are you kidding me!" yelled Ygo. "Peanut, come now!"

Instead of asking, Cuss knew to wait.

Ygo told him, "Her capsule has a homemade docking adapter. We'll need to build a companion piece before we can get to her."

When two spacecraft docked, their mating seal had to be airtight before the hatches could be opened. Standard docking adapters did this well. But if one half of an adapter was a custom design, something incompatible with any of the standards, then the other half needed to be fabricated to match.

"Can't I go over in a suit?"

"You won't fit."

"Oh, for… How can I help?"

"Let's see. You could make the bolt pins while Peanut builds the ring frame."

Fabrication took the full ninety minutes of travel time to the prison canister, plus forty more minutes floating next to it while they assembled the pieces. Finally, Peanut floated from the *Nelly Marie* carrying the custom adapter. Using a power wrench, he joined the two craft together.

Ygo approved the connection, and with Peanut still outside waiting to disconnect the two vessels, Cuss opened the hatch into the canister.

"Aurora?" he called.

No answer.

He poked his head into the opening. "It's me, Cuss."

The air was so cold that his breath fogged, the chill stinging his face and hands. He amplified the dim light with his lens and then used thermal imaging to scan the cramped interior.

He spotted her ahead and to his right, wrapped around a warm square near the cylinder wall.

"Aurora!" he shouted. "Wake up!"

She didn't respond.

He floated to her and shook her shoulder. Nothing.

She was ensconced in a sleeping bag, her nose poking out through the opening at the top. Her abdomen was pressed against what Cuss presumed was the heating element for the capsule. She was bent around it, hugging it for warmth.

A thermal image normally showed red, orange, and yellow temperature contours running through a body. But he was seeing lots of green and even blues. Too cold to support life.

"Is she alive?" he asked Ygo.

"Barely," said Ygo. "Here."

In his lens, Cuss saw a live stream of Aurora's heart pumping at a weak thirty-four beats per minute.

He moved quickly after that, prying her free from the heating element and floating her to the center of the cylinder. Tugging open the top of the sleeping bag, he examined her face.

Her skin had a pale, glassy texture, except for the tip of her nose, which was turning a whitish blue. Her pupils were dilated, her eyes unseeing. Her lips were also blue, pressed together as if she were trying to restrict breathing to her nose.

"Wake up, Aurora," he called as he jostled her.

She still didn't respond.

Moving quickly, he floated around her, grabbed a handful of sleeping bag, and backed out of the cylinder feet first, pulling her with him toward the warmth of the *Nelly Marie*. But when she reached the opening, she wouldn't fit because her knees were pulled up near her chest. He pushed her back into the canister, moved next to her, and spoke reassuring words as he repositioned her in the sleeping bag.

He began to shiver himself. The capsule was *cold*.

When she was mostly straight, the sight of her floating on her back like she was lying on a bed gave him an inspiration.

"The rejuv!" he called to Ygo. "Fire it up. We're on our way."

He pulled her into the *Nelly Marie*, closed the hatches so Peanut could wrench the two craft apart, and floated with her up to the middeck.

Hovering next to the rejuv, he unzipped the sleeping bag and peeled it off her.

She looked bigger than he remembered, and then he realized her girth was from multiple layers of sweatpants and sweatshirts.

Ygo said, "You need to get her out of those clothes for the rejuv to work."

Undressing himself in weightlessness was a trial. Undressing someone else was close to impossible. When he tugged on a piece of clothing, she floated in the direction he pulled. He tried pushing her away and then jerking back against her momentum, but it didn't work in reality the way it did in his head.

He searched for a tool and settled on handheld power clippers he found in Peanut's closet. Holding the tool up, he turned it on and off to observe the cutting action. Deciding it was safe enough, he got to work, cutting through layers of clothing, feeling a bit like a farmer shearing sheep.

He made good progress and soon had her down to panties and a sports bra. There was a red abrasion on her thigh, a fresh wound. He figured he'd scraped her with the power clippers at some point.

"This has to be good enough," he said to Ygo.

"Perfect. Now give her an infusion."

He looked up, uncertain what he was supposed to do.

"In the med closet."

Cuss pulled Aurora over to the medical stores closet and opened the door. Drawers down the center held a variety of supplies. Shelves along either side held medical appliances that Ygo could control from his den. One was an infusion prep machine. The machine's ready light was green.

"What's in it?" Cuss asked as he lifted the handheld part of the infuser from its holder.

"Meds to help with her circulation, oxygenation, blood pressure, heart rate, and pain. She'll think her skin is on fire once she surfaces. Give a dose in each thigh and each shoulder. Four in all."

Cuss began with the thigh nearest him. He pressed the infuser tip against her skin, pushed the button on the side of the device with his thumb, and heard a click. He turned her in the air and repeated the procedure on a shoulder.

"Her circulation is weak," explained Ygo while Cuss used the infuser. "This will distribute the meds faster."

When Cuss had completed the sequence, he floated her over to the rejuv.

"Peanut's back inside, so I'm getting us underway. Hold her over the patient platform and steady yourself."

Cuss heard the Paulson drives fire, and then a gentle acceleration created a light gravity. He was able to remain standing while he guided Aurora down onto her back in the middle of the rejuv platform. He positioned her arms at her sides and then straightened her legs, noting as he did that two of the toes on her right foot showed a blueish white that matched the tip of her nose. He finished by placing a protective pad over her eyes.

The silver box he'd positioned above her began sending healing rays across her body. He watched her vital signs in a display above the rejuv, expecting the rays and infusions to change things around. But so far, she was barely hanging on.

Ygo said, "I've asked Peanut to insert an IV."

Cuss had thought he was alone and turned to see the bot climbing the ladder up from the command deck.

Peanut went to the same medical closet that Cuss had used. Inside, a different appliance had loaded an IV bag full of clear liquid. Peanut connected a line to the bag, carried the assembly to the rejuv, hung the bag on a hook designed for that purpose, and inserted the needle at the other end of the line into a vein in the crook of Aurora's right arm.

Happy that Peanut was available for the more technical tasks, Cuss made himself useful by putting a dollop of ointment on an applicator, which he then used to coat the wound he'd made on Aurora's thigh.

Cuss didn't know if it was the rejuv or the infusions finally kicking in, or if it was the IV that made the difference. Maybe it was the ointment. Whatever the cause, her vital signs began to strengthen.

"She's doing well," he said when the trend upward seemed clear, hoping Ygo would agree.

"I'm very optimistic."

Over the next minutes, her skin began to develop color. Her chest rose and fell in a slow rhythm as her breathing strengthened. And for the first time, Cuss saw her as a young woman lying before him, exposed in a way that would mortify her.

He looked her up and down and then looked away. "Would a blanket be a problem?"

"Your blue bedsheet is lightweight cotton. Spread it evenly and we should be okay."

Cuss sent Peanut to retrieve it and then covered her from chin to toe, taking care not to dislodge the IV.

He set up a chair next to her after that and watched her numbers climb. "How's your optimism now?"

"You've saved her. My only concern at this point is possible damage from frostbite, and psychological trauma from her time in the cylinder."

"*We* saved her, pal, and you know it. You did good."

They didn't talk about it after that. Instead, Cuss started on a long string of calls.

He began with Georgio, who broke down in tears, crying even harder when Cuss showed him a view of Aurora lying in the rejuv.

"She's doing well," he assured Georgio. "She'll be in a Nova Terra hospital in a couple of hours."

Georgio had an endless series of questions, but Cuss didn't have the time. "I called you first, Georgio. Which means I have other calls to make."

He called Arron and Sara, who were both giddy, and not just because he and Ygo had saved their victim. The bigger news from their view was that the contents of the white ball had solved their space piracy case.

"The silo that glowed on the far end of the ball is some sort of reactor-oven contraption," said Arron. "It cooks the equipment in an energy bath that scrambles the ID tags."

Sara grinned. "It's a great day for the Interworld Marshals Service."

Cuss surprised himself by calling Julie next. She'd been an important part of the team, had made substantive contributions, and deserved an update. But the real reason, plain and simple, was because he missed her. He wanted to hear her voice.

She listened intently as he told the tale, gasping at the part where the errant laser cut across the small pirate's chest.

When Cuss wound down, she said, "I get that Royale lost his wife's fortune and panicked. But solving the problem by becoming a pirate, kidnapper, and killer doesn't make sense."

"I've learned a few things about him," Ygo told Cuss privately.

Cuss said aloud, "Ygo, are you there? Do you have insights on what drove Royale?"

"I do," said Ygo. "Hi Julie."

She returned his greeting, and then he began.

"When Gurby-Dent was laying the groundwork for their project, Royale got wind of it and was enamored by the benefits to Nova Terra. To convince his wife to invest, he explained that water not only provides the liquid of life, but since it's made of oxygen and hydrogen, it also provides breathable atmosphere. He claimed the project was good for their portfolio, but even more important, was vital for Nova Terra's future. He finished by tugging on one of her personal passions, suggesting that the expanded air supply might allow the ugly vines covering the buildings to be pulled away, elevating the discussion on lunar architecture."

"So he's just a misunderstood patron of the arts," said Cuss, sarcasm dripping from his words. "What a guy."

Chapter 28

C uss sat with Aurora in her apartment on Deck 9 of Hermes. It was a modest place. Bedroom, bathroom, and a living area with a small kitchen at the back. The rooms were decorated with personal bits. Pictures of family and friends. Keepsakes from her youth. Souvenirs from her travels.

It had been four days since her rescue. He was there for a special thank-you meal.

He studied her from across the table and thought she looked wonderful. Her hair was washed and brushed. Her face freshly scrubbed. Light makeup except for her lips: they were a glossy red, which was also the color of the tip of her nose. There was no lasting damage, but the skin needed time to heal from its brush with frostbite.

He teased her about looking like Rudolph. When she didn't laugh, he apologized for his insensitivity.

"I did lose the tip of the little toe on my right foot," she said. "But it doesn't affect how I walk or anything."

Though she looked great on the outside, her eyes told a different story. There was a sadness. A dark emptiness where once there'd been life. Every so often she'd drift away, eyes unfocused, staring at nothing.

When they finished the meal, they moved to the couch. She sat right next to him, so close their thighs touched. She smelled like a fresh spring day.

On the coffee table, she spread out scraps of paper and explained they were ideas for tattoos. "I'm still working on Moby's tribute. And here are ideas for Mom and Dad."

In just over a week, her grandfather, father, and mother had been murdered in two separate attacks. She'd been kidnapped and imprisoned in horrific conditions. And she'd had her own brush with death. She needed time to process it all. It would be a long and difficult journey, one that would require professional help. When she came out the other end, she'd be a different person.

"They're not like the one you got for Georgio's dad," said Cuss. That one was simple linework. A circle, triangle, and Christian cross. The new tattoo ideas were richer. Complex with imagery. Dark things like a club with blood dripping off the end. Another had a skull and what looked like a person in a pressure suit being shot by a laser.

"Georgio arrives tomorrow and I'll get his input. But what do *you* think?"

He thought they were awful. "More important is what you think. Is this how you want to remember your folks?"

She fingered the one for her father, the ugliest of the lot. "I don't want to think of him as a bad guy. But he was involved with them. How do I accept that?"

Cuss shook his head. "It wasn't like that. He accepted their early engine orders thinking they were honest customers and he'd stumbled onto a good thing. When he and Moby figured out they were helping a piracy ring, they rebelled, maybe even threatened the bad guys, and it cost them their lives."

He paused to let her digest his words before continuing. "And the two who actually did the killing, the same two who kidnapped you and put you in the capsule, have paid the price with their lives. The rest are in custody awaiting trial.

"Thank you for that." She kissed him on the cheek and rested her head on his shoulder.

She'd been overly attentive since his arrival. Complimenting him. Touching him repeatedly. Laughing at his lighter comments. He'd seen the behavior before. Rescuer adulation. Hero worship. Savior attachment. It had lots of names.

He prodded her to talk about her childhood and fond memories of her folks. Her mind was in turmoil and she rambled, laughing and crying within seconds of each other. He let her go until she went quiet.

It was time to leave, and he moved to the door.

She hugged him. A long embrace. "Can I see you tomorrow?"

Standing in front of her, he moved a strand of hair off her face with his finger and looked into her sad eyes. "I would love to spend time with you, Aurora. But your doctor counsels that I step away and let you heal."

"Forever?"

"Months, anyway. Healing is a slow process."

"That's not fair. Maybe next week?" She sounded hopeful.

He shook his head. "When your doctor says you're ready, contact me if you're still interested."

She protested some more. He remained firm. She began to cry, though she didn't really have any tears left to shed. He gently peeled her grip from his arm.

As he stepped out the door, he said over his shoulder, "Good luck, sweetie. I'll be thinking of you."

He didn't look back as he walked down the hall. Finally, the door closed. When it did, he said to Ygo, "Why does the right thing feel so wrong?"

"She's had a rough go of it. No question."

When he reached the pedestrian thoroughfare, he boarded a pod and rode in silence down to Luna Deck. From there he made for the shuttle station, where he'd catch a ride down to the spaceport and the *Nelly Marie*.

When he arrived at the shuttle station plaza, a noisy tour group was just getting into line. Rather than wait behind them, he walked to a park bench in a quiet corner of the plaza and chose a seat that let him watch the progress of the tour group as they boarded the shuttles, ten passengers at a time.

He thought about Julie and messaged her, explaining that he was killing time and if she felt like chatting, he'd love to hear her voice.

"Ten minutes," was her response.

He went to a food kiosk, got a cup of pistachio ice cream, and was just finishing when she called.

"How are you doing?" she began.

"Good. I'm on desk duty for the next week so I can help the Lagrange MA put together their case."

After some light chitchat, he told her the news.

"I've been invited to serve on the advisory board for Chaparral. That's the Marshals Service training school in Seattle. There's a board meeting next month, and they want us there in person so we can walk the grounds, look at buildings, meet instructors. Like that. Anyway, I can take a week off either before or after the meeting, and I wondered if you might like to spend that time together? Maybe take a drive and explore the Pacific Coast?"

She blushed. He loved that about her.

Holding up a finger, she looked down at what he presumed was her calendar. After a quick frown, she looked up. "I'll have to shuffle some things, but I think I can make one of them work. Give me a few days?"

They chatted some more, exchanging ideas about what to see on the trip and places to stay. He was excited that she was excited.

They kept at it for twenty minutes, and then she had another appointment. The shuttle line had long since thinned. He stood with a contented sigh.

"Cuss!" He heard a woman's voice and looked around. "Marshal Abbott!"

He picked her out of the crowd. Chik Gambier. She was coming toward him, taking the long strides of someone accustomed to lunar gravity.

She had a small bouquet of flowers in one hand. Daisies. She held them out for him with a self-conscious smile. "I got you these. I was on my way down to deliver them."

"How nice."

"I'm not drunk."

"Congratulations."

"Haven't had a drink in over a month. It's given me lots of time to think."

"Thinking is good."

"I'm interested."

"Wonderful. In what?"

"You. You said to tell you if I was interested when I was sober and you'd respond in kind." She grinned from ear to ear. "Here I am."

"Oh Lord," said Ygo.

From the Author

Thanks for reading. If you enjoyed the book, please consider telling others about it with a rating or review on Amazon. Reviews are the lifeblood of an author, and reader excitement motivates us to write!

Also by Doug J. Cooper

The Crystal Series

The Crystal Series is four books of action and suspense involving AI, spies, romance, and battles in space!

Crystal Deception (Book 1)
Crystal Conquest (Book 2)
Crystal Rebellion (Book 3)
Crystal Escape (Book 4)

Readers' Praise for The Crystal Series (Amazon Reviews):

★★★★★ "Characters that feel like real people, who behave in ways that make sense and you can empathize with."

★★★★★ "It has all the features of Anne McCaffrey 's Dragon Riders of Pern series. Strong characters, sentient improbability and interesting plots."

★★★★★ "Nicely done hard sci-fi. I am a fan of this kind of story line so it sucked me right in."

★★★★★ "A tale of intrigue, action, a touch of romance and heartbreak."

For info and purchases, visit: crystalseries.com

Free Story!

Crystal Horizon – Prequel to the Crystal Series

The Crystal Series is four full-length books where the emergence of self-aware AI and alien first contact occur at the same time.

Sample this popular space opera for free by downloading Crystal Horizon, the prequel.

In book 1 of the series, Crystal Deception, Cheryl is captain of the military space cruiser Alliance, and Sid is a covert warrior for the Defense Specialists Agency. We learn that the two have a shared history, and in particular, a romantic relationship that has somehow gone awry.

In the prequel, we get their backstory. We join Sid and Cheryl on the day they first meet, and experience that shared history with them.

Crystal Horizon is offered free to newsletter subscribers.

To obtain this free book, visit: crystalseries.com

Adventures in Time
With a Sinister AI

Bump Time Trilogy

On his twenty-fifth birthday, Diesel Lagerford is visited by a twenty-six-year-old version of himself. His look-alike spins impossible tales of their shared future, claiming they have dozens of "brothers" from parallel timelines who can visit each other using a T-box, a machine they bankroll with lottery winnings. He introduces Diesel to the incredible Lilah Spencer, the T-box operator, and Diesel falls head-over-heels in love. But during his travels across timelines, Diesel learns that Lilah will soon die under suspicious circumstances. Devastated, he joins his brothers in a race to save her. Can they solve the mystery of her death before it's too late? And will their unusual solution play out over time in the ways they had anticipated?

For info and purchases, visit: crystalseries.com